Dewey
Decimated

Dewey Decimated

A HAUNTED LIBRARY MYSTERY

Allison Brook

NEW YORK

Copyright © 2022 by Marilyn Levinson

All rights reserved.

Published in the United States by Crooked Lane Books, an imprint of The Quick Brown Fox & Company LLC.

Crooked Lane Books and its logo are trademarks of The Quick Brown Fox & Company LLC.

Library of Congress Catalog-in-Publication data available upon request.

ISBN (hardcover): 978-1-63910-090-3
ISBN (ebook): 978-1-63910-091-0

Cover illustration by Griesbach/Martucci

Printed in the United States.

www.crookedlanebooks.com

Crooked Lane Books
34 West 27th St., 10th Floor
New York, NY 10001

First Edition: September 2022

10 9 8 7 6 5 4 3 2 1

For my grandson Jack Andrew Levinson
who is learning to read: you have a
lifetime of reading wonderful books
before you!

Chapter One

"Thanks, Aunt Harriet. Dinner was delicious as always," I said.

"You're most welcome, Carrie dear. You know I'm always delighted to have your company. While I'm glad your Uncle Bosco is civic-minded, I wish so many of his meetings weren't scheduled at dinnertime."

I stood to bring my dishes to the sink, but my great-aunt put her hand on my shoulder. "I'll do that. Sit down and relax a few minutes before you head home. You must be tired after putting in a full day at the library." She started loading the dishwasher.

I didn't mean to, but a huge sigh escaped my lips.

Aunt Harriet turned around, a look of distress on her face. "Is something worrying you? You've been quiet all evening."

"I suppose being here reminds me of how simple my life was a year ago when I was living with you and Uncle Bosco."

That brought on a roar of laughter. "Carrie, love, you've forgotten how miserable you were last September—doing little more than shelving books in the library and having no social life to speak of. Look at all you've accomplished in the past year—a satisfying job, many friends. And best of all, you're engaged to a wonderful fella."

"Right."

Even to my ears, my answer sounded glum. Aunt Harriet lifted my chin so she could peer into my eyes. "Are you and Dylan having problems?" She looked anxious. My aunt cared about Dylan almost as much as she loved me.

Impulsively, I hugged her. "Don't worry. Dylan and I are fine. It's just . . ."

"I know." She stroked my back. "Getting engaged, agreeing to join the town council. It takes a lot of adjusting."

I shrugged, longing to open up yet reluctant to talk about what was troubling me. Best simply to agree.

"I suppose that's it. I'm feeling nervous about all the new things in my life, though Dylan promised not to pressure me about setting a wedding date."

"And I'm doing my best to keep your Uncle Bosco from doing the same."

Her kindness touched me, and I found myself spilling out what had been bothering me for some time now.

"I love Dylan. I want to spend the rest of my life with him, but there's something that I didn't think much about until we got engaged. Then it began to loom larger and larger."

I paused to draw in a deep breath. I'd never uttered aloud what I was about to say to Aunt Harriet—not to Dylan or to my newly wedded best friend Angela—but it was time I got it off my chest.

"Whenever I ask Dylan something about his parents, he brushes me off. I've tried several times. He shuts up like a clam, and if I persist he turns distant. Curt. The way he was that first time I went to look at the cottage."

I stared into Aunt Harriet's eyes and held fast so she wouldn't try to evade my questions. "You and Uncle Bosco knew Dylan's parents. In fact, you ended up selling them the Singleton Farm because you couldn't afford to keep it and resented that the Averys took advantage of your situation and bought it at a low price."

"And if you'll remember, I once told you that selling when we did turned out to be for the best. The farm had stopped paying for itself and Bosco and I were getting too old to run it. Yes, Cal and Estelle offered us less than we'd asked for, but I urged your uncle to take it. The Averys updated and expanded the farmhouse, sold it, and now it's a successful B and B. Lucky for us, your uncle and I were able to bid on this house as soon as it came on the market. The opportunity to buy a house on the Green is as rare as hen's teeth."

"Getting back to Cal and Estelle, did they do something awful, something Dylan's afraid or ashamed to tell me?"

It was Aunt Harriet's turn to exhale a loud gush of air. "Not that I know of, but I'm afraid they weren't the most congenial people. Oh, they were sociable enough—throwing large parties once or twice a year and inviting everyone to their big house. Bosco and I went to a few of their shindigs.

"Cal was cordial enough when you took care of bank business. He played the role of bank vice president just right—asking about your health, the health of your spouse. Until you asked for a loan. Then he was tough as nails." Aunt Harriet chuckled. "And how Estelle loved to play her role of wealthy lady about town. She and Cal owned buildings here and in New Haven. They had other businesses, too. They thrived on buying and selling properties. Making investments.

"As for Dylan, I'm not aware of anything either of them ever did to harm him intentionally, but they didn't spend much time with him, either. The poor child was pretty much left to himself while his parents worked and socialized. I used to invite him over when you and Jordan came to stay with us. As you know, he and Jordan became fast friends."

I smiled when she mentioned my older brother, whom we'd lost eight years ago. Not a day passed that he wasn't in my thoughts.

"Dylan continued to come to the farm even after you and Jordan went home to the city. Your uncle gave him chores to do, which he seemed to like, and he sometimes had dinner with us."

"Dylan never said," I murmured. "He doesn't talk much about his life before we met, except to tell me about some of his investigations, chasing after stolen artwork and gems all over the world." I was already dating Dylan when his boss, Mac, made him a partner in the company. Then Dylan had opened the office in New Haven and began handling more local and less exotic cases.

"Has he ever mentioned any relatives?" Aunt Harriet asked.

"No. When we got engaged in July, I asked Dylan if he was planning to call family members to tell them our news. He said there was really no one to call. That he liked my relatives and was happy to share them with me."

"I'm sorry I can't be more helpful," Aunt Harriet said. "I suggest you talk to Dylan, let him know what's on your mind."

"And if he continues to avoid talking about it?"

"Then I suggest you be patient. Knowing the kind of relationship you two have, I'm sure he'll share everything in time."

I stood and hugged her. Though she hadn't told me much more than I already knew, Aunt Harriet had succeeded in making me feel better. I took her unspoken message to be that while there might be mysteries in Dylan's past, they neither reflected badly on Dylan nor would they have a negative impact on our future together.

I scooped up Smoky Joe, who had wandered into the kitchen to join us. My furry feline had appeared one morning last fall as I was about to drive to work. He was probably one of the barn cats from the farm on the other side of the woods from my cottage. Half-grown, he'd jumped into my car, and I had no choice but to bring him into the library, where he instantly became the library cat. He had proven to be a most sociable creature and was a favorite of patrons young and old.

Smoky Joe started purring and reached up to lick my nose.

"Time to put you in your carrier, boy, and drive us home. It's been a long day."

* * *

Dylan called me as I was pulling in front of the cottage. It was situated on the Avery property about a quarter of a mile past the large house I thought of as the manor. I'd rented the cottage from Dylan almost a year ago, and now we spent most of our time here together. He'd worked late tonight, which was one of the reasons I'd accepted Aunt Harriet's dinner invitation.

"Hi, babe, have a good home-cooked dinner?"

"I sure did, though I make home-cooked dinners all the time."

Dylan laughed. "I don't think bringing home takeout from the Gourmet Market is considered home cooked."

"Did you eat?"

"Gary ran out to the deli down the block and got us a few sandwiches." Gary was Dylan's new assistant who was helping him with new cases. He seemed to be settling in well.

"Where are you?" I asked.

"Ten minutes from home. I need to stop by the house to check my mail and pick up a few things. Want me to come over, or is it too late?"

"Sure, come on over. It's only eight thirty."

Once inside the cottage I released Smoky Joe from his carrier and he dashed over to his bowl. I poured in some kibble along with a few treats the way he liked it and filled his water dish. After I changed into jeans and a T-shirt, I returned to the kitchen to see what I had in the fridge.

Dylan arrived a few minutes later. As I suspected, when asked if he'd like a small snack, he was all for it. I heated up the left-over chicken parm from the Gourmet Market that he liked so much and served it with some cold pasta salad. While Dylan ate, we chatted about our days, then moved on to the living room to watch TV.

We cuddled on the couch and caught a segment of the news. When a commercial came on, I clicked off the TV. Dylan cast me a questioning glance.

I swallowed. "I wanted to talk to you about something that's been on my mind."

"Oh?" His eyebrows shot up.

I felt nervous but forced myself to continue. "Dylan, I don't want us to have any secrets from each other."

I hadn't meant to blurt it out that way, but Dylan didn't seem to mind. He grinned. "Do you think I'm seeing someone else when I stay late at the office? Because believe me, the cases are piling up. I'm happy to work as hard as I can for us."

I stroked his arm. "It's not that. I want our life together to be one of sharing. And one of the things we share are the people we love. You know everyone important to me. You know my friends.

My family." I paused. "And I know so little about your parents. About when you were little."

I felt his muscles tense. "There's not much to tell. My parents weren't the warmest people. In fact, they probably never should have had children, given the way they raised me."

"I'm sorry."

"I'm happy to share your family—Jim and Merry, Bosco and Harriet. Your cousin Randy and his family."

"And my mother?" I asked with a smile.

Dylan grimaced. "Can't leave out Linda, difficult as she is."

"But your parents—were they really that awful?"

Dylan frowned. "Let's put it this way: they didn't beat me or forget to feed me. But they weren't there for me like other parents are for their kids. Usually," he added when he caught my expression.

My father had spent a good deal of time away from home during my growing-up years, either in prison for one of his heists or just . . . away. My mother was self-centered and not at all maternal. My older brother, Jordan, had been my one constant, and he'd lost his life in his mid-twenties in an automobile accident.

"I'm not saying they were the worst parents," Dylan went on. "They just weren't parental. They were completely wrapped up in work and in themselves. As I got older, my resentment grew, and after high school I chose to cut myself off from them." He gave a little laugh. "I went away to college, spending a year in England, and rarely came home during vacations. They didn't seem to notice."

"I'm sorry," I said. "Your childhood was as bad as mine. At least I had Jordan."

"Jordan," Dylan echoed. "Those summers you guys came to visit are my best memories. And after you went back to the city I kept on visiting your aunt and uncle."

"Aunt Harriet told me."

"They were always so kind to me." He sniffed. "I used to pretend they were my aunt and uncle, too."

"And now they are," I whispered and held him in my arms. "You must have aunts and uncles and cousins," I said a minute later.

"When I was ten we went to a family reunion in Pennsylvania. My parents left me with the other kids and went to join the adults. Even though they were different ages, from six to fifteen, the cousins all knew one another. I was very shy in those days. I finally got up the courage to approach a boy who looked to be my age but he turned away. They soon broke up into small groups and took off in different directions. I went inside and stayed in the kitchen till my parents came looking for me hours later. At least the woman whose house we were in was kindhearted and didn't try to make me go out and play with the other kids."

He scoffed. "My parents didn't even ask what I'd been doing all afternoon or if I had a good time. They spent the entire drive home tearing apart the people at the reunion—all relatives, but you'd never know it, judging by their comments:

"'I had to stop myself from grabbing Doris's hand when she reached for another cookie. Clearly, she hasn't seen herself in a mirror in years or she'd tape her mouth shut when they brought out the desserts.'

"'Your cousin Jimmy never stopped bragging about his new Cadillac. His brother-in-law told me Jimmy's already behind making payments.'

"Riding home that evening, I told myself that as soon as I was old enough, I would create my own life and have nothing to do with my parents ever again."

Chapter Two

The following morning I drove to the library on autopilot as I mulled over what Dylan had told me about his early life. I'd had no idea that his parents were the way he'd described them. Sure, I knew there had to be a good reason why he hadn't wanted to talk about them, but their selfish self-absorption and their greed to make more and more money was shocking. They had virtually ignored their child and his needs as if he were no more than a piece of furniture in their elegant home. I believed the term was *benign neglect*.

And all the time we'd been dating, I hadn't had an inkling of what Dylan had lived through. I smiled, remembering how supportive he'd been when I'd faced rough patches with each of my parents. How had he acquired the compassion and understanding to see me through those difficult times when he hadn't been given such care and attention while he was growing up? Tears welled up in my eyes and I promised myself I'd give Dylan the same support when he needed it.

Though we had barely touched on the extent of the damage Cal and Estelle had wrought, I decided to drop the subject for now. I'd leave it to Dylan to tell me more about his parents, but only when he was ready to do so.

My mind had been so completely occupied with Dylan, I'd all but forgotten that the work on the library's new addition was scheduled to begin today, the second Wednesday in September. This fact was rudely brought to my attention when I found myself driving around the library's parking lot in search of a spot. Though it was only five to nine and the library had yet to open, I finally managed to snag the last available spot in the lot.

The reason soon became obvious. The workers had removed the fence separating the library parking lot from the lot of the adjacent building soon to become part of the library. Now their many trucks and large pieces of machinery sprawled across half if not more of our lot.

Seriously? In addition to the noise and disturbance, we're expected to do without half our parking spaces for the months of construction ahead of us? I don't think so.

As I exited my car, I heard raised voices coming from the other lot. I hurried over to investigate and managed to get close enough to observe what was going on. In the midst of trucks and equipment, Sally Prescott, the library director, stood arguing with a large, burly man who appeared to be in charge while four or five workers watched in amusement as if it were a Netflix show.

"Yes. Go ahead and call Sean Powell," Sally said. "I made it very clear to him that our parking area was not to be used to store your equipment."

"Will do," the foreman said, "but I know what he's going to say."

I wouldn't bet on it, I thought, knowing Sally's capabilities, and returned to my car to get Smoky Joe. As soon as I entered the library, I released him from his carrier and off he zoomed, bushy tail in the air, ready to greet his many fans when they arrived while I headed for my office.

I had two part-time assistants who were as different as any two assistants could be. Trish Templeton was a short, round brunette—a dynamo of a worker I could count on to carry out any plan or project I came up with and then some. Trish came in at ten or ten thirty Monday through Friday and stayed for five hours.

Susan Roberts worked late afternoons and evenings. When I'd become head of programs and events last October, I had found Susan to be passive and lackadaisical. But asking for her suggestions regarding the library's Halloween party had been like turning on a flood light, and I quickly discovered just how talented and creative she really was. Now Susan's crafts and posters were in evidence all around the library, and her drawings graced our newsletter. The Gallery on the Green soon became aware of her talent and started selling her artwork for more money than she had ever dreamed of making.

I glanced through my email, responded to those that needed answers, and was about to stop by the programs that had just begun to make sure they were running smoothly when Sally called and asked me to stop by her office.

"I saw their equipment in our parking lot," I said as I sat in one of the chairs facing her desk. Sally's face was blotchy with emotion and she appeared frazzled, so unlike her usually calm demeanor.

"I came in early today just as they were filling up half our lot with their monster machines. This, after Sean told me they wouldn't be infringing on our parking space." She sighed. "We don't have enough parking spots for patrons as it is."

"Isn't there enough room in the parking lot behind the other building?" I asked.

"They claim it's full of ruts and bad for the machinery. I told them to park their trucks in the street that runs behind that parking lot, but they didn't go for that idea. They said our patrons could park on the street. I said no way, José. The foreman called Sean Powell and he showed up right away."

Sean Powell owned Powell Construction Company, which had won the bid to renovate the building next to the library. I knew Sean because he was also a member of the Clover Ridge Town Council, which I'd joined earlier in the month.

"What did Sean say?" I asked.

"I reminded him that he'd agreed the workers wouldn't use our lot for their machinery. He met with his men and came back to say they'd pull back some of their equipment, but he was sorry that he miscalculated when he promised not to infringe on our parking lot. The truth was they'll be needing to use a quarter of our lot, even half on some days, and he promised never to exceed half of our lot!"

"What did you say to that?" I asked.

Sally shrugged. "What could I say? Sean was agreeable and courteous as always. I knew it was a losing battle."

"We discussed using part of the Green for the equipment at our last council meeting," I said, "but one member in particular refused to even consider it. Said it was unsightly."

"That must have been Babette." Sally scrunched up her face like she smelled something awful when she mentioned the high school art teacher's name. "Always the *artiste* concerned with *aesthetics*. There's a time when we have to be practical."

"At least we're being allowed to hold the Fall Festival on the Green," I pointed out.

"True." Sally sank back into her chair, the wind gone out of her sails. "I shouldn't get upset over something like this. When we acquired the building next door and started raising money to help pay for the new addition, I told myself that we were in for a difficult few months before we had exactly what we wanted—more space for our collections, a stadium-seating auditorium for events, and rooms for more programs. I'll try to focus on that."

I left her in a calmer frame of mind and returned to my office. I'd no sooner sat down at my computer when Evelyn Havers appeared.

"I see Sally's had her first skirmish with the construction people," my ghostly friend said by way of a greeting. "All that equipment and machinery! You'd think we were preparing for war."

"I'm sure they need it all," I said, "or why would they have brought it here?"

"Why, indeed?"

I nodded approvingly at my visitor's early fall outfit—a brown pencil skirt and a white blouse with sprigs of flowers under a tan jacket. Evelyn Havers was the library ghost, though as far as I knew I was one of only two people who could see and talk to her—the other person being my little cousin Tacey. Now and forever in her mid-sixties, Evelyn had worked as an aide at the Clover Ridge Library for many years. In the eleven months I'd been head of programs and events, we had shared many adventures.

"I've been getting an earful from Sally," I said. "She's upset because the workers tried to commandeer half our parking lot for their equipment. I'm afraid we're in for a rough few months."

"Sally had better cool her jets," Evelyn said. "Being in the midst of construction is never fun, and I've a feeling this library extension is going to involve some additional surprises."

I fixed my gaze on Evelyn, who sat perched on the corner of my assistants' desk, her favorite spot in the office. "Are you saying we're in for some problems with this new addition?"

She shrugged. "Just a feeling. Do you know the history of the building next door?"

"Only a bit. I know it was built in the late seventeen hundreds—the home and workshop of a silversmith. After that, it belonged to a candlemaker, a carpenter, a milliner, and finally was turned into a tavern. Most recently, it became the property of three heirs."

"That's right," Evelyn said. "A brother and a sister—James and Marcella Whitehead—and their cousin Albert inherited it about twelve years ago. By then, the property had been neglected and the interior was in shambles. The three cousins couldn't agree on what to do with it. While none wanted to buy out the other two and turn it into a livable home, they couldn't agree on selling it, either. And since all the buildings facing the Green have landmark status, tearing it down was out of the question.

"The only thing James, Marcella, and Albert did jointly was pay the taxes on the building and maintain the exterior walls as required by a town ordinance. James, the oldest and most contentious of the three, died about eighteen months ago. Shortly after, Marcella and Albert agreed to sell the building to the town."

"While I'm not glad that someone died, I am happy the library had the chance to acquire the building," I said. "We need more space, and since we're located on a corner of the Green, there are very few ways we can expand. Converting it into our much-needed addition turned out to be the perfect solution."

"So one would hope," Evelyn said, looking solemn.

A tingle of apprehension ran down my spine. "Why do you say that?"

Evelyn shook her head as if to dispel her thoughts. "The building has had a history of bad luck. Some say its first owner cursed it when he was forced to sell it for less than its worth because his business failed. Others say he was a good silversmith but foolish when it came to money matters. At any rate, whoever bought the property afterwards had little financial success and ended up selling it at a loss."

"That sounds like an old wives' tale," I said.

"I sincerely hope that's the case," Evelyn said and promptly disappeared.

Chapter Three

I puzzled over Evelyn's words, wondering if she was simply being gloomy (which she sometimes was), predicting a calamity of some sort, or if she knew something bad was about to happen. I was fond of Evelyn, as she was of me, and while I knew something of her earlier years, I knew nothing about her "life" after death. Not even the simplest bits of information. Like where did she keep her lovely wardrobe of clothes? Or how did she spend her time when she wasn't here with me? I'd asked often enough, but Evelyn always evaded my questions like a seasoned grifter avoided arrest.

I heard the sound of machinery start up and figured the construction crew must have finished moving some of it from our lot and were beginning their day's work. I had no knowledge of their schedule and, frankly, I wasn't interested in knowing the details— except when it came to questions regarding the new auditorium and rooms.

After visiting the ongoing programs, I returned a call to a local chef scheduled to present a cooking demonstration that evening. He'd decided to make a change in his Autumn Dinner menu and would be preparing an apple crumble rather than the carrot cake he'd originally asked us to mention in our newsletter and flyers.

I posted the change on our Facebook page and left a copy of the apple crumble recipe he'd just emailed me on my assistants' desk. When Trish came in, I'd ask her to print out enough copies to hand out to everyone attending the food presentation. Then I walked across the reading room to say hello to my best friend, Angela Prisco, who worked at the circulation desk.

Tall and slender with dark curly hair, Angela was a look-alike for Angie Harmon. She was a bride of three months and still had the glow of a newlywed. I waited while she checked out a few items for a patron, then asked if she'd had trouble parking that morning.

Angela frowned. "I ended up parking on the street. I thought we weren't going to lose our parking lot while construction was going on."

I told her the result of Sally's chat with Sean Powell.

"So, Sean isn't following through on what he promised." She winked. "Maybe now that you're on the town council with him, you can convince him to keep all of his workers' equipment off our lot."

"Right. I've been on the council all of two weeks and attended one meeting so far. I've met Sean exactly three times. You probably know him better."

"I suppose so, since his construction company updated my parents' bathrooms and kitchen a few years ago."

Curious, I asked, "Were they pleased with the job?"

"Yes, very," Angela said, "but I remember first they had to shoot down some of his more grandiose suggestions."

"I suppose all businesspeople try to make as much money as they can," I said.

Angela laughed. "Aren't you a well-informed consumer?"

"I try to be," I wisecracked back. "Meet you at noon?"

"Of course."

Our usual lunch date set, I headed back to work. Smoky Joe scampered over and accompanied me to the office, where he curled up on my assistants' chair and promptly went to sleep.

* * *

An hour later, Trish came bursting through the door, her face alive with excitement. "Guess what? They found a body in the old building next door."

"For real? Is this a joke?"

"Of course it's for real! The workers were told to stop what they were doing and exit the building. And you should see the crowd!"

I went outside via the library's front entrance facing the Green, which I rarely used. Sure enough, word of the gruesome discovery had gotten out, and a mob swarmed the front of the building next door, spilling into the street and onto the Green. An ambulance and a police car were parked in the road, blocking all traffic. I spotted the tall, spare figure of John Mathers talking to one of the EMTs. I wasn't the least bit surprised to see he was already on the case.

Eager as I was to find out more information, I knew better than to approach him now. While I had helped John solve a few murders and considered him and his wife, Sylvia, to be dear friends, our police lieutenant drew the line when it involved what he considered police business. Translated, that meant he expected me to share whatever I found out regarding a victim and his or her suspects, while I wasn't to expect any such reciprocity.

I was astounded to learn that a dead person had been lying in the long-abandoned building next to my workplace for an indefinite period of time. Days? Months? Years? And I wondered why none of the workers had noticed it until now since there had been a thorough inspection of the building before the purchase went through. Unless, of course, someone had dropped off the body when no one was looking and had hidden it in a dark corner that had already been inspected.

But my curiosity was limited for a variety of reasons. This past year I'd had enough close encounters with homicides to last me the rest of my life. And at the present moment, there was more than enough going on in my life to keep me busy. I'd recently gotten engaged, I was busy at the library, and as a newly appointed member of the town council I had plenty to learn about town issues. And so I returned to my office and concentrated on library work until it was time to meet Angela and walk over to the Cozy Corner Café.

Angela, on the other hand, was all agog about the dead body they'd found next door. She was up-to-date on new developments in the case, courtesy of her cell phone and the efforts of Julie Theron. Our persistent, often in-your-face, local TV investigative reporter had appeared on the scene shortly after I'd returned to work.

Julie was in her early twenties and looked even younger—petite, with big blue eyes and cropped blonde hair that gave her a gamine look. That is until she started speaking and her take-charge manner commanded everyone's attention. She'd managed to evoke comments from Buzz Coleman, the burly crew foreman; from an EMT; and even from John. Angela shared all this with me as we walked the three short blocks to the café.

"They found it in a corner of the basement," she told me with glee. "When asked why they'd never noticed it earlier, the foreman said it was under a shelf and in the dim lighting had remained out of sight."

"Did they ever think of using a flashlight," I murmured, "to check out nooks and crannies like they were supposed to?"

Angela waved away this boring detail. "The technician said a dark wool blanket was wrapped around the body. A male body, from the looks of it."

"Ugh! Too much information," I protested.

"Just think, Carrie," my best friend crowed, "a man was murdered and hidden in the abandoned building attached to the library." Her dark eyes shone with excitement. "It could have been there for years and nobody knew."

I shook my head in disapproval. "From the way you're talking, no one would guess that a few members of your family recently met the same fate."

Angela had the grace to look ashamed. "You're right. I got carried away because this time neither I nor anyone I know is connected to the dead person."

"That you know of," I said darkly.

Angela sighed. "I suppose you're right, but Julie Theron said there was no ID on the remains. No wallet or papers. Except for a hundred-dollar bill found folded up real small in an inside jacket pocket."

"Money for unexpected expenses," I mused. "You would know better than me if anyone local has been reported missing in the last few years."

"No one I can think of," Angela said. "Julie announced she's checking into missing persons in the area. So far nothing's come up."

"Interesting," I murmured.

Dewey Decimated

"Are you going to investigate?" Angela asked. "Find out who this person is? Why he was murdered?"

"Of course not. I've got better things to do with my life." By this point, we'd reached the café, and I pulled open the door. "Let's go eat. I'm starving."

Chapter Four

By the time we walked back to the library, we could hear the sound of the construction crew tearing down the interior walls of the building next door. The crowd, having nothing more to gawp at, had dispersed. I was surprised that work had resumed and had expected to see yellow tape strung across the building declaring it off limits. Then again, since the death had taken place so long ago, I supposed that after the crime team photographed the area and the body was removed, there was no need for that.

Trish and I worked on the December-January newsletter. I held up the sketches Susan had made—one of kids having a snowball fight, the other of people skating on a pond—and asked Trish which one she liked better.

She studied them for a while, then said, "Sorry, I can't decide. I like them both."

"Then we'll use both. One on the first page, the other on the last page."

"That girl is so talented," Trish said.

"Don't I know it. I keep waiting for her to tell me she's leaving us."

"I doubt that will happen," Trish said. "Susan considers you the person responsible for giving her the confidence to launch her art career."

I grinned. "Maybe we'll be lucky and she'll stay with us a while longer."

We got most of the newsletter in shape by the time Trish left at three thirty. Our two usual delinquents—Marion Marshall, the children's librarian, and Harvey Kirk, the head of the computer department—each still owed me a short news update regarding their sections. Marion was a friend, so I had no problem urging her to send her article along, but Harvey, though a whiz when it came to computer skills, was cantankerous. Also, he resented me for once suspecting him of murdering one of our colleagues. I'd ask Trish to deal with him tomorrow.

I walked over to the children's section and wasn't at all surprised to find Smoky Joe there, receiving lots of attention from the young children sitting cross-legged in a circle while Gayle, Marion's assistant, read them a story.

Gayle jerked her head, indicating that Marion was in their office. I smiled and went inside.

Marion looked up from whatever she'd been working on as I sat down. "Can you believe it! Another Clover Ridge murder, and this time it happened in our new library addition. Are you going to find out who did it?"

"I doubt it," I said. "I don't even know who was murdered."

"Neither do the police. Your friend John Mathers is here in the library talking to Sally."

"Is he? I'm not surprised he's asking questions, though I can't imagine what Sally would know."

"He should be talking to the Whitehead cousins who owned the property for years." She scoffed. "Though the most likely murderer is James, and he's dead."

"Why James?" I asked.

Marion cast me one of those looks that meant I was totally uninformed, which in this case I was. "James Whitehead was an arrogant, nasty piece of work. His sister and his cousin Albert were too terrified to do anything without his say-so."

"And James is dead."

"Exactly!" Marion said with relish. "Meaning we'll never find out who this person is and why James murdered him."

"John Mathers is capable of investigating the situation," I said. "And I need your article for the next newsletter ASAP."

"Oh." Marion looked at me in surprise, as if this were the first she was hearing about it.

"Is there a problem?" I asked. "All you have to do is write a few lines about what you've been doing recently and upcoming plans. Like the Fall Festival. I suppose you could ask Gayle to do it." *Again*, I thought.

Marion made a face. "No, I told myself I'd take care of it this time. Sorry, Carrie, but for some reason, I find it difficult to sit down and write something. I've no idea why."

I smiled at Marion, who was usually a very efficient person. "You're sitting right now, so this might be the perfect time to get it done. I'd love to have it by tomorrow."

"You're a tough taskmaster," she complained.

"Tomorrow," I repeated and stood.

I returned to my office and gave a start to find John Mathers sitting in my assistants' chair checking messages on his phone.

"I heard you were in the building," I said, sitting down to face him.

"It looks like the body was there for years, so I don't expect anyone working here to know much about it. Still, I'd be remiss if I didn't talk to the entire library staff."

"And talk to the people who own and work in the Sweet Shoppe on the other side."

"Of course I will, though the Sweet Shoppe changed hands three years ago, which was after the body was placed there."

"What do they know about it?" I asked.

"The forensic inspector thinks male. Age undetermined but probably middle-aged or even older."

"How long does he think it's been there?" I asked.

"His rough guess is between five and eight years." John laughed. "Why all the questions? Are you planning to look into the case?"

I pursed my lips. "Just natural curiosity. I want no part of this investigation."

"Music to my ears." John stretched out his long legs and took out his small notepad. "Have you ever been inside the building next door?"

"Yes. Twice. The first time was when we got word that the library board was considering buying the building. When it was deemed safe to walk around, we went inside with the architect to get a sense of the size of the place and how we could best make use of the space."

"Did you go downstairs to the basement?"

"Yes." My body tensed up as I remembered the basement. "It smelled dank and the lighting wasn't great, so I took a quick look around, then hurried back upstairs."

"Do you remember if anyone spent more time down in the basement than the others?"

I shook my head. "Why would they? It was creepy."

John cocked his head. "Creepy?" When I simply shrugged, he asked, "And the second visit?"

"That was almost two months ago. By then we had actual measurements of the interior space and the basic plan. Sally asked us to focus on what we wanted for our departments and to be as specific as possible regarding size, etcetera, for when we met with the architect. I wanted a stadium-seating auditorium and additional rooms for programs and classes. I went down to the basement with Marion for a quick look around—this time with a flashlight—but I never noticed a body."

"It had been tucked under a shelf in an out-of-the way corner," John said.

"Which means someone placed it there and didn't want it to be found too easily."

"Exactly."

"But he or she must have known that it would be discovered eventually," I said.

"And I'll take it from here." John shut his notebook and got to his feet.

"That's it for the questions?" I said.

"Unless you have something to offer on the subject."

"I don't."

He smiled. "Thank you for your time and cooperation, Ms. Singleton."

I smiled back at him. "Always, Lieutenant Mathers."

* * *

As soon as John closed the door, Evelyn materialized, an excited expression on her face. "It seems a body has been discovered in the basement of our future addition."

"Yes—probably male, middle-aged or older, ID unknown."

"I told you that building had a history of bad luck."

"So you did. According to forensics, the person died five to eight years ago. That's around the time—" I stopped, not sure of the proper way to refer to Evelyn's own demise.

She laughed. "No need to search for a sensitive way of describing my departure from this plane. The murder—if that's what it was—took place shortly before my death or soon after."

"So it seems. Do you remember news of anyone disappearing at the time?"

"Let me think." There was no sound as Evelyn drummed her fingers on my assistants' desk. Finally, she shook her head. "I don't think so."

"Was the building abandoned at the time?" I asked.

"As far as I can remember."

"So there would be no reason for a tourist or visitor to enter the building."

"Unless he or she was thinking of buying it," Evelyn pointed out.

"What about vagrants?"

Evelyn thought. "Since the Green is the pride of Clover Ridge, I'm quite sure that, though the building was abandoned, if a local resident noticed someone entering it, he or she wouldn't hesitate to call the police."

"When we inspected the building, we didn't see any evidence of squatters having lived there," I said. "Did you know the previous owners of the building?"

"The Whiteheads," Evelyn mused. "Everyone knew who they were since they were one of the richest families in the area." She pursed her lips. "And of course I saw them when they came into the library."

"You didn't much like them."

"They didn't make themselves likable. James acted like he was lord of the manor—giving out orders as though we were his servants." Evelyn giggled. "Some years ago he stopped by the reference desk and asked my niece Dorothy to gather books and print out information about an exotic island he and his wife were planning to visit. He said he'd be back in two hours. Dorothy got busy with other patrons and hadn't managed to do what James requested. When he returned to the library and discovered Dorothy was just starting to do what he'd asked, he shouted at her, saying what a lazy so-and-so she was and he was going to get her fired."

I laughed, remembering what a tough cookie Dorothy had been.

"Well, Dorothy never permitted anyone talk to her that way. She let James have it with both barrels. She began by calling him arrogant and rude, egotistical and entitled. She ended by mentioning a few of his crooked business deals."

"I suppose James Whitehead had no idea that Dorothy collected dirt about everyone in town."

Evelyn frowned at me. Even with Dorothy gone, Evelyn hated to hear a bad word spoken about her favorite niece. "She couldn't collect dirt about a person unless there was dirt to begin with."

"What did he do? Complain to Sally about Dorothy?"

"I have no idea. Dorothy never said. All we knew was that the man never set foot in the library again."

"What about his sister, Marcella, and their cousin Albert? What were they like?"

"Marcella was quiet. Plain looking. Reminded me of a sparrow. But that might be because she never bothered to fix her hair or put on lipstick. She always fell in line with whatever James decreed." Evelyn put a finger to her cheek as she thought. "Now she must be close to eighty-six."

"About nine years older than my uncle Bosco," I said.

"She loved reading romances. Reserved her favorite authors before the books came in. Often she was the first person to read a new book."

"And Albert?"

"Albert reminded me of a rat—pointy nose, receding chin, and those glittering eyes flicking from side to side, always looking for an angle, an in—and never to be trusted.

"He had the worst business sense. The only money he made was when James and Marcella invited him to take part in a few enterprises. From what I heard, James won over the other two by playing the heavy. Once in a while Albert and Marcella banded together and managed to work a deal their way, but that was rare."

"After James died, Albert and Marcella had no trouble selling the building they all owned," I said. "Why didn't they sell it sooner, when James was alive?"

"Probably because he was holding out for more money. James knew that even though the building was in bad shape, it had value because of its location. Both Marcella and Albert needed money, so they were quick to sell when James died. The way the will was set up, his third automatically went to them."

"Do they still live in Clover Ridge?"

"They're residents of the Clover Ridge Home for Seniors. Both Marcella and Albert have fallen on hard times, and neither is in the best of health. Marcella has a bad heart, and Albert suffers from a variety of conditions."

"I wonder if they know anything about the body that was hidden away in the building that they owned."

"Or be willing to fess up that a Whitehead murdered him," she mused.

"Evelyn!" I remonstrated. "You have no proof that any of them is guilty."

"Just saying aloud what I was thinking."

Chapter Five

The next two days proved to be uneventful, except for the constant racket coming from the demolition work in the building next door. The discovery of the body in the abandoned building was the topic of everyone's conversation. The dead man's identity continued to be a mystery, as Julie Theron reminded us several times on TV. Though, knowing John, I was certain he was making good use of NamUs—the National Missing and Unidentified Persons System—as well as every database available to the police and the FBI.

On Thursday, I left work at five and drove to my aunt and uncle's house on the far side of the Green, where I was having dinner for the second time that week.

"It's the least we can do—offer you a meal and a place to leave Smoky Joe on the nights you have a council meeting," Uncle Bosco had said when I'd told him I'd finally decided to fill in for Jeannette Rivers, who was moving out of state.

"Much appreciated," I'd told him, "but you don't need to feel guilty for urging me to join the council. It was my decision to take it on—at least until Jeannette's term is up next November."

"Nonsense! We did our best to convince you to join," Aunt Harriet said. "Besides, it's a great excuse to have you come for dinner twice a month."

I wasn't about to argue when tonight's menu was her salmon croquettes, stuffed baked potatoes, and a beet salad. When I stood to leave, Smoky Joe was too busy playing with his new toy mouse filled with catnip, a gift from Uncle Bosco, to notice.

"Bye, Smoky Joe. See you in two hours," I called to him.

He barely glanced my way. So much for feline loyalty.

I arrived at Town Hall a few minutes early and headed for the small room where the council met. The three male board members stood near the head of the table that took up most of the room and were engaged in an animated discussion. Mayor Alvin Tripp and Reggie Williams were firing questions at Sean Powell.

"What I don't get," Al was saying, "is how you and your crew missed seeing the body. I mean, you were supposed to examine every inch of that building to make sure it was sound."

Sean's hands shot up in self-defense. He was in his mid-seventies—slender and in good shape from a lifetime of construction work and playing tennis.

"Hey, as I explained to the police, the lighting's very poor in that basement. The rug or whatever the body was wrapped in blended in with the wall. And don't forget it was tucked under a shelf. Both Rafe Torres, the architect, and the engineer he hired missed seeing it as well."

"Come on, Sean. This was a human being we're talking about," Reggie said, flashing his beautiful teeth. He was a handsome black man in his fifties, an executive at a PR company, and the only man here wearing a sports jacket.

Sean shrugged. "Could be someone stashed it there after the inspection. The locks on the front and back doors aren't the greatest."

"However that body got there, it's bad publicity for our town," Al said. "We don't want to get the reputation of being the Cabot Cove of Connecticut."

"Let's not forget that a person died. There must be people somewhere who are missing him," I said.

They all gave a start when they saw me standing in the doorway. Al, ever gracious, waved me closer. "Hello, Carrie. Come and join us."

We exchanged greetings. The comment I was expecting came like clockwork.

"You're good friends with John Mathers," Al said. "Have the police discovered anything new about the—er, dead man?"

"Not that I'm aware. There wasn't any ID on the body, so I imagine they're waiting for DNA tests to come back as well as missing persons reports from around the country."

"He's not from around here," Sean said. "No one's reported a missing person."

"I wonder how long he's been dead," Reggie said. "Once they know that, they'll have a better idea of who went missing nationwide around that time."

"Hopefully, the forensic test results will provide some answers," I said.

"Sorry I'm late!" a female voice trilled as Babette Fisher traipsed into the room, her wispy blonde hair creating a halo around her face. Her big blue eyes and rosy cheeks added to her angelic appearance.

Though only from a distance. Babette liked to come across as a winsome ingénue—flighty and flirtatious—when she was closer to fifty than twenty. And though I'd only attended one council meeting before this one, I noticed she was always asking questions that showed she hadn't bothered to read whatever reports the various boards and groups had sent to the council members requiring our stamp of approval.

And she always arrived late.

Al called the meeting to order and handed out copies of the night's agenda. Babette opened her iPad and began taking minutes. Until I attended my first meeting two weeks ago, I had no idea of the many groups, departments, and boards that reported to the council. Among them were the board of education, the police department, the fire department, housing, building and land use, parks and social services, planning and zoning commission, the water board, the library, and various committees.

Roads, bridges, and the like were often under the jurisdiction of the county, state, or federal government. They required authorization for repairs and usually went begging for funds. Beneath it all, the steady influx of moneys and revenue supported and allowed for the smooth running of our town's day-to-day activities. The financial web was complicated, and I doubted that I'd ever completely understand it.

The good thing was that Al, Sean, and Reggie were familiar with the many components that made up Clover Ridge's infrastructure. All three men struck me as intelligent and seemed willing to view each proposal with fairness and give it its proper attention. Even Babette, when she dropped her act, was insightful. And being a high school art teacher, she was knowledgeable in the realm of education.

The meetings always began at seven sharp and ended between eight thirty and nine, never later. If there were topics we didn't get to that required discussion, they were tabled until the following meeting or, if they were urgent enough, discussed via emails and video chats.

Tonight there were a few matters that required no more than rubber stamping—allotting a certain amount of town money for the upcoming holiday decorations on the Green, demolishing an abandoned gas station, and giving the council's approval to the housing and zoning requests. I was surprised at how smoothly it all went.

Sean brought us up to date on the renovations of the library's new addition. Now that I was giving him my full attention, I noticed that he'd lost weight since I'd first met him during the summer. And why those pauses for deep breaths? When it came to mentioning the corpse discovered in the building's basement, Sean merely said the police were looking into it. No one made a comment.

I glanced down at tonight's agenda as Al said, "Well, that just about covers everything. Unless someone has something urgent to discuss, I'll bring the meeting to a close."

Reggie stood. "Since it's only twenty to nine, I'd like to introduce a subject—the Seabrook property."

Sean let out a groan. "Come on, Reg. It's getting late for this old contractor. Besides, the preserve's scheduled for our next meeting."

"I know that, Sean, but this is a major issue, and since we've got time now I'd like to open the discussion," Reggie said.

Al shrugged. He glanced at Babette and me. When we both nodded, he turned to Sean. "The majority has it."

"Okay." His arms crossed, Sean leaned back in his chair. He looked tired, but then his workday started early. His face had an ashen pallor, though—surprising for a man who spent a lot of time outdoors.

Al riffled through his briefcase and pulled out a folder. Without so much as glancing at it, he said, "The parcel of land known as the Seabrook Preserve, donated to the town of Clover Ridge fifty years ago, loses its sanctuary status in three months. These sixty-seven acres are located three-quarters of a mile south of the Green with twenty of its acres bordering the Long Island Sound. We are expected to make our recommendation regarding the future of the property by midnight, October twenty-first.

"The Parks Department would like to turn it into a family park that offers town residents swimming and boating, along with a picnic-barbecue area and a playground. The Seabrook Preserve conservatorship wants to keep it as is, and Building and Development have been contacted by a company that builds condominiums all over the east. Lighthouse Builders would like to buy the property and turn it into an upscale gated community."

"Just what we need," Sean mumbled, just loud enough for us to hear. "More housing for the uber rich."

Babette cackled. "Since when do you have a gripe against the wealthy? I seem to remember it was only six months ago that your company put up those four McMansions for over two mil each."

Sean shrugged. "I just think a park would be nice—for family outings. Or even keeping the preserve as it is."

"Financially speaking, a gated community on the Sound is a great idea," Reggie said. "The sale of the property alone will bring in plenty of moolah, along with the revenue via property taxes, which we could certainly use. The other two choices will cost us.

The park more so, but even the preserve is in need of an overhaul. The parking area's a mess, and the last few storms have knocked down trees, some of which have fallen across the walking trails. It's been years since the preserve has received the attention it needs."

"Personally, I like the park idea," Babette said. "It will cost money, of course, but I think it can end up being a money maker."

"Only if there's a big entrance fee," Reggie said.

"Residents already have the option to pay an annual park fee," Al reminded them. "That should cover any entrance fee."

"To cover costs, they would have to pay for certain activities," Reggie pointed out. "Like boating."

"After getting a free ride for fifty years, it's only right that the Parks Department pay to spruce up the preserve," Al said. "Repave the parking lot, remove the fallen trees, perhaps install a cafeteria and a gift shop. And perhaps charge nonresidents an entrance fee. Eventually the preserve could even bring in revenue."

"We could give it a facelift and see how it goes," Sean pointed out. "Then say in five years, maybe do something different with the property."

"Or we can keep part of the preserve and sell the remainder of the property to a building company and create a smaller condo community," Reggie added.

"Breaking up the preserve isn't an option," Al said. "Nor is doing something else with it further down the line. We have to decide by the deadline what's to be done with the property."

Since I didn't know anything at all about the Seabrook Preserve, I listened as Reggie, Sean, and Babette expressed their thoughts regarding the future of the property. Aside from presenting facts and clarifying misinformation, Al withheld his opinion.

"It's nine o'clock," he finally announced. "Let's stop now and pick this up at our next meeting."

I stood and gathered my iPad and pocketbook and slipped into my cardigan. We said good night to one another and Sean was the first out the door. Babette and Reggie followed more slowly, deep in conversation.

Al had taken his time gathering up his papers. I got the feeling he wanted to talk to me, and I wasn't wrong when he asked me what I made of our recent discussion regarding the Seabrook Preserve.

"I remember you, Reggie, and Sean talking about it in July, the day I met you all for brunch."

"Good memory!" Al said.

"And today Reggie brought it up earlier than scheduled."

He nodded.

"For some reason, Sean is against the condo project. Reggie thinks it could be a good thing for Clover Ridge because it would bring in revenue. And Babette prefers the park idea."

"You've been paying attention," Al said proudly.

I didn't appreciate being treated like a school girl. "But you didn't say much about how *you* think the property should be used," I pointed out.

"I didn't weigh in because we're too far apart. We have to present our decision as one we all agree upon—at least in the majority—no later than the deadline." He shuffled through his briefcase and pulled out a bundle of papers. "Here's the information about the property along with the proposal Lighthouse Builders have sent us. Read it and then tell me what you think."

I took the papers and stood. "I'll go through them, but first I'd like you to tell me what Sean, Reggie, and Babette have in the game."

Al grimaced at me the way John Mathers sometimes did—a look that expressed exasperation, defeat, and a grudging respect.

"All right. Take a seat. This may take a while."

I sat down again, as did Al, his brow furrowed as he gathered his thoughts.

"Sean is against the condo for personal reasons. We all know it but don't want to make too much noise about it in hopes that he'll come around. Not necessarily vote in favor of the building project, but consider it fairly as required of a member of the town council. Reggie, Babette, and I have worked with Sean long enough to know that he'll do the right thing for the benefit of Clover Ridge."

I raised my eyebrows but remained silent.

Al exhaled loudly. "Sean's son took a job with Lighthouse Builders. The company's owned by a man named Timothy Fisk, and it's been growing by leaps and bounds. Kevin Powell got a job with them a few years ago. It was Kevin who told Fisk the Seabrook Preserve was up for grabs and would make a great place to build a condo community. Fisk came and looked and decided he wanted to buy the property."

"I don't get it. Isn't Sean glad his son has a good job?"

"So you'd think, but that's not how the story goes. Sean and Kevin have butted heads for years, especially when Kevin was working at Powell Construction. Then a few years ago, he and his father got into a zinger of a fight. I have no idea what it was about—no one does—but my wife told me Pat was sick over it. She and their daughter-in-law had to pull the two men apart."

"That's too bad." I still didn't quite understand the problem. "I don't see Sean's construction company being large enough to buy the property and build a condo community."

"Of course it isn't. And wasting time and energy resenting Lighthouse Builders because they're a bigger company should be the last thing on Sean's agenda. Especially now."

"What do you mean, especially now?"

Al looked uncomfortable. "Well, he's getting older, isn't he? Turns seventy-eight in a few months."

Something told me that wasn't the whole story, but pushing for information wouldn't get me anywhere. "What about Babette and Reggie?"

Al leaned back in his chair. "Reggie's a go-getter and very savvy when it comes to sensing good business deals. If the condo deal were to be approved and went through, I wouldn't be surprised if he invested in the project.

"We've done some research into Lighthouse Builders. They use good architects and construct sound, attractive units. They get top ratings and have satisfied customers. Of course they'd have to put in their bid like any other company, but there's a good chance they'd get it."

"And Babette?"

Al bit his lower lip. "She seems to favor the park idea. Babette appears flighty, but when it comes down to making a final decision about something as important as this, she makes it her business to find out everything there is to know about the subject under discussion."

"I plan to do the same. I've started reading the reports and proposals you gave me at the last meeting."

"And I've just given you more." Al smiled. "You'll soon discover there's never a shortage of reports and proposals we have to read."

"And where do you stand regarding the Seabrook Preserve?"

"I'd rather not say at this point. I'm not being coy or secretive, but I'd like you to read up on the three options and form your own opinion. Our next meeting is open to the public so they can hear proposals of all three plans and share their thoughts with us." He gave a little laugh. "I imagine their preferences will be as varied as the ones aired earlier.

"The final decision regarding the Seabrook Preserve rests with the council. We're in for a hot and heavy debate regarding the future of the property. When three of us are agreement, then we can go full steam ahead with the project of our choice."

"And if we can't get a majority to agree?" I asked.

"We're in big trouble."

Chapter Six

I picked up Smoky Joe at my aunt and uncle's and drove home slowly, wondering why the future of the Seabrook property was such a major issue. It had been a preserve for fifty years. At the rate land all around us was being built on, I saw the benefits of keeping it in its natural state for another fifty years. A park would be nice, though Clover Ridge didn't lack for parks. And there were already plenty of upscale gated communities in the area.

The financial side of things was another story. New upscale housing would bring in plenty of money, but more residents meant a possible strain on utilities and services like the school system and the fire department. I shook my head. There was a lot to consider. I had to read all the various proposals and review our current projects before I could begin to form an opinion. And I intended to talk to people in the know.

* * *

The next day was Friday, and I had no time to think about the Seabrook Preserve or the body—identity still unknown—that had been discovered in the basement next door. Like everyone else on staff, I was involved in preparations for the Fall Festival the following day. This was only the second year the festival was being held. There would be several food trucks and activities for children, including a pony ride, as well as booths selling local crafts and farm produce. The Friends of the Library were holding a used book sale. While the library would remain open, both my assistants and I planned to spend the day at the festival helping to make sure that everything ran smoothly.

I was glad this year we'd been given permission to hold the festival on the Green. Last year it was held in the parking lot. Even with a fraction of the activities going on then, the setting had been much too crowded. The weather forecast for today was a perfect sunny September day in the mid-seventies. And I was grateful that no noise would be coming from our new addition as the workers were off on the weekend.

The vendors and rides began arriving Friday afternoon, quickly occupying a large section of the Green across from the library. Sally had given all of us diagrams of where everything was to go, and either she, Marion, Harvey, Fran Kessler, or I were expected to be out there directing everyone to their appointed location while our two custodians set up booths and tables and signs. At five o'clock we all went outside to help out and by nine that evening managed to have everything in place.

Saturday morning I put on jeans and a T-shirt, slathered my face and arms in sunscreen, and made a mental note to bring along a hat when I left the cottage. After breakfast, Smoky Joe rushed to the door, expecting me to carry him out to the car in his carrier.

"Sorry, boy, today you stay home." I left an extra supply of treats in his dish. Dylan had errands to run that day, but he'd promised to stop in and feed Smoky Joe and play with him. The day would be hectic, and I was looking forward to our dinner out that evening with Angela and Steve.

At the time of last year's Fall Festival, I'd been working in the library at a low-level position, doing little more than re-shelving books and helping out wherever I was needed. This year would be very different. Now I had a library position that I loved and I was an active member of the community.

People started arriving at ten when the festival opened, and by eleven our section of the Green was crowded and in full swing. I walked around, asking vendors and craftspeople if they needed anything, and was pleased that everything seemed to be running smoothly. Library patrons stopped to talk. Many asked questions about the construction; even more asked about the body, and a few wanted to know how I liked being on the town council.

I had just finished chatting with Uncle Bosco, who was a member of the library board, when I spotted my cousin-in-law Julia waving at me. I waved back and grinned as her young daughter came running toward me. Five-year-old Tacey was the only other person I knew who could communicate with Evelyn. I swept her up in my arms and swung her around.

"Wow, you're getting heavy," I said as I set her down.

"That's 'cause I'm getting bigger, Cousin Carrie. I'm in kindergarten now."

"I know that. You must be learning a lot."

"We're studying money," she said proudly. "Daddy gave me a quarter and a nickel and dime and a penny to bring to school. And he said I could keep it."

Just then Tacey's eight-year-old brother and their father, my cousin Randy, joined us. Mark paused midstream while listing the reasons why he should be allowed to go around the festival with his friends, just long enough to give me a hug.

Randy grinned at me. "Be nice to Cousin Carrie because she's now an important and powerful member of the town council." He winked. "We need her approval if we want to build that treehouse you guys want."

I rolled my eyes. "There are restrictions and regulations regarding treehouses that have nothing to do with me. The roof can't be higher than thirteen feet, and no part of the treehouse can be within ten feet of your property line."

Randy roared with laugher, then grabbed me in a bear hug. I hugged him back, knowing his teasing was good-hearted, something I'd learned since we were kids.

"Dad!" Mark said. "Can I go?"

Julia and Randy exchanged glances. Then Randy said, "All right, but I'll be a few feet behind you."

Julia and I watched father and son take off.

"So how does it feel to be an engaged woman?" she asked.

I shrugged, suddenly self-conscious. "I don't know. The same. We haven't made any plans."

Julie looked concerned. "I didn't mean to put you on the spot. I only wanted to say how happy Randy and I are that you're going to marry Dylan."

"Thanks. It's just that with me suddenly on the council and Dylan setting up his new office, we're not rushing into making wedding plans."

"Of course. I hope you haven't forgotten that Randy and I want to give you guys an engagement party. You'll let me know when you're ready."

"Absolutely. That's so kind of you both," I said, meaning it.

"Well, Randy's very fond of his kid cousin, and I feel like we've known each other forever."

An entertainer on stilts walked by. Tacey giggled. "Look, Mommy. Isn't he funny?"

"Let's meet for lunch," I said. "I'll call you next week and we'll set up a date."

Julia beamed. "I'd like that very much."

* * *

Dylan stopped by at lunchtime. We bought salads and spanako-pitas at the Greek food truck and found a half-empty table in the eating area, which we shared with a couple and their small children. They'd no sooner left when Babette slid onto the bench next to me. A slender, bearded man who appeared to be about five years younger than me hovered behind her. He carried a paper plate filled with food in each hand.

"Is it all right if we join you?" he asked.

"Just sit down, Graham," Babette ordered. "This is a festival, not a formal dinner. Carrie and I are old friends."

Old friends? "Of course. Join us," I said, feeling sorry for the guy whose ears were now flaming red with embarrassment. "I'm Carrie Singleton and this is my fiancé, Dylan Avery."

"Thank you," he mumbled as he sat down next to Dylan and placed one plate in front of Babette.

Babette thrust out her hand to Dylan. "Nice to meet you, Dylan. I'm Babette Fisher, artist and art teacher, and this is Graham Tolliver, who's with the prestigious architectural Waterford Group."

Artist. Prestigious architectural group, I thought as we all smiled and exchanged greetings.

Dylan stood. "Excuse me, but I need to get some coffee. Carrie, would you like something to drink?"

"Lemonade, it they have it. If not, anything cold."

"Sure. Be right back."

"Handsome, isn't he?" Babette commented as she watched Dylan stride toward the food trucks.

And what is Babette doing with someone twenty-five tops, young enough to be her son? I turned to Graham. "So you're an architect. Were you one of Babette's art students when you were in high school?"

That brought on gales of laughter from Babette and more blushing from Graham.

"I'm older than I look," he said, "and you can call me a designer, as I don't have my architectural license quite yet."

"Sorry. What kind of buildings do you design?" I asked quickly.

"The Waterford Group specializes in landscapes and parks—mostly any outdoor structure other than buildings and bridges."

"How interesting," I said. "Kind of like the park the town is considering—if that's what we decide to do with the Seabrook Preserve."

"Exactly!" Graham's eyes lit up. "Such a gorgeous piece of property right on the Long Island Sound! The perfect site for a park that includes a beach and a boat basin."

"So you've seen it."

"Of course. I'm on the committee that's been working on the project to create the most fantastic park. I have the honor of presenting it at the town council's next meeting."

"I had no idea." I turned to Babette. "But I suppose this isn't news to you."

"Graham's so enthusiastic about the project," she said before taking a bite of her sandwich.

"Have you seen the plans Graham's company drew up?" I asked.

"Just a few early sketches," Babette said between bites. "They're awesome."

"Really? Has anyone else on the council seen them?"

She glanced away. "Maybe not yet."

I stared at Babette until she met my gaze. "Care to explain?"

She shrugged. "It's no biggie. I figured if that group Kevin Powell works for could draw up a proposal to build condos on the preserve property, I'd find the best landscape architects to design a park. Graham's company liked the idea. And that's where things stand."

So that's how the presenting groups got chosen! Someone knew someone and they got on the roster. Something Al failed to explain. I looked at Graham, who was out of architectural school two-three years max, and back again at Babette. "I still can't figure how Graham comes into it?"

She blinked her eyes, trying for a look of innocence. "When I contacted the company, they sent Graham to look over the property."

"I was the one who gave them the news that the preserve was now open to other uses, one of them being a large park," Graham said.

"Oh!" I pretended not to have an inkling of what was coming next. "And you happened to know that because?"

Graham grinned, clearly proud of himself. "Easy. Babette told me 'cause she's my cousin."

* * *

48

Babette and her young cousin finished their meal in silence, then murmured goodbyes as they scooted off.

Dylan shot me an inquiring glance as he watched them go. "What was that all about? The air was as thick as pea soup when I returned."

"Babette wants the Seabrook property to be turned into a park. She contacted her cousin, who works for a big architectural firm that designs landscapes and parks. He's not even an architect, but they probably let him join the committee to draw up plans for the park because he brought in the possible commission."

"Is that bad?" Dylan asked. "Sounds logical to me."

"Sounds sneaky to me when a council member tells a relative about a possible project so the firm he works for gets a jump on other companies. Not that the companies doing the presentations are guaranteed to get the job. There's the whole bidding business to deal with. Still, it seems to me that the architectural firm that does the initial presentation has a leg up."

Dylan laughed. "You'll find out soon enough that everyone on the council has an agenda and will try to push something through involving a personal connection."

"Or try to block it. Sean Powell is against Lighthouse Builders building condos on the property because his son now works for them."

"The politics of small towns," Dylan said, shaking his head. "They can be more cutthroat than the shenanigans on the national scene."

I drew back in a huff. "I would never take advantage of my position on the board for a pet project."

"Really? Let's see how you vote when it comes to an issue that doesn't favor the library."

"Well, of course I'd vote for what's in the library's best interest."

"As I'd expect. And I suspect everyone on the board has a favorite service or utility, be it the hospital, the fire department, or building new condos."

I nodded. I was beginning to understand the dynamics of the group of which I was now a member, and my concerns about joining the council came flooding back. I might care more about the library than other town institutions, but it wasn't for personal reasons. Like voting for a town project for the sake of a relative's career. Or not voting for one because my son worked for the competition.

I was beginning to think I had made a mistake when I'd said yes to Al Tripp. I wasn't politically motivated or out for personal gain. The Seabrook property was clearly going to be a source of conflict, and I didn't want any part of that.

* * *

After Dylan left, I went into the library to freshen up in the bathroom and to check on the few ongoing programs. Trish had already started the afternoon movie. In the reading room I ran into Max, our senior custodian. He was taking a break from making sure the festival's refuse pails were emptied before they overflowed with garbage and that the grounds of the Green remained clear of debris.

"Big crowd," he commented. "Good thing Sally approved hiring three men to help out today. Too big a job for just Pete and me."

"And the festival's even busier now than it was this morning."

Max gestured with his chin toward the building that was to be our new addition. "Frankly, I was surprised Sally went ahead with the festival, given the mess that place is in." He lowered his voice. "And then finding a body."

"She considered canceling it this year, but so many patrons said they were looking forward to it, she didn't want to disappoint them, especially since the council said we could hold it on the Green."

"Good thing too, since it's at least twice the size of last year's festival. I hope they continue to let us hold it on the Green from now on," Max said. "There's no way our parking lot could handle it, even after it's extended to include the parking area of the new addition."

I agreed with Max and headed outside. I was about to cross the street and return to the festival when someone rammed into me with such force, I stumbled to the ground.

"Oh my God, I'm so sorry!"

I looked up at Buzz Coleman, the burly construction foreman, an expression of distress on his face. He reached out a hand to help me up. "Are you okay?"

"I think so," I said, brushing off the knees of my jeans.

"You're one of the librarians, aren't you?" he said.

"Yes. Carrie Singleton."

"I'm so sorry, Carrie. Buzz Coleman. I should have been looking where I was going." He shook his head. "I was just so . . ."

My curiosity was aroused. "So what?" I asked.

"Nothing. It's stupid." Buzz blinked and started walking away.

"Were you at the work site just now?" I asked.

"I was." He turned slowly. "I went in to check on something. It was the weirdest thing."

"What?" I urged.

"No one was in the building. I know because I locked the door behind me. When I went into a room at the back of the house—right above where we found that body in the basement—I got this feeling I wasn't alone. No one was there, but I swear something passed right by me, chilling me to the bones."

Like a ghost, I thought.

I wondered if I'd spoken aloud, because Buzz chortled. "There ain't such things as ghosts. It must have been a draft coming from a broken window. I'll check every window first thing Monday morning. Sorry again, Carrie, for running into you like that."

Chapter Seven

The rest of the weekend couldn't have been more perfect. What made it so special was that Dylan started to include childhood anecdotes in our conversations, something he rarely did before I'd opened up the discussion about his parents. It validated my belief that I'd been right to raise questions about this difficult subject. Now Dylan was willing to share some painful memories. I hoped that talking about them washed some of the hurt away.

Saturday night, we met Angela and Steve at a local restaurant for hamburgers and beer. We spent Sunday morning working out at the gym, then went apple picking at a nearby farm in the afternoon. We ended up with a large amount of eating apples for us and a bagful of cooking apples for Aunt Harriet, who loved to bake. When we stopped by to drop them off, she and Uncle Bosco insisted that we stay for dinner, which we did.

I let out a contented sigh as we headed home to the cottage. "Today was lovely. It felt like a mini vacation."

Dylan patted my leg. "I agree. A good break from work. I'm slammed the next few days."

"And I have that noisy racket to look forward to."

"I wonder if John's made any headway ID'ing the dead man," he mused. "Given the condition of the body, they only have his teeth to work with, and that's only a help if they can track down his dentist for X-rays and records."

"They can use it to match DNA, can't they?" I asked.

"Sure. But only to the DNA of people already in the system. Lots of people aren't."

"I'm still puzzling over Buzz Coleman's state of mind when he ran into me on Saturday," I said. "He's a big, brawny guy. Not the type to be easily frightened."

Dylan glanced at me. "You think he saw a ghost, don't you?"

I nodded, knowing he wasn't being snarky. I'd told Dylan about my relationship with Evelyn a few months ago. I had to because he often wondered where I'd gotten various bits of information, and I didn't want to lie. More importantly, Dylan had become my significant other and I didn't want to keep such a large secret from him. Of course I shouldn't have told him when he was driving because he almost ran us off the road. But he'd eventually settled down and accepted Evelyn's presence in the library and in my life.

"I think he may have sensed the presence of a ghost. I don't really know that much about ghosts, and Evelyn's no help when it comes to the subject—why they remain on this plane, who can see them."

"Maybe it's the ghost of the dead man they found the other day," Dylan said.

"Or the ghost of someone who lived in that building sometime in the past. Evelyn told me the place was cursed."

"James Whitehead, the most contentious of the three former owners, died recently. Maybe he's haunting the place."

"Could be." I bit my lip as I thought. "Or maybe Evelyn paid a visit to the building next door and Buzz happens to be sensitive to ghosts."

"Good idea. Ask her," Dylan said as he turned onto the private Avery road.

"I will," I said. "Though she may very well avoid answering."

* * *

I drove to work Monday morning, hoping that Evelyn would show up as soon as I arrived at the library. She knew my assistants' schedules and stopped by when they weren't in the building or were on duty at the hospitality desk. She usually knew when was a good time to find me—in or out of my office—and sensed when I needed to talk to her, but not today.

Sally had called a meeting at ten o'clock to discuss the Fall Festival. We had cleared a nice sum of money, all of which was going toward expenses for our new addition, and everyone agreed it had been a huge success. I did some paperwork in my office, then went to talk to Norman Tobin, the reference librarian, about a problem I'd been having with my laptop.

I was about to head back to my office when I ran into Rafael Torres exiting the Historical Room where we housed books, newspapers, and all memorabilia related to Clover Ridge's history. Rafe was the architect who had designed the interior of the library's new addition. He was a handsome man in his mid-forties. He was of medium height, in good physical shape, and always dressed well. Right now he had a broad grin on his face.

"You look like you've had a fun time doing research," I said.

"You could say that! I unearthed a pile of old magazines featuring houses built in the seventeenth and eighteenth centuries with some wonderful photos."

"That's great," I said. Rafe was writing an article about old houses in Clover Ridge for an architectural magazine. "As you know, the Historical Room will have larger quarters in the new addition. I promised Norman I'd help him categorize everything properly as soon as the renovations are finished, so you'll have an easier time finding what you need."

"That will be helpful since I'm thinking the article might eventually turn into a book. There are so many wonderful old houses in this area."

"That sounds exciting," I said. "I've never considered writing a book."

As Rafe started to move on, I asked, "How is the construction going?"

"Fine. I just stopped by. Just the few minor snags you'll find on any job. The work is progressing pretty close to schedule."

Minor snags? Rafe's grim expression made me ask, "Is there a problem?"

"You mean besides a dead body turning up the first day of work?"

"It must have been well hidden," I said, "since neither you nor the engineer saw it when you examined the building."

Rafe's ears reddened. "Buzz is still razzing me for missing it. Have the police found out any more about the victim?"

"Not that I know of," I said. Geez! Did everyone in town know I was pals with John Mathers and had helped solve a few homicides?

Rafe shrugged. "Well, I suppose we'll hear soon enough. With all the sophisticated computer programs the police have, they're sure to identify him before long."

"And hopefully find out why he was murdered," I added.

* * *

It wasn't until four that afternoon that Evelyn made her appearance. As usual, she perched on the corner of my assistants' desk. She was eager to hear how the Fall Festival had gone.

"Sally called us in for a brief meeting this morning to tell us it was a huge success. Most of the proceeds will go toward furniture and equipment for the new addition."

"I'm glad to hear it." Evelyn adjusted the gray cardigan that draped from her shoulders. "And how is the new addition coming along?"

"They've pretty much finished ripping out all of the interior walls and most of the flooring. I ran into the architect earlier. Rafe said they're close to schedule, despite coming across that corpse in the basement."

Evelyn shivered. "How unpleasant that must have been. Has John Mathers been able to find out who the poor soul is?"

"Not yet," I said, "which leads me to think that he probably didn't come from around here. Certainly not Clover Ridge."

"I wonder if John talked to Marcella and Albert Whitehead," Evelyn mused. "They were the last owners."

"I have no idea, though I imagine he would have. You know John doesn't fill me in on his cases, especially when I have nothing to do with them."

Evelyn shot me a look of disbelief. "Carrie, it's unlike you to take such little interest in solving a mystery right on your doorstep, so to speak."

That wasn't quite true, but I chose not to correct her. When I made no response, she went on, "Of course, if anyone had dealings with the dead man, it would have been James Whitehead, since he handled the property."

"And he's dead," I said, which reminded me. "Evelyn?"

"Yes, dear?"

"Did you, by any chance, happen to stop by the building next door to see how the work was coming along?"

"I don't believe I ever entered that building—in my previous incarnation or more recently."

"Oh."

My disappointment must have showed. "That was a strange question, Carrie. What made you ask it?"

"Saturday afternoon, I was walking back to the festival from the library when Buzz Coleman, the foreman, came barreling into me and knocked me down."

"Oh, dear!"

I waved my hand. "I was fine. Really. But the thing is, Buzz was badly shaken. Which was why he wasn't looking where he was going. He'd gone into the building for something—I forget what. Anyway, he suddenly got the sensation someone was there, and a waft of cold air swept past him."

Evelyn released a loud peal of laughter.

"Shhh," I cautioned, afraid someone would hear her.

She waved away my concern. "You know that you and darling little Tacey are the only people who can see me or hear me."

I stared at her. "Then it was another ghost that frightened Buzz?"

"I really couldn't say," Evelyn said. "But I haven't seen any lurking around."

She stretched out her hand as if to pat my shoulder, then thought better of it. "Carrie, the place next door has been neglected for years. And with the men working away on the walls, they could very well have broken through to the outside. For all we know, what Buzz felt was a draft coming through a break in the wood or a shattered window."

"I never thought of that," I said, "though Buzz thought that was a possibility."

"Of course you didn't," Evelyn said, sounding a bit testy. "You always go for the dramatic."

After she left, I decided that Evelyn was right. Not that I went for the dramatic, as she put it, but that there could be another explanation for Buzz's reaction on Saturday. He might have mistaken the sensation of a breeze for a ghost. Sure, he was a big tough guy. But who was to say he didn't have some fears left over from childhood or a bad experience?

I wondered, too, if perhaps I was secretly hoping to discover that a ghost was haunting the new addition. Because if that was the case, I was the perfect person to deal with the situation. After all, I was the only adult who had contact with Evelyn, the library's resident ghost.

Or was I simply looking for a new mystery to solve? While I was curious about the body the workers had found in the house next door—whom I secretly called Mr. Bones—I had no personal reason to get involved in this particular homicide, or a reason to find out who the poor man was that had ended up dead and hidden away for years.

* * *

Tuesday was a late day for me. In the morning, I ran a few errands in Merrivale, the town just west of us, ate a quick lunch at home, then Smoky Joe and I set out for the library.

As soon as I stepped inside and released him from his carrier, I knew something was wrong. A number of staff members and patrons had gathered near the reference and computer areas, but I had no idea what the problem was.

Suddenly the crowd turned around and began walking toward me. I caught sight of Angela and rushed over to her.

"What on earth happened?" I asked.

Angela shook her head. "The workers broke through the common wall. They made such a commotion we ran over thinking they'd brought the whole building down."

"Oh, no! Another problem," I said.

"You're not kidding. The opening set off an avalanche of debris. You should see the computer room. There's rubble and pieces of the wall all over the floor."

"Were any of the computers damaged?" I asked.

"I don't think so, but Harvey was ranting like a maniac," Angela said. "He took the mess as a personal affront."

We both burst out laughing. Harvey Kirk was not a favorite of ours.

"It's not funny," I said, but I averted my eyes for fear of laughing again.

"Good thing Sean happened to be on site. He told Buzz to have the men clear up the mess, then put up one of those blue tarps to cover the opening until they could repair the wall. And he told us to keep out of the area so we won't breathe in the debris."

"Aren't they building an archway to connect the two buildings?" I asked.

"They are, but not in the computer room."

I went to my office and started checking my emails. Trish joined me a few minutes later.

"I suppose you've heard what happened," she said.

"Yes. The workers broke through the common wall. An accident, I suppose, since they're tearing down all the interior walls."

"I wonder," Trish said.

I glanced up, noting her serious expression. "Why do you say that?"

"My dad thinks we never should have bought that building. He insists it's cursed."

"Really?" Trish's father, Roy Peters, knew most of the older people in town and had helped me in a few of my investigations.

Trish shook her head. "I told Dad not to be silly, but he said families that lived there had unhappy lives. Businesses failed. Even worse, there were a few tragedies. And he didn't much like James Whitehead, the last person that owned the property."

"Well, so did his sister and their cousin."

"They did, but it was known all over town that Marcella and Albert kowtowed to James and went along with whatever he said. Dad said he was a bully and always pulling all sorts of shady deals."

"I heard he was a bully," I said, "but what kind of shady deals?"

"Mortgage fraud, for one thing," Trish said. "Insider trading for another. If James was involved you could be sure it was bad business."

* * *

I checked on the programs in progress, then settled down to do some paperwork. It wasn't easy because now the noise coming from the new addition was louder than ever. And I'd started musing about James Whitehead. Not a very nice guy, according to everyone who mentioned him. When I had some free time, I planned to see what I could find out about him in old newspaper articles and town records.

Had he lured Mr. Bones into the house for some reason and murdered him? I supposed we'd never find out since James Whitehead was dead. Many homicides were never solved for a variety of reasons.

Trish left for the day and Evelyn appeared.

"The workers accidentally broke through the adjoining wall," I told her. "The noise is deafening."

"I noticed the blue tarp," Evelyn said. "These things happen."

"You don't think it's because the building is cursed?" I asked.

Evelyn thought a moment. "Difficult to say. The library is for the benefit of our community and emits positive vibrations strong enough, I'd imagine, to defeat a centuries-old curse."

"Glad to hear it," I said.

"Any news on the identity of the remains?" she asked.

"Not as far as I know."

Evelyn tsk-tsked. "So sad to think someone disappeared and no one seems to miss him."

"I agree."

"And what are your thoughts regarding the future of the Seabrook Preserve?"

"I've been reading up on it, and the truth is I can see the property being used for any of the three purposes: a nature preserve, a park, or a condo community. I'm looking forward to hearing the various proposals at the next meeting."

Evelyn cocked her head. "Have you ever been to the preserve?"

"No."

She smiled. "I think you might consider spending an afternoon there. Perhaps then you'll have a sense of how the property would best be used."

"I'll do that," I said. "It bothers me that Babette is in favor of a park so her cousin can design it, and Sean is against the condo idea because the company his son works for has a good chance of winning the contract."

"People often vote on a project for personal reasons."

"Not me," I said.

"Glad to hear it."

As soon as Evelyn disappeared, I decided to see how Sally was faring after this latest mishap. I'd no sooner stepped out of my office when a strong breeze tousled my hair. A man in his mid-fifties came stumbling toward me. He wore a tan blazer, beneath which his striped shirt hung outside his pants. His clothes were wrinkled and soiled. What's more, one of his shoes was missing.

I approached him cautiously, not certain what I was about to say or do. If he was drunk, I needed to find Max. If he was ill . . .

"Can I help you?" I asked when I was a few feet from him.

He kept on walking. I stepped aside, afraid he would run into me, and was grateful when he suddenly halted. Closer, I noticed his eyes darting from side to side.

The air current had grown strong enough to turn the pages of a book propped open on a shelf.

Is he causing this?

"Where am I?" he asked.

"In the Clover Ridge Library," I said, doing my best to remain calm.

"How did I get here?"

"I have no idea. I suppose through one of the doors."

As he moved past me I felt a chill. It was the kind of sensation I felt when Evelyn came too close to me. No! He couldn't be . . .

I covered my mouth to keep from shouting "Stop!" as he wandered into the reading room, bumping into chairs and brushing by people. A magazine fell to the ground. Then another. Patrons stared after him as he passed, expressions of puzzlement or fear on their faces. I realized that they couldn't see him, but they felt the air current he was causing, sensed an eerie presence that disturbed their peace of mind.

So this was the ghost that Buzz Coleman had encountered! I had to stop him from wreaking havoc in the library. I also wanted to help him, but I hadn't the slightest idea what to do.

Panic was building inside me as the apparition only I could see bumbled toward the circulation desk where several people stood waiting to have their books, movies, and tapes checked out. It was impossible to grab hold of him and lead him away. And calling to him would make people think I'd lost it. From the way patrons touched their ruffled hair and stared at papers fluttering to the ground, I knew they were wondering what on earth was happening.

What to do! What to do!

Suddenly Evelyn appeared. I'd never been so happy to see her! I watched as she took hold of the ghost's arm and, a finger to her lips, urged him to turn around and walk toward me.

"Carrie, is your office empty?" she whispered when they came closer.

I nodded.

"Let's go there now and figure out what to do with Charlie over here."

"His name is Charlie?" I asked.

She rolled her eyes. "It is for the time being."

Chapter Eight

"**I** still can't figure out how I ended up in your library," Charlie said for the eighth time. Or was it the twelfth? I had no idea, since that was how he responded to every question Evelyn and I asked him, even after we'd explained repeatedly that we were assuming he belonged to the body recently discovered next door, and that he'd entered the library through the break in the wall.

He was either dazed at having found himself in unfamiliar surroundings or had suffered some form of amnesia. Which was a big disappointment. I'd expected Charlie to tell us who he was and how he'd ended up in the building next door. And while I appreciated the way Evelyn had managed to convince our visitor to accompany us to my office, she wasn't any more successful than me. Didn't all ghosts function on the same level? Observe the same protocol? Clearly this wasn't the case, judging from her lack of results.

"Charlie," I began. "Can we call you Charlie until we find out your real name?"

He nodded. "Okay. I guess. Why not?"

I exhaled loudly. He seemed calmer. Still very confused but definitely calmer. And the gusts of wind had died down.

"Okay. Our library bought the building next door so we could expand. The building has been abandoned for years. Last week a body wrapped in a blanket was discovered in the basement. They think it's been there at least five, maybe eight years. Recently, one of the workers broke through the adjoining wall. We think that's how you came to wander into the library."

Charlie nodded as he thought this over. "And you think that body is—was me?"

"It could be. Do you remember entering that building?"

"No."

"What do you remember?" Evelyn asked.

Charlie stared at her. "You're like me, aren't you?"

Evelyn, who had been perched on the corner of my assistants' desk, came to stand in front of him and drew back her shoulders. "If you mean that your body and mine have both left this corporal plane, the answer is yes. Other than that, we are worlds apart."

"Sorry," Charlie said quickly.

"No need to apologize," Evelyn said, her tone warming. "Carrie and I want to help you get where you belong."

"Much appreciated," Charlie said. "As to your question, I wish I had a good answer for you. My mind is fuzzy when I try to remember my life. My history. I get flashes of places I recognize, people I knew, but nothing more." He sighed. "I can't even tell you my name."

"That's all right," I said quickly. "Just tell us what you can remember."

"Being in that place next door," Charlie said. "I remember lurking in that dark, dismal building. Hearing the workers making a racket as they set about breaking up the place." He laughed. "And I must have scared that big guy a while ago when he came in on his own. I didn't mean to, but I was moving around trying to figure out how to get out. He sure took off in a hurry."

"That was Buzz, the foreman," I said. "He couldn't see you but he sure sensed your presence and the stir you caused around you."

"I didn't mean to scare him," Charlie said. He cocked his head and stared at me. "Why aren't you afraid of me?"

I laughed. "Because Evelyn's a ghost, and she's a good friend of mine."

"Isn't Susan due to come in soon?" Evelyn asked.

I nodded

"Then I think we'd better concentrate on finding a place for Charlie to stay while we figure out—several things," Evelyn said.

"What about the attic?" I suggested. "It's kind of a mess, I'm afraid, but it's the only safe place I can think of. No one ever goes up there." I smiled at Charlie. "If you wander around the library, you'll frighten the patrons."

Charlie looked at Evelyn. "Can't I stay with you?"

"I'm afraid not. But you'll be safe upstairs in the attic. I spent many wonderful hours up there before it became the storage space for discarded furniture. I'll accompany you there if you like."

I watched them disappear, thinking that this was one of the strangest experiences of my life.

* * *

I waited until we'd finished dinner and were enjoying bowlfuls of pistachio ice cream to tell Dylan about Charlie showing up at the library. So far, he was the only person I could talk to about seeing ghosts. I kept meaning to tell Angela about Evelyn but never found the right time or place.

"How weird is that," he said shaking his head as he pictured the scene.

"I was so happy when Evelyn came along and convinced him to go with us to my office. Though neither of us could get him to tell us how he ended up in that basement. Poor Charlie was so out of it. He has no idea why he came to Clover Ridge. He can't remember anything about his life."

"His name is Charlie?"

I laughed. "That's what Evelyn named him for the time being, until we find out his real name."

"And you think he's the ghost of the body they discovered in the basement last week?" Dylan asked.

"It's the only thing that makes sense. And he remembers being there."

Dylan pursed his lips as he thought. "So you stashed him up in the attic for now. Do you think he'll stay there?"

"I hope so," I said. "Patrons can't see him, but he practically blows up a storm as he wanders through the library. Not like Evelyn, who manages to dart about without anyone noticing her. Except for little Tacey, if she happens to be in the building."

"That's probably because Evelyn spent years working in the library. This poor guy ended up dead in an abandoned building. Who knows where he's from."

"I hope John finds that out real soon," I said.

"So do I, babe," Dylan said, eating a spoonful of his melting ice cream. "So do I."

* * *

I arrived at the library Wednesday morning, wondering what to do about Charlie. It wasn't like I could hide him in the attic indefinitely. But neither could I have him wandering around the library, stirring the air and unnerving the patrons. I had to keep him far away from Smoky Joe. I'd seen him hiss and meow in Evelyn's company and could only imagine the scene he would make if he encountered Charlie.

I found Evelyn and Charlie waiting for me in my office. Charlie looked as if he'd had a good night's sleep, if ghosts ever slept. The important thing was he was calmer. Calmer but still totally ignorant of who he was and how he ended up dead in the building next door.

"Is there anything you remember?" I asked.

He thought a minute, then shook his head.

"Anyone you remember talking to?"

Charlie cocked his head to one side, then the other. Finally, he said, "Kind of."

"What does 'kind of' mean, exactly?" Evelyn said.

I frowned at my ghostly friend. Sometimes Evelyn could be a tad impatient, though she had been kind enough to spend hours with Charlie.

Charlie glanced at her apologetically. "I'm sorry, Evelyn. All night I tried to remember something, anything, but it's like a fog is blanketing my memory." He turned to me. "I remember talking to two men, but whether it was in that place next door or somewhere else . . ." He turned up his palms. "I can't say."

"Two men," I mused. I thought immediately of James and Albert Whitehead. "Would you recognize their names if I mentioned a few?"

He shook his head. "I doubt it."

"Do you know what you talked about?"

"Money."

Evelyn laughed. "Well, that came quick enough."

I felt a sense of accomplishment until I caught the pained expression on Charlie's face.

"Sorry for pressuring you for answers, Charlie," I said.

"I'm trying my best to remember, but it's no use. Can I stay here with you, Carrie?" he asked.

"I wish you could, but I have two assistants who work with me part of every weekday." I looked at Evelyn. "Can't you take him with you when you leave here and go—wherever you go?"

"That's impossible," Evelyn said.

Charlie hunched up his shoulders and looked extremely unhappy. "I'm not going back to that awful place on the other side of the wall."

"We'll think of something," I said.

In the end, I realized there were no movies or programs planned for the large meeting room. He could stay there all day and keep his distance if anyone happened to enter the room. Or he could go back up to the attic, if he liked.

Evelyn offered to keep him company for a while. As they disappeared and went silently down to the meeting room, I wondered why they couldn't simply go outside. But somehow I felt that wasn't an option, since Evelyn would have suggested it otherwise.

* * *

At twelve noon, Angela and I set out on the three-block walk to the Cozy Corner Café for lunch. She was repeating a funny story that a patron had told her when she stopped walking. I continued a few steps until I realized she wasn't at my side.

"What's wrong?" I asked.

"My question exactly," Angela said.

"What do you mean?"

"You haven't heard a word I said," she complained. We continued walking.

"Sorry, I've been thinking about something," I said, which was true. I was thinking about Charlie and wondering how to help him.

"Care to tell me what you've been thinking about?" Angela asked.

"Well . . ." I began. How to explain Charlie? Evelyn?

"Have you started investigating another murder, maybe the body they discovered in the new addition?"

"No, of course not!"

"Wow, that sounds like a resounding lie."

I turned to Angela. Her face was red with emotion. "Why would I lie to you?"

"That's what I'm wondering," she said.

When I didn't respond, she said, "You know what? I'm not hungry. I'm going back to the library."

She turned around and starting walking fast. I had to run to catch up. "Angela, I'm sorry."

She kept going.

I grabbed her arm. "All right, I'll tell you."

As she slowed down, I looked for a place where we could sit down. I pointed to a low wall running along the front of a shop. "Let's sit here while I explain."

"Why do we have to sit down? I'm hungry."

I refrained from pointing out that she'd just insisted she wasn't hungry. "Because what I have to tell you is shocking."

"This better be good," she grumbled.
We sat down and I started talking.

* * *

Twenty minutes later, a subdued and pensive Angela walked beside me to the café. We were running late but fortunately managed to get seated immediately. Angela picked up her menu, then set it down on the table.

"You've known Evelyn since the day Sally offered you the job," she said for the third time. Clearly, she was having trouble absorbing what I'd just told her.

"Yes. I would have turned it down if it weren't for Evelyn."

"I remember Evelyn from when she worked in the library."

"Yes, she was an aide."

"And now there's another ghost, but no one but you and Evelyn can see him."

I nodded.

Jilly, our waitress, appeared with a smile on her face. "Ready to order?"

"BLT," Angela mumbled.

"Chicken salad on rye," I said.

"And to drink?" Jilly asked.

"Coffee," I said.

"Coke," Angela said.

"Coming right up!" Jilly left.

"And you wouldn't have told me if I hadn't forced you to," Angela said.

"Not true. I was waiting for the right time. It's a lot to take in."

Angela nodded and sipped her water. "This is weirder than people in my family getting murdered," she said.

"I suppose."

Jilly brought our food and we ate in silence. I was afraid that I'd caused a shock to Angela's system, but I had to finish my spiel. "You can't tell anyone, Angela."

"Not even Steve?"

"Let me think about that."

"I bet Dylan knows."

I felt guilty as I nodded.

"I won't tell Steve until you say I can."

"All right. But if he knows, that's the limit. I mean it."

"Who would I tell?" Angela said, sounding like herself. But when she caught my grim expression she added, "I can see why you want to keep this quiet."

Now I was offended. "Being able to see ghosts isn't something shameful, Ange. The problem is most people find it scary and react the way you did."

She gave me a sheepish grin by way of an apology. "How did Dylan react when you told him?"

"Nearly crashed the car into some bushes."

We both laughed, and suddenly things between us were back to normal.

* * *

The rest of my work day moved along smoothly. I spent time filling out the monthly expense form for my department, then sat at the hospitality desk for an hour, chatting with patrons as I signed them up for programs. The workers repaired the hole they'd managed to create, and the noise level was back to what it had been before the mishap. I must have gotten used to the din, because eventually I managed to tune it out.

But Charlie the Ghost hovered in the back of my mind. It looked like he was a fixture in the library for the time being. What was going to happen when he got tired of hiding out in unused rooms? I shuddered to think of the havoc his presence would cause among the patrons.

Evelyn stopped by my office to tell me she had to leave for a while and that Charlie would remain downstairs in the meeting room as he'd promised. But for how long? Now he couldn't even return to the other building, not that I wanted him to stay in a place he feared and hated.

Then Susan arrived. After we chatted a minute or two, she cleared off the desk she shared with Trish, got out her art supplies, and began working on Halloween decorations. Susan's handiwork was unique and much appreciated by everyone who came into our library. For the children's room, she'd created a huge jack-o'-lantern made of wood and oak tag. The kids loved to play with its movable parts. She was working on a large witch sitting on a broomstick, also with movable parts. I couldn't wait to place it on the wall for the patrons to see.

Susan was too engrossed in her work to wonder what I was doing, for which I was grateful. Because I was looking up everything I could find online about the Whiteheads.

I started with James. There were several newspaper articles available, among them his obituary. The newspaper articles referred to various businesses and enterprises he'd been involved in over the years. Most were Connecticut-based, but I was surprised to see that two of them were based in Chicago.

I skimmed over the houses he had owned—one in Florida, a ski lodge in Aspen, as well as a home outside of Clover Ridge—and focused on his family. His wife was deceased and his two children,

Chloe and Andrew, were both married and lived in neighboring towns. James, his obituary reported, had died of congestive heart failure at the age of eighty-nine. A year and a half ago.

A year and a half ago. Perhaps Charlie had come to do business with James. They got into an argument. James killed him and stashed the body in the basement of his abandoned property. Then he himself died a few years later and never got the chance to get rid—

"Carrie."

I gave a start. "Yes?"

Susan laughed. "I didn't mean to scare you."

"You didn't," I fibbed.

She shrugged. "Did you happen to hear Julie Theron's interview with Lieutenant Mathers?"

"No. When was this?"

"At one this afternoon outside the police station. She questioned him about the body they found in the building next door."

My ears perked up. "Did John report any new developments?"

"No, which pissed Julie off. She made a few digs about him and the police department, saying maybe it was time they brought in a special investigator."

"Oh, no! The case is hardly a week old. She's just trying to bring attention to herself."

"It gets worse," Susan said, her eyes shining with excitement. "Julie mentioned *you*."

I bit my lip, knowing I was going to hate what I was about to hear.

"She said that you were responsible for solving all the homicides this past year and John should consider resigning."

"Poor John. What did he say to that?"

Susan nodded appreciatively. "He handled himself very well. He said they were actively pursuing the case and Ms. Theron would be one of the first to hear when there was something to report. Then he turned his back on her and her crew and went inside the station."

"Good for him. The reporter who had the job before her was never this snarky."

"Well, Julie Theron's another breed. She announced that since the police were doing nothing to solve the case of the unidentified body, she planned to do it herself!"

Chapter Nine

Susan's news upset me. John Mathers was a good friend of mine. Yes, I had played a role in solving some of his cases, but he was a good detective and did solid police work. Whenever I landed in a spot of trouble, he always had my back. Though John sometimes got annoyed at what he called my interference, over time he'd learned to appreciate whatever I managed to uncover about suspects. But now he had to contend with Julie Theron, a brash young investigative reporter who was yanking his chain.

I didn't much like that she'd brought me into the picture. I had been totally out of the loop regarding this investigation—as far as she knew. And now she intended to do some sleuthing on her own. That thought put an end to my musings. Not that I was in competition with Julie Theron, but I wanted to talk to James's sister and cousin, Marcella and Albert Whitehead. Surely they could tell me something about James and the building next door.

As soon as Susan left the office to spend an hour at the hospitality desk, Evelyn paid me a visit.

"How's Charlie?" I asked.

"Fine. Resting. Have the police made any headway?"

I filled her in on what Susan just told me.

"So, Clover Ridge has another Nancy Drew," she teased.

"Right now I'm checking out the three Whiteheads who owned the property next door. I've read up on James and I'm about to find out what I can about his sister and his cousin."

"I doubt you'll find very much," Evelyn said. "Albert was a dud when it came to making money. He lived on whatever funds he could cadge from his relatives and the few business enterprises they allowed him to join.

"And, as I told you, Marcella was totally dominated by her brother. Their father died when James and Marcella were probably fourteen and ten. James quickly made himself the man of the house, bossing his mother and sister about."

"Marcella never married," I mused.

"No one met James's approval."

I squashed my retort about chauvinistic males and googled Marcella Whitehead. To my surprise, a few sites came up. They referred to *The Best Blueberry Bake Book* and to a small community herb garden that she had sponsored and helped to create years ago and that was still flourishing.

"And you said both Marcella and Albert are currently residents of the Clover Ridge Home for Seniors." I looked up the address. It was right outside of town.

"Why don't you call Marcella?" Evelyn suggested. She'd been peering over my shoulder, careful to keep enough distance so I wouldn't get chilled.

"And say what? 'A body has been discovered in the building you used to own. I'm trying to find out the victim's name. And by the way, do you know if your brother murdered him?'"

Evelyn laughed. "Some questions are more tactful than others. You want information, right? Why not start with that?"

Why not? I thought as I dialed the senior residence's number and asked to speak to Marcella Whitehead.

I was almost surprised when the operator connected me to Marcella's room and she answered in a surprisingly chipper voice. "Hello, who is this?"

"Hello, Marcella. Miss Whitehead. My name is Carrie Singleton. I'm the head of programs and events at the Clover Ridge Library."

"Ah. Not so long ago, the library was one of my all-time favorite places. I suppose you're calling about the body they found in the building that we sold to the town."

"Well, yes, I am," I said, surprised at how coherent and alert Marcella sounded. Not at all like the timid woman Evelyn had described. "I'm curious about the history of the building. And I was hoping you could tell me a bit about your brother, James."

"Ah, James." Was that derision, sadness, or dislike I'd heard? More likely a combination of all three.

"Would it be all right if I came and talked to you some time?"

"How about later—after dinner?" Marcella said. "Say, five thirty?"

Five thirty is after dinner? "That would be fine. I get off work at five, but I'll have Smoky Joe with me. He's the library cat, but he actually belongs to me. Or I could drop him off at my aunt and uncle's house."

"By all means, bring him along. It will be nice to have an animal in the place for a change."

"Okay, I will. I'll see you later."

I was about to mention Albert when Marcella said, "I'll ask my cousin Albert to join us, if you don't mind."

"I'd love that," I said.

"I must run," Marcella said. "I want to get to the dining room early enough to snag the table beside the fireplace. I so hate when my friends and I have to eat in the center of the room."

I turned to Evelyn. "She didn't sound at all like a timid sparrow."

"No, she didn't," Evelyn agreed. "Being set free of her brother's control seems to have made a big difference."

* * *

As I drove to the senior residence, I wondered what other surprises were in store for me. I'd called Dylan to let him know I had something to do after work and he should eat on his own. As it turned out, Dylan was glad to have the opportunity to take Gary, his new assistant, out to dinner. I was relieved when he didn't ask me what I was doing. I would have told him, of course, but he wouldn't have liked to hear I was sleuthing again, even though tonight's outing was perfectly safe and there was little chance I'd be ruffling any feathers.

I managed to find a parking space close to the entrance of the Clover Ridge Home for Seniors, which was much appreciated since I was bringing Smoky Joe's carrier inside. Residents oohed and aahed when they caught sight of him peering out at them. I walked over to the desk and was asking the receptionist to call Marcella when a woman in her mid-eighties approached, her hand outstretched.

"Hello! You must be Carrie Singleton."

"I am."

"Welcome! Welcome! I'm Marcella Whitehead." She bent down to peer into the carrier. "And you must be Smoky Joe!"

Smoky Joe responded with a meow.

Marcella was petite and birdlike, as Evelyn had described, but there was a glint in her blue eyes. I found it difficult to believe that her brother had browbeaten her all her life.

"So nice to meet you both," she said. "Follow me to the elevator and we'll go up to my apartment. Albert will join us momentarily."

We rode up to three, which was the top floor, and walked along a carpeted hallway to Marcella's apartment. Once inside, she glanced at the small kitchen area to our right. "Can I get you something to drink? Soda? Coffee? Beer? Wine?"

"No, thanks. I'm good."

She glanced at the cat carrier I was holding. "If Smoky Joe's well behaved, you can let him out."

"He is," I said, hoping this would be the case. Though he spent most days in the library and had been to several people's homes, I couldn't swear to his good behavior.

I opened the carrier's door. Smoky Joe took his time sniffing the air before stepping out gingerly and peering around. Marcella led me to the living room just beyond the small hallway. She gestured to the sofa. "Why don't you have a seat? I'll join you in a minute."

Just then, the doorbell rang. "That must be Albert," she said and went to let him in.

I heard them speak in voices too low for me to make out any words. A minute later, Albert walked slowly into the living room, leaning heavily on his cane.

"Hello! Hello! So nice to meet you, Carrie." He offered me his hand and we shook.

"Nice to meet you, too, Albert."

He sank into what appeared to be his usual chair and stretched out a leg on the accompanying hassock. Like his cousin, he was short, but where Marcella was thin, almost frail, he was portly. They were first cousins and I discerned a family resemblance, but Albert's pointy nose and recessive chin made me think of a rat, just as Evelyn had said.

Marcella joined us a minute later. She handed Albert a glass containing what looked to be beer. Holding a glass of wine in her other hand, she sat down in the wing chair facing me.

"This seems like a very nice place," I said, stroking Smoky Joe, who had just climbed onto my lap, having finished investigating the apartment.

"It's not bad, though the food's not up to par," Albert said. "They advertise they have a gourmet kitchen. Hah! What a joke."

Marcella shot him a sharp glance. "Carrie hasn't come to listen to your complaints."

"You're right. Sorry." Albert gulped down half his glass of beer.

"How long have you been living here?" I asked, genuinely curious.

"Albert's been here a year. I moved in six months ago," Marcella said.

"Can you tell me something about the building that you owned until recently?"

Albert glanced at Marcella, and she gave him the tiniest of nods before sipping her wine.

"My mother, Marcella's father, and our aunt Agnes were siblings. Aunt Agnes and Uncle Barney never had any children. The property next to the library was one of Uncle Barney's real estate steals. That's what he called his deals that were practically give-aways. He died, and when Aunt Agnes died, she left it to James, Marcella, and me—her niece and two nephews."

"We were, none of us, thrilled," Marcella said. "The house, or whatever it was in its last phase, was a mess. I was all for unloading it as soon as possible, but big brother had other ideas." She scoffed. "James thought that being situated on the Green meant it was worth a lot of money and we should hold out for a big number."

"Only no one saw it like James did," Albert said, his tone sour, "or at least no one ever agreed to his terms."

"But the two of you seem to be in accord," I said. "That's two versus one."

Albert pursed his lips. "You don't know what James was like. Bossy. Intimidating. We had a few offers, but none were high enough to suit him. And believe me, I could have used the money years ago."

Marcella grimaced, her expression very much like her cousin's. "It was impossible to argue with James. He always managed to cow Albert and me until we agreed to see things his way. And since, of the three of us, he was the only one with connections in the business world, we left it to James to deal with the sale of the building. Only that never came to be while he was alive."

"Did your brother let you know when someone was interested in buying the building?" I asked.

Albert made a scoffing sound. "You mean, did James allow us to have input regarding offers we received? The answer is no. He thought women didn't have a head for business. And I was no better in his eyes since the few times I undertook a commercial venture, for some reason, it always ended up going bust."

"I do remember James getting excited about a possible sale." Marcella squinted as she tried to recall the details. "Maybe five years ago? No, more like six." She turned to her cousin.

"You're right. He was smiling and happy because finally someone was willing to pay his asking price."

Six years ago! My spine was tingling. That was well within the period of time the medical examiner thought Charlie had been murdered and placed in the basement. "So what happened?"

"Nothing," Albert said. "Absolutely nothing. When I asked James about the deal a few days later, he snarled at me and said the deal fell through."

"Did he say why?" I asked.

"No. Just spat out a few choice words and mumbled something about the curse on the building being real."

"Which is a lot of nonsense," Marcella quickly added as she glanced at me. "It's just a coincidence that some of the people who owned it before us had a run of bad luck. And unfortunately there were a few fatal accidents. But this is a centuries-old building we're talking about. I'm certain the library patrons will make good use of the new addition once the renovations are finished."

I could have hugged her for being so solicitous about my feelings. Or was Marcella worried that something unforeseen was bound to be discovered and the town would demand a refund—if that was even possible?

"I'm looking forward to our new, enlarged library," I said. "We have several plans for the new rooms and the stadium-seating auditorium. You both must come and see it for yourself when all the work is complete."

And we must have a dedication to honor you both, I thought. *Perhaps name a room after you.*

"Thank you. We sure would like that. Wouldn't we, Albert?"

"Most definitely." Albert laughed. "I'm thinking how none of this would have ever happened but for Aunt Agnes's clever stipulation in her will."

Marcella nodded. "As soon as James died, his son and daughter came around asking what we were willing to pay them for their third of the property. We told them zip. Were they pissed!"

"I'm surprised their father never explained the terms of the property to them," Albert said.

"Or they thought we were plum ignorant," Marcella said with some heat. "We knew that Aunt Agnes's will stated that if one of us were to die before we sold the property, his or her share went to the two surviving heirs. And that's what the judge told my niece and nephew."

"Several months later," Albert said, sounding bitter. "It held up the sale."

I cleared my throat. "I'd like to backtrack a bit and ask you both something you might have trouble talking about."

"Shoot," Albert said, looking interested.

Marcella burst out laughing. "You want to know if we think James might have killed that poor guy found wrapped in a blanket in the basement of the house."

"Yes, I do," I said, astonished by her candor.

"James had quite a temper," Albert said. "I wouldn't put it past him."

"Me, neither," Marcella said. Observing my expression, she added. "Maybe you'd like to reconsider and have a bit of wine."

"I think I'd like that," I said as I leaned comfortably back against the sofa.

Chapter Ten

I chuckled as I drove home from the Clover Ridge Home for Seniors and mentally replayed my conversation with Marcella and Albert Whitehead. They'd been so forthright about their opinion of James, admitting quite openly that they could see him killing someone who had reneged after agreeing to buy their white elephant for a good price.

It was hard to reconcile Evelyn's description of Marcella Whitehead with the woman I'd just visited. Clearly, her brother's death had freed her from living under his oppressive thumb and she now gave free rein to her outspoken nature.

It occurred to me that I ought to share what I'd learned with John, but immediately dismissed the idea. For one thing, he would be annoyed that I'd gone to see the cousins, proof that I was investigating the murder. For another, what Marcella and Albert had expressed was merely their opinion and not even hearsay. James was dead and, according to what they told me, he had never said anything to lead them to believe he'd met Charlie, much less murdered him.

Besides, for all I knew, John had already interviewed them. Neither Marcella nor Albert had mentioned being questioned by the police. But it could be they'd forgotten or hadn't considered it important enough to tell me. The crucial point to consider was whether James Whitehead had murdered Charlie. Charlie remembered discussing money, so there was a good possibility it was he who had agreed to buy the building then decided against it. The timing was right. And who besides James had access to that building?

I let out a sigh of exasperation. With James dead, we might never find out who had murdered Charlie!

I was starving when I arrived home. I heated up some leftovers I found in the fridge, then called Dylan.

"You're quite the local celeb," he said by way of a greeting.

"What do you mean?"

"I caught what Julie Theron had to say about you on the six o'clock news."

"Oh, that." In the excitement of meeting with the Whiteheads, I'd forgotten about Julie Theron's comments. "She's just trying to drum up a story for herself."

"She's doing a good job of it," Dylan said. "I happened to talk to John earlier today about a case. The poor guy's been getting calls, texts, and emails from people demanding to know why the mystery man remains unidentified. Don't be surprised if Julie Theron contacts you."

"She'd better not," I said.

"Where did you go after work? Or is it confidential?"

"Why would someplace I go be confidential?" I asked.

"Maybe it's code for something related to town council business."

I laughed. "Actually it had to do with library business—indirectly. I went to have a chat with Marcella and Albert Whitehead."

There was a silence, then, "So you've gotten involved in this case after all."

"I did it for Charlie. He wants to know who he is, but he can't remember anything—how he ended up in that building, how he died. He only knows it involved money and he vaguely remembers being with two people, though he can't swear they had anything to do with his death."

"What did you learn from the Whiteheads?"

"They didn't much like James. Said he was bossy and controlling and insisted on handling the sale of the property himself. They remembered he had a potential buyer for the building about six years ago, but the deal fell through." I snorted. "They both thought he was capable of murder."

"Still, that's a big stretch to linking him to the body they found in the basement."

"The lost sale and the murder are in the same time frame. The dead man could very well have gotten excited about buying a property on the Green, then, after thinking it over, changed his mind."

Dylan laughed. "From what I remember about James Whitehead, I doubt he'd be dumb enough to kill someone and leave the body on his property."

I sighed. "I suppose you're right."

"And proving that one dead man killed another is close to impossible. According to the autopsy, cause of death was blunt force trauma, but no weapon was discovered in the basement. Even if they manage to get fingerprints off your Charlie's clothing or the blanket he was wrapped in, how would they go about getting James Whitehead's prints?"

We chatted a bit more before saying good night. Though he didn't say it, I could tell that Dylan wasn't happy that I'd started looking into Charlie's murder. But all I had done was talk to two of the people who had owned the property before selling it to the town. And that would probably be the end of it, since I didn't have any further leads to follow. But I was glad I'd told Dylan where I'd gone after work and we were able to discuss it. Transparency was essential in a relationship. And keeping secrets from a loved one took its toll.

* * *

I caught sight of the TV van as soon as I drove into the library parking lot the following morning. *Oh, no! She'd better not be here for me.* My first thought was to turn around and fly out of the lot. But why should I have to run? Instead, I killed the motor and reached for the handle of Smoky Joe's carrier as I did every day I came to work.

I was closing the car door when Julie Theron came striding toward me, mic in her hand, a grin on her face. She was about five four, an inch or two shorter than me, and had a trim, sturdy build which led me to believe she'd played sports in high school and college. Contact sports, no doubt, and always a fierce competitor.

Her blue eyes glinted in anticipation as she focused the considerable force of her personality on her target: me. Behind Julie, a young bearded guy had me in the sights of his camera while someone else held up a light. I squinted as it shone in my face.

I raised my hand to ward off the glare. "Please let me through." I started walking toward the library.

I heard a mumbled apology, and the light disappeared. But Julie kept pace beside me, her mouth going a mile a minute.

"And here we have the true law and order gal, the woman who sees to it that Clover Ridge streets are safe from murderers. What do you have to say to your public, Ms. Singleton?"

I stopped dead in my tracks. So did Julie and the photographer. I decided it was better to say what I thought than run away like a scared rabbit. "Lieutenant John Mathers is our police chief. I place my trust in his hands." I glared at Julie. "And I think you should, too, Ms. Theron."

"But you've solved many of the homicides that have recently plagued our little town. Are you planning to find out who murdered the unfortunate person whose remains were discovered in the building next door to the library?"

"I certainly am not!" I declared and continued on my way.

To my relief, Julie Theron didn't follow me. But I cringed when I heard her say, "I bet many of you would love to see me team up with Carrie Singleton and solve this crime. Working together, we'll not only discover the poor man's name and why his life was snuffed out, his body left like trash in an abandoned building, but we'll also find his murderer and make sure that he's punished."

As soon as I entered the library, I released Smoky Joe and stomped off to my office. I was steaming mad. How dare she accost me like that! How dare she put out the image of us as crimefighters like—like Rizzoli and Isles!

I switched on my computer to read the emails waiting for me, but my concentration was shot. The words might as well have been hieroglyphics for all the meaning they conveyed. I was glad when Evelyn and Charlie made an appearance a few minutes later. I put my computer to sleep and gave them my full attention.

"Have you learned anything new?" Charlie asked. "Did you find out who I am?"

I shook my head. "Sorry, but I did speak to two of the people who owned the building where you were found."

"Did they kill me?"

I imagined Marcella and Albert as murderers and smiled. "No! Why would you think that?"

"Because they owned the property where Charlie was found," Evelyn said, sounding like a teacher whose student had sorely tried her patience.

"Well, of course, but they aren't the type to murder anyone. Besides, they weren't involved with selling the place until recently. Marcella's brother, James, handled that until his death three years ago. It seems six years ago he had a buyer and then he didn't, which made him angry. Both his sister and his cousin Albert think James was capable of killing someone—not that they have proof that he ever met you, much less murdered you."

"So there's a chance James might have killed me because I backed out of the deal." Charlie shook his head. "I can't imagine wanting to buy that building. It's terribly run-down."

"For an investment, perhaps," Evelyn suggested. "It is a valuable piece of property—located right on the Green."

I had an idea. "Would you recognize James Whitehead if I showed you his photograph?"

Charlie shrugged. "Maybe. Maybe not."

"It's worth a try," Evelyn said.

I turned on my computer and found one of the newspaper articles that included a photo of James Whitehead. Charlie leaned over my shoulder, sending a shiver up my spine. I moved out of his range of vision. He stared and stared.

"He does look familiar," he finally said. He glanced at me, then at Evelyn. "I think I knew him. Or met him a few times. Do you think he murdered me?"

What a strange question. "Unfortunately, I can't talk to him because he's dead."

"What about the other man?"

"What other man?" Evelyn asked.

"I told you there were two men." Charlie blinked. "Or maybe I'm remembering something that has nothing to do with my death."

Since the meeting room was in use for the rest of the day, Charlie agreed to go back upstairs to the attic. "I don't think I can take much more of this," he grumbled.

"I can only stay with him a while," Evelyn whispered. "I have things that need looking after."

"I understand. Thanks for keeping him company," I whispered back as I watched them fade from sight. Alone again, I wondered how Charlie had become my responsibility.

I managed to get through my emails and phone calls that required my attention. Trish arrived at ten and we discussed our plans for the Halloween party scheduled at the end of October. I'd organized a costume party with entertainers last year, and since it had been such a success, Sally and I both agreed it would make a wonderful yearly tradition.

Julie Theron called me on my library extension, but I let it go to voice mail. Her message was simple: "Please call me" with her phone number. I wished the woman would stop hounding me.

Babette texted me, asking if I'd had a chance to look at the park plans for the Seabrook Preserve property that Graham had left with me and saying she hoped that I would before our meeting tonight.

Meeting tonight? How could I have forgotten? Tonight the contractors were making presentations at the open council meeting. Of course I hadn't had a moment to even glance at Graham's firm's proposal or to read much of what was in the packet of information that Al had given me the previous week. And I didn't even have it with me, so I couldn't look it over during the day. Which meant I'd have to rush home from work and grab something to eat for dinner as I read what I could before driving to the meeting. I was feeling overwhelmed, to say the least.

Chapter Eleven

"I can't believe how stressful my life has become," I complained to Angela as she turned on to Mercer Street and we headed for lunch at our favorite Indian restaurant. We'd agreed we needed a change of scenery, and I was terrified of being ambushed again by Julie Theron. "I have to worry about the comfort of an unhappy ghost, being stalked by Julie Theron, and I haven't even read through the proposals for the meeting tonight. What kind of a council member am I turning out to be?"

"I'm sure the people who are making the proposals tonight will be very thorough in their presentations." Angela grinned. "Later, you board members will pick them apart and seek out flaws and hidden expenses and problems. You don't have to vote on this yet, do you?"

"No. That's next week."

"See! Problem solved."

"And what about Charlie?" I said. "So far there's no word about who he is. Evelyn's been wonderful, but she can't keep on playing nursemaid to him. And frankly, I feel awful, hiding him away like he's done something shameful."

"I'm sure John is working hard to find out who he is," Angela said.

"I suppose," I agreed without much enthusiasm.

We stopped at a red light and she turned to me, her eyes shining with glee. "Can you imagine what Ms. Theron would have to say if she knew you were in communication with the victim's ghost? It would scare the pants off her."

I scoffed. "I doubt it. She'd probably interview Charlie. I wish she'd stop hounding me. If she's so intent on playing detective, you'd think she'd want to solve the mystery herself instead of wanting to be my partner." I spit out the last word like it was poison.

Angela winked. "That's the price you pay for being our local Nancy Drew."

* * *

For all her teasing, Angela managed to calm me down, and I thoroughly enjoyed the Indian buffet, eating much more than I should have. By the time we were on our way back to work, I'd come to a few realizations. The police were bound to find out who Charlie was sooner or later; I'd learn everything I needed to know about the three proposals tonight via the presentations and discussions; and all I had to do regarding Julie Theron was ignore her calls.

When we returned to the library, I called Aunt Harriet to tell her that though there was a council meeting that evening, I'd be going home after work instead of coming by for dinner since I'd eaten a big lunch. Smoky Joe must have sensed I was back in the building because I heard him meowing outside my office door.

I welcomed him inside and watched him scarf down his food as quickly as any dog.

I realized that, with everything going on, I'd never phoned Julia to make a lunch date as I'd promised. I called her on her cell, knowing she was at work. Julia was an interior decorator. She'd been working part-time, but now that Tacey was in kindergarten, she was putting in a full week.

"Hello, Carrie." She sounded out of breath.

"Hi, Julia. Is this a bad time?"

"I was just dealing with the client from hell, and now I'm late for my next appointment." The calm, take-charge Julia I knew was stressed out.

"Sorry. I called to make a date for lunch, but if this is a bad time we can talk another time."

"No, I definitely want to set something up with you. We keep saying we'll get together, and the days slip by. It's just that lately every appointment runs overtime. I didn't think working full-time would make my life so hectic."

I had an idea. "Dylan and I have no plans this weekend. If you're free, why don't you and Randy come for dinner Saturday night?"

"Oh!"

I suddenly felt foolish. "I suppose you guys are busy or you need to plan ahead and get a sitter—"

Julia gave a little laugh. "Randy and I haven't been out on a date in ages. We could both use some 'us' time. I'd love to come for dinner, though I hate to make you cook on a Saturday night."

"Not to worry. Our meal will come straight from the Gourmet Market." We both laughed. "Shall we say seven o'clock?"

"I'm looking forward to it. So will Randy, when I tell him the news," Julia said, sounding considerably calmer.

"Will you have a problem getting a sitter?"

"Are you kidding? Aunt Harriet and Uncle Bosco will be thrilled to stay with the kids. I'll call her right now."

And Aunt Harriet and Uncle Bosco would be happy to hear that Dylan and I were getting together with Randy and Julia. And planning our dinner would take my mind off the stresses in my life. I smiled as I settled down to do some paperwork and finished it earlier than expected. I walked over to the hospitality desk where Trish was helping patrons sign up for programs.

"'Make Your Own Jewelry' is filled and so is 'Let's Talk About Witches,'" she told me.

"That's nice."

"Not so nice," Trish said, looking worried. She lowered her voice. "Veronica Briar carried on when I told her the jewelry class was closed. She said we have some nerve, advertising a program then not having enough places for everyone who wants to attend. Sally heard and came over to calm her down."

"Veronica Briar," I mused. "How many times has she demanded we refund her money after not showing up for a program?"

"Twice since you've been here," Trish said. "A few times before that."

"And our 'no refund' policy is printed on every newsletter, every receipt. Consider the patron. I wouldn't give her a second thought."

Trish shot me a big smile. "Thanks, Carrie."

I told her I'd be checking on the programs in progress then helping out at the food presentation. At two o'clock a local Latin restaurant owner and chef was presenting a menu of soup, salad, and empanadas. That meant he'd be arriving soon to set up in the meeting room downstairs. Every food presenter brought the ingredients and cooking utensils for his or her program. I liked to be available at least twenty minutes before the patrons sat down to make sure he had everything he needed and to hand out copies of the recipes he'd be preparing. Then I stayed to help serve the food.

It was an exhausting day, and I was tired by the time Smoky Joe and I headed for home. I spoke to Dylan as I drove, filling him in on the events of my day, including the arrangements I'd made with Julia.

"I miss you, babe," he told me.

"I miss you too." *A lot*, I realized when I disconnected. I was glad tomorrow was Friday and we would soon be together until Monday morning.

I fed Smoky Joe and changed his kitty litter, then found a few leftovers to tide me over. I skimmed through every brochure in the packet Al had given me. Then it was time to freshen my makeup and drive back to town.

The sun was sinking as I pulled into the Town Hall parking lot. Though it was only a quarter to seven, the parking lot was already half-filled. This was an open meeting, and many civic-minded residents were expected to attend to hear about the proposed plans for the Seabrook Preserve property and voice their opinions. Reggie pulled into the spot beside me and slid out of his car while talking on his cell phone. He ended his call and smiled when he saw me. We walked together toward the entrance.

"We can expect a big crowd tonight," he said, gesturing at the two cars driving onto the lot. "And plenty of shouting."

"You really think so?" I said.

"Absolutely. There are three options, and the residents who show up all have an agenda. There are the nature lovers who want to keep the preserve, the family-minded in favor of the park, and those with the foresight to keep Clover Ridge a growing, thriving community."

Translated: the condo plan you like so much. "In the end, it's the five of us who get to decide," I said.

Reggie pulled open the door and stepped back to let me enter. "Yes it is, Carrie, so listen carefully to what everyone is really saying and cast your intelligent vote."

Strange advice, I thought as Reggie left me to join a group of four men and two women standing in a circle. I felt a moment of anxiety as I glanced around the room filled with chairs for at least seventy people and was relieved to spot my uncle Bosco talking to Al Tripp and Jeannette Rivers, whose place I was filling on the council because she and her husband were moving out of state. They had gathered at the far end of the room near the dais. I hurried over to join them.

We all exchanged greetings. Uncle Bosco put an arm around me and kissed my cheek. "Be prepared for fireworks tonight."

I heard a burst of laugher and glanced at the group of people standing a few feet away. There was Babette and her cousin Graham with a striking gray-haired woman and two dapper-looking men.

Al followed my gaze. "The park contingent."

I nodded. "I met Babette's cousin Graham at the Fall Festival on Saturday."

"And what did you think of the Waterford Group's proposal?"

I turned to find Sean Powell behind me. Al, Uncle Bosco, and I stepped back so he could join us.

"I haven't decided," I hedged. "I thought I'd wait until I heard what everyone had to say before making up my mind."

"You'll hear a bunch of exaggerations and downright lies. Mostly from people out to cash in at the town's expense."

Sean had spun around to glare at the group across the way, the group that Reggie had joined. "And to think my own son is responsible for it all."

It was easy to spot Kevin Powell. He was a younger, taller version of his father—slender and handsome, but with a pulsating restlessness that was noticeable even from where I stood.

"Come on, Sean," Al said, resting his hand on Sean's arm. "You can't blame Kevin for encouraging Lighthouse Builders to make a bid for the property. It happens to be the perfect place for an upscale condo community guaranteed to bring in lots of revenue."

Sean scowled. "And Reggie's all for it. Are you, Al?" He turned to me. "And you, Carrie?"

Jeannette said, "There's no need to make this personal, Sean."

"Everything's personal, Jeannette." Sean spun on his heel and took off.

"Sean's angry because Kevin went to work for Lighthouse Builders," Jeannette said.

"So Al told me," I said.

"A double whammy since Sean and Tim were once partners. When they split up, Tim got a job at Lighthouse Builders and worked his way up till he reached the top. He's largely responsible for where the company is now—building condos and senior retirement communities in three states." She lowered her voice. "While Sean stayed local, doing okay but nothing compared to his old partner."

"Did Sean hope Kevin would take over his business?"

Al shrugged. "Depends on who's telling the story. According to Sean, Kevin was a handful growing up. He got into trouble. Nothing too serious—he went joyriding in a stolen car; he and his friends got drunk and trashed a bar. He straightened out when he was nineteen, twenty and went to work for his father—never doing more than the bare minimum. A few years ago, he asked to be made partner in the company. Sean said he had to earn a partnership. According to a few of Kevin's friends, Sean hemmed and hawed, so Kevin got angry and quit, then went to work for Lighthouse."

"There's more to the story," Jeannette said. "Sean told me that when Kevin worked for him, he still had some rough edges— sometimes arriving late or hungover to a job, getting into arguments with the other workers. Sean had his doubts about making him a partner and for good reason."

"Regardless of their past history, it's time the two of them made up," Uncle Bosco said.

He and Jeannette went to sit down. The room had filled up. Soon every chair was occupied.

Al looked at me then gestured up at the dais. "Time to take our seats."

"I hope we don't have to answer any questions," I said.

"Don't worry. You won't have to say a word. The open meeting is to give residents an idea of what could be done with the Seabrook Preserve property and for us to hear their thoughts on the matter."

I started to follow Al up the three steps to the platform when someone tapped me on the shoulder.

"Hi there, Carrie."

I turned around, startled to see Julie Theron grinning at me.

"What are you doing here?" I demanded.

"Attending the town meeting, just like you."

Chapter Twelve

Al brought the meeting to attention and introduced the evening's agenda.

"The property known as the Seabrook Preserve has been a favorite destination of nature lovers these past fifty years. The town can now decide to keep it as a preserve or use it for another purpose that will benefit Clover Ridge in some respect—either financially, aesthetically, or culturally.

"After much discussion, the council has decided on two possible alternatives. A park that offers activities for all ages, including swimming and boating, is one. The construction of a gated condo community is another. Tonight we will hear presentations of all three options. I ask that you show each speaker respect and remain silent when someone has the floor. Residents will have plenty of opportunities to express comments or concerns. Callouts and interruptions will not be tolerated. Do so, and you'll be asked to leave the meeting."

Al smiled at me as he sat down, once again the congenial, friendly mayor I knew him to be. His warning regarding protocol reminded me that he was a lot tougher than he often appeared.

Someone wheeled a projector into the room. We board members were asked to move our chairs to either side of the stage so the screen behind us was visible to everyone.

Julie, I noticed, was texting away at lightning speed on her cell phone. She looked up as the lights were dimmed and caught me studying her. A broad grin spread across her face and she gave me a thumbs up. Now what was she scheming?

A young man introduced himself as a forestry graduate student and a part-time worker at the preserve. He presented a short slide show of the preserve's history. There were several beautiful woodland shots, including a few of the Sound at sunset.

"Our goal is to keep this property as it is—pristine as nature meant it to be. Too much of our land in the northeast is overdeveloped with buildings, shops, and housing. Clover Ridge residents need a sanctuary where they can be at one with the natural world."

When the lights came on again, he fielded a few questions—about overgrowth, fallen trees, and if the preserve intended to update the shabby restrooms. Julie didn't appear to be listening to the young man's detailed answers, but kept her eyes on her cell phone.

Al stood and thanked the young man. "Next we'll hear from the award-winning Waterford Group, an architectural firm that specializes in outdoor creations and public spaces. They're here to present their vision of a town park that would include a beach for swimming and sunning, a boat basin where boats could be rented, and a small restaurant."

The man sitting next to Graham approached the projector and showed us a PowerPoint presentation of a park that seemed to include every attraction except a zoo.

"How much would that cost us?" a man called out.

"Bruce, let's save the questions for later," Al responded.

"You allowed questions to be asked about the preserve," Bruce shot back.

"So I did, but further discussion will continue after all the speakers have given their presentation." Al eyed Bruce meaningfully.

Bruce must have known that Al meant business about throwing out hecklers because he didn't say another word. *Yay, Al!* I was relieved. Tonight's meeting revolved around a topic that could very well turn into a volatile situation.

When the park presentation ended, Al said, "And now the Lighthouse Builders will show us what the Seabrook Preserve might look like should the property become a condo community. Please remember, while the Waterford Group and the Lighthouse Builders have been kind enough to share their creative visions with us, if we decide to go with one of the two alternate plans, other architectural firms will also be considered."

Kevin Powell approached the projector. He seemed to be having difficulty getting started. He grimaced and called to one of his colleagues, who joined him and must have resolved the problem because he sat down again as Kevin began his spiel.

"Sorry for the delay, folks. We included a few last minute additions and whoever put them in didn't know what he or she was doing."

Nice put down, I thought.

The first image was an overview plan of the property under discussion as a condo community.

"As you can see, most of the units will be townhouses, four in a pod, with a sprinkling of villas and a handful of individual homes. They will be built in free-form circles around four artificial lakes. The clubhouse will face the Sound and house a restaurant, a gym, and an indoor pool. Adjoining it: an outdoor pool, tennis and pickleball courts."

Admiring sounds issued from around the room. I was among those totally bowled over by this dream creation.

The next shot was a sketch of a few pods surrounded by trees. "We might include piers or a marina for residents who own boats."

The two-story clubhouse, with its floor-to-ceiling windows facing the Sound, evoked more oohs and aahs. It was followed by four different interior plans.

"Do they start at a million and end at three?" Bruce asked.

Laughter rippled through the audience.

When Kevin finished, the lights were turned on, the projector was removed, and the three presenters joined the members of the board on the dais where additional chairs had been provided.

Al stepped to the front of the platform and waited for the chatting to die down. "Now you've seen and listened to detailed reports of the three options being considered for the property known as the Seabrook Preserve: keeping the preserve and making some necessary improvements; erecting a multi-use park with a playground, a picnic area, a beach for swimming, and a boat basin; and lastly, building a gated community of three hundred or so townhouses and villas.

"Again, I want to remind you that the last two presentations are *examples* of what we have in mind for a park and a condo community. Once we decide which of the three projects we're going with, other architectural groups will be invited to offer proposals. Our final decision will be based on cost efficiency, design, and our community's needs."

Several hands shot up. Al cleared his throat.

"Before we open the agenda to questions, I'm going to ask the three presenters to tell us how their proposal would benefit our town and give us a ballpark figure of estimated financial costs. Why don't we go in reverse order. Kevin?"

Kevin Powell stepped up to the platform. He placed a thick packet of paper on the lectern and began talking.

"Clover Woods on the Sound, as we've named the community we would love to build for you, would be a most desirable development guaranteed to draw the most desirable people."

"You mean rich," someone called out, earning him a burst of laughter.

"Yes, affluent people will fall in love with our units and with its unique location. We are willing to pay a hefty amount of money for the property. Let me see . . ."

He shuffled through the papers before him, then named an enormous figure. I heard gasps. A few chuckles.

"Yes, Clover Ridge, my hometown, will benefit greatly if we build this community. Think of the taxes Clover Woods will generate."

Kevin offered a few more comments, including that the local tradespeople would profit were Lighthouse Builders to undertake the project.

Someone asked how much the units would cost. Kevin hemmed and hawed and finally said they would begin at eight hundred thousand dollars for the smallest, no-frills unit.

"Will Lighthouse Builders be getting a tax deferment if they win the bid?" Bruce asked.

"Too soon to say at this point."

"Or you won't say," another man shouted.

Other voices called out comments.

Al came to stand next to Kevin. "We will not tolerate shouting and disorder. You will have your chance to ask questions after we've heard from our next two speakers. Another outburst and this meeting will come to an end."

I glanced at Julie. Her eyes were fixed on her cell phone, her mouth open in amazement.

The Waterford Group's representative stood and began spouting figures. "While the township of Clover Ridge would be paying us to develop the park we've described, you will be gaining a beautiful parkland that will add prestige and delight to your historic town. Much of the cost of our fee will be regained through your entrance fee and the additional charges for services like boat rentals."

The young man from the Seabrook Preserve emphasized that unlike the other proposals, maintaining the preserve was cost efficient. "More importantly, land in its natural condition is rare in these parts and becoming rarer. There's a great benefit in keeping the Seabrook Preserve property a preserve."

The questions came fast and furious then. Most of them involved money—the cost of each project. Where would the money to improve the preserve or build the park come from? Would taxes be going up if either of those options was chosen?

A number of residents aired their resentment that the council was considering another high-end complex to be built. Why another park? someone else demanded. My mind was spinning from all the questions and comments, but I jotted them down as best I could. These were Clover Ridge residents giving voice to their opinions regarding the land under discussion. I was duty bound to consider their wishes when I cast my vote for one of the projects.

After an hour of animated discussion, Al drew the session to a close. He thanked the three presenters and their colleagues for coming and announced that we would carefully consider the many comments we'd heard that evening when we made our final decision regarding the future of the Seabrook Preserve.

I'd gotten so caught up in the discussion, I lost track of Julie. She was gone! When had she taken off? Had she left because someone had sent her an important message? The large room emptied slowly as friends and neighbors continued to tell each other why they supported or hated a particular proposal.

"I'd like us to have a short meeting," Al said as we five council members got to our feet.

"Now?" Babette asked, as if he'd said we'd be pulling an all-nighter.

"It won't take long, I promise," Al said.

He ushered us into the smaller room where we usually met. None of us was happy about this. It was after ten, and most of us had to be up early to go to work. Al began immediately.

"We're meeting next week to discuss and then vote for the project we regard as the best choice for our town. This is a big decision. What I'd like from everyone now is a brief report on your general view of the three proposals—which one you're leaning toward and why."

Babette smiled. "Easy enough. I like the park idea. And not just because my cousin Graham worked on the Waterford Group's presentation," she quickly added. "I think many Clover Ridge residents would make use of a park like the one the group designed.

And the property would still be accessible to residents, unlike the condo idea."

"As long as they paid a steep price to use the park's facilities," Reggie said. "And I imagine we'd have to open the park to outsiders if we hope to recoup the money we'd be laying out for the high-priced design and the work involved."

"Is that such a bad idea?" Babette asked. "Letting other people pay an entry fee to use the park?"

"I thought Clover Ridge residents were to benefit from whatever we decide," Reggie said calmly.

From the glances Al and Sean exchanged, I gathered that Babette and Reggie often squabbled.

"Thank you, Babette," Al said. "Reggie, care to share your thoughts regarding the three projects?"

"With pleasure." Reggie smiled at each of us in turn. "I'm all for going with an upscale condo community like the one the Lighthouse Builders presented. You saw how impressed everyone was when they saw those sketches of Clover Woods. Frankly, I wouldn't mind living there, and I imagine plenty of older couples with empty nests would like it as well. Clover Woods, or a place like it, can only enhance our community."

"And Clover Ridge residents would lose access to the Sound," I found myself saying.

Reggie shrugged. "I suppose. But there must be plenty of other local sites on the Sound they could visit."

"Unfortunately, there are very few open to the public," Al said.

"The condo proposal favors the wealthy," Sean said. "I don't like the idea of Clover Ridge being known as a town for the rich."

"Are you sure you don't have a personal vendetta against the condo idea?" Reggie asked.

Sean glared at him. "What about your personal reason for liking it so much?"

"We have to rise above our personal reasons and agendas when we vote on this project," Al said.

"What are your thoughts, Al?" Babette asked.

Al smiled. "I can see all three projects flourishing on that beautiful piece of property, but unless I'm convinced otherwise, the Seabrook Preserve has my vote."

We all stared at him, but Al didn't seem to notice.

"I agree with the young fellow. Every year we lose more and more undeveloped land. Our preserve is special. I checked the map. It's the only natural area in a fifty-mile radius. I think it could do with a good cleanup. And the bathrooms definitely need a facelift. But that shouldn't cost a bundle."

"But by keeping the property a preserve, we lose revenue," Reggie pointed out. "The way I see it, it's a huge piece of waterfront property lying fallow. The condo development can bring us money we sure can use."

We discussed the matter for ten more minutes, then Al brought our meeting to an end. Sean, Babette, and Reggie flew out the door. I turned to Al.

"Thanks for not asking me what I think should be done with the property."

He grinned. "Since you've just joined us, I thought I'd give you a break—unless you'd like to share your thoughts with me."

I laughed. "Like you, I can see all three possibilities. I'm not sure, but I think I'd like to see the land remain a preserve."

"That puts us in the majority," Al said. "All we need is one more vote and it remains the Seabrook Preserve."

I grimaced. "Sean's against the condos, and Reggie and Babette have agendas. I bet that's how they'll vote."

"Maybe Sean will come through for the preserve. If not, even people with agendas have been known to change their mind."

Chapter Thirteen

It was close to eleven when I arrived home, but I was too restless to go to sleep. I played with Smoky Joe until he conked out, then, knowing I'd have no success in shutting them out, I gave my thoughts free rein.

It seemed to me that everyone on the council had a definite opinion regarding what should be done with the property known as the Seabrook Preserve. Everyone but me. Al said he wanted to keep the preserve, but I wondered if that was because he didn't like the other two options. Or he was playing it close to the chest and would go with whichever decision seemed most popular?

If I was being honest, I wasn't sure which I favored, either. The condo project was great if you were rich and wanted to move into a brand new home on the Sound and enjoy a life of leisure. The park idea sounded nice, but I had a feeling it was going to cost much more to create than the numbers the architectural firm had shared with us. Maybe leaving the preserve as a preserve was the best option after all.

I finally drifted off to sleep without bothering to set the alarm since Friday was a late day. I was dreaming away when Smoky Joe woke me at six for his morning feeding. Bleary-eyed, I stumbled into the kitchen, fed him, and crept back into bed. When I awakened, the sun was peering in through the bedroom curtains.

I leaped out of bed, surprised that I'd slept so late. But I managed to calm myself down. There was nothing wrong with sleeping in once in a while when my work day began at one in the afternoon. I made myself breakfast and called Dylan. Rosemary told he was talking to a client and would call me when he was free.

I carried my second cup of coffee into the living room and turned on the TV. The local news channel was running commercials, so I picked up my cell phone to check out my emails and texts. Angela had sent me a funny joke that had me laughing out loud. I was about to look at the library's Facebook page when I heard a familiar voice. Not Julie again! She was everywhere, every minute of the day. And there she was on TV, surrounded by a crowd of people in front of the Clover Ridge Police Station.

". . . once again, I am happy to announce that my crew and I have discovered the name of the man whose remains were discovered in the basement of the building undergoing renovations next to the Clover Ridge Library. As I speak, members of my crew are trying to local Alec Dunmore's relatives so they can give the poor man a decent burial."

"How did you manage to find out who he is when the police didn't have a clue?" a young man asked.

"Good investigative teamwork," Julie said and went on to mention a few of the nationwide missing persons sites she and her crew had combed through. "We know that he lived in or near Chicago."

Someone shouted out a question. The only word I could make out was "police."

Julie's face took on a smug expression. "Of course we hope the police will find Alec Dunmore's murderer. But judging by the fact that *we* discovered his identity, I'm not counting on that happening any time soon."

Poor John! I thought. A homicide investigation was difficult enough, but having someone like Julie shooting zingers at you on television made matters triply worse.

"Will you be investigating his murder?" someone asked.

"If I see that the police aren't making progress any time soon, I'll be obliged to start my own investigation."

I clicked the remote, removing Julie's smug face from my sight. As much as I hated that she was responsible for finding out who the man was, I couldn't wait to tell Charlie the news.

Smoky Joe and I arrived at the library around eleven o'clock. Sally saw me as I was releasing him from his carrier. "What are you doing here so early? Today's a late day for you—or did you forget?"

"I didn't forget, but I had nothing urgent to do at home so I thought I'd come in early."

She hooked her arm through mine. "I'm glad you're here. Sean and Rafe are coming by soon to give an update on the renovations next door. I'd love to have you join us."

Uh-oh! I was about to find out just what adjustments Sean and Buzz had to make to the original plans. "Sure. Let me just stop by my office first."

Sally smiled as though she were giving me a break instead of having just involved me in a meeting I hadn't expected or planned for. "Relax. Take your time. I'll call you when they're in the building."

I entered my office and found Trish speaking to someone on the phone. When their conversation came to an end she told me,

"That was a woman asking if we'd be interested in having her group of belly dancers perform when the new stadium-seating auditorium is built."

"What did you tell her?" I asked.

"To call back when you're here."

"Did she give you any references?" I asked.

"She said they'd performed at several libraries in the area." Trish glanced at her notes and rattled off a few names.

"Could you please call those librarians and find out what they thought of the group?"

"Sure."

"Thanks. Everything running smoothly?" I asked.

"So far," Trish said.

I went through my messages while Trish called the various libraries. Nothing required my immediate attention. Which was a good thing, because I couldn't concentrate on anything other than telling Charlie that we now knew his name.

And then what? I asked myself. What good is knowing your name when you don't know anything about yourself—the important people in your life; your likes and dislikes?

And why hadn't anyone been looking for Charlie, I mean Alec, all these years? But maybe knowing his name would jar his memory and it would all come back to him—who he was and how he'd ended up in that dilapidated building.

Sally called me on the library phone. "They're all here! Come and join us."

All? "Sure, but who is 'all of them'?"

"Sean, Rafe, and Buzz Coleman."

"Oh. I didn't realize Buzz was coming."

"I didn't either, but the more the merrier. We'll start as soon as you get here."

Sally didn't sound merry. In fact, her voice sounded strained, which gave me a frisson of anxiety. What could be the matter?

"I'm on my way," I said and hurried to find out.

I found Sally at her desk, chatting with the three men who sat facing her. I greeted them and took the empty chair beside Sally's so that we formed a rough circle.

The men were munching away, making serious inroads in the platter of cookies Sally had brought over from the library coffee shop for the occasion. I wasn't hungry, but couldn't resist reaching for one of Katie's homemade chocolate-peanut butter cookies. Sally, I noticed, wasn't eating.

"Rafe, Sean, and Buzz have discovered a few problems that require our immediate attention. If we want to get the renovations done close to schedule, we'll have to issue additional work authorizations that will cost a good deal more money."

"Oh," I said.

"It seems that stripping an old building down to its bare bones often reveals problems like dry rot and mold," Sally said.

"But wasn't that figured in when you gave us your price?" I asked Sean.

"Of course it was. We quoted you what we figured was a good estimate."

A low estimate, which was why it was decided you were the best company to do the job, I thought.

"But we weren't prepared for what we uncovered," Buzz said. "And there are problems with the foundation that need to be taken care of first and foremost."

Sean glared at Rafe. "All of which we based on Rafe's plans and his engineer's report, which we now see was full of holes!"

Rafe opened his mouth to speak, then thought better of it.

"So what does this mean for the library? How are we supposed to get the money to cover the new expenses at this late date?" I asked.

"The money we made from the Fall Festival will help, but it's nowhere near what's needed," Sally said.

"We'll have to bring it up at the council," Sean said. "Perhaps ask for an advance on the library's budget for next year. We should be able to cover part of it that way."

"But not all," Buzz added.

I turned to Sally. "What exactly does that mean?"

She cleared her throat. "The four of us were discussing it, and the only solution we came up with is to make the auditorium a bit smaller than planned. Or forget about having stadium seating and keep the original number of seats."

"Smaller? How much smaller?" I croaked.

For a minute, no one spoke. "We figure forty seats have to go," Buzz finally said. "That's partly because of new handicap regulations—for the nearby bathrooms and widening the ramps in the auditorium itself." He turned to Rafe. "Something else that wasn't factored in."

"Oh," was all I could manage.

"Since the auditorium's your baby, I thought it best to let you decide," Sally said.

I mumbled that I'd think about it and get back to them and stumbled from the room. Forty seats! That was one-eighth of the seats we'd planned for. How could this happen? I knew that unforeseen problems could always present themselves during renovations. Sean and Buzz blamed Rafe and his engineer for not spotting them. But Sean had known the building was in bad shape. Had he simply lowballed the estimate to get the job? Difficult to say since the town council, which I wasn't on at the time, and the library board had studied the numbers.

The proposed changes regarding the new auditorium were devastating. A small part of my mind told me I was overreacting. Three hundred and twenty seats down to two hundred and eighty was considerably larger than what we had now. But our library was almost doubling in size. I'd studied figures and layouts before offering my input, and I knew I'd come up with the best plan for an imposing auditorium that could be utilized for lectures, large meetings, performances, and plays. Surely something could be done to keep the original plan.

Or should I be realistic and tell them that standard seating would be okay? The floor would be slightly sloped. No, I was standing firm on stadium seating, my original plan. I'd reached my office and was about to go inside when someone called my name.

I blinked as Evelyn manifested beside me. She looked upset.

"You have to do something about Charlie," she said. "He's growing more and more anxious and refuses to stay out of sight." She shook her head in dismay. "Earlier this morning he tore through the reading room like a madman. Books and magazines tumbled to the floor. Good thing only a few people noticed."

"Where is he?" I asked.

"In one of the small rooms downstairs. He promised to stay there while I went to look for you."

We hurried down the stairs to the lower level. I followed Evelyn into a small room often used for one-on-one tutoring. I let out a gasp of surprise. Charlie was pacing three feet above the ground.

When he saw us, he collapsed into a chair and dropped his head in his hands.

"Charlie, I'm sorry you're so distressed," I said.

He looked at me mournfully. "I can't take much more of this. I keep asking Evelyn to take me with her when she leaves this plane, but she won't. She insists I'll go where I'm meant to go when everything falls into place. Now what does that mean?"

"I don't know, but I have some news I hope will be helpful. Your name is Alec Dunmore. Does that sound familiar?"

"Alec Dunmore," he said slowly. "Actually, it does."

"Wonderful!" I clapped my hands. "And they think that you lived in or near Chicago."

He nodded. "If you say so, but I don't get any vibes."

"What else did John find out about Alec?" Evelyn asked.

"It was a TV reporter named Julie Theron who found out who Alec is—was," I said. It felt funny calling Charlie Alec. "She has it in for John." I turned to Alec. "Maybe now that the police know who you are and where you're from, they'll be able to find out why somebody wanted to kill you."

Evelyn nodded. "Finding out what happened to you will help bring back your memory. And then I'm quite sure you'll be sent where you're meant to be."

Alec released a deep sigh. "I sure hope you're right about that."

I left them a few minutes later. Since the room we'd been using was scheduled to be occupied very soon, Evelyn agreed to accompany Alec up to the attic and spend some time with him there. Alec promised to keep out of sight and try to remain patient and calm.

When I returned to my office, Trish told me that Dylan had called me on the library phone. That was unusual. He always texted or called me on my cell. "And he said not to bother calling him back because he was busy all afternoon, but he'd stop by the library around six thirty and bring you dinner."

"Really? I wonder why."

Trish laughed. "I wouldn't wonder if my fiancé offered to bring me dinner when I was working late."

"Did Dylan say anything else?"

"No, just what I told you."

I tucked away my misgivings and told Trish about my meeting with Sally, Sean, Rafe, and Buzz.

"That stinks!" Trish declared when I'd finished. "Cutting down the size of the auditorium because of expenses and larger bathrooms. Maybe you can talk to Al Tripp about getting more town funds to cover the new costs. You're on the council. Maybe he can give us more money to keep the original plans."

"They probably will give us some funds, but I doubt it will be enough."

"Oh."

"Sean blamed Rafe for the discrepancy, but it seems to me he should have known about the potential problems since the building was so dilapidated. Do you think Sean deliberately lowballed the cost, knowing this would happen?"

Trish shrugged. "If you asked me this a few years ago, I would have said I wouldn't put it past him. In fact, I would have expected Sean Powell to pull a fast one to get the job. But not lately. He's hard working and sees that his workers are too. I hope the company remains in reliable hands when he retires."

"Sean's retiring!" I exclaimed. "I had no idea."

Trish raised her eyebrows. "Don't you people on the council talk to one another?"

"Of course, but—how did you know?"

Trish covered her mouth. "My bad. Dad ran into Sean a few days ago and they got to talking. They used to be good friends when they were neighbors but drifted apart when Sean and Pat moved to their big house. Sean said to keep it under his hat because he was still working out the details."

"Did he tell your father who'll be taking over his company?"

"No."

"I won't say anything. But I wonder why Sean is keeping this a secret."

Chapter Fourteen

D ylan entered my office at precisely six thirty. My fiancé took pride in being on time, and tonight was no exception. He greeted Susan with a smile and me with a kiss as he plonked down a plastic bag from the Gourmet Market on my desk.

Susan stood. "Good to see you, Dylan. I'll give you guys some privacy and the use of my chair."

"Thanks, Susan," I called after her.

Smoky Joe dashed into the office as she left. He rubbed up against Dylan's leg, then came over to me, letting loose a loud meow.

"Give me a minute and I'll feed you," I told him, opening the cabinet where I kept his kibble.

When he was gobbling down his dinner, purring all the while, I turned to Dylan, who was placing containers and tinfoil-covered dishes on the section of my desk that he'd covered with napkins.

"And what delicacies have you brought for our dinner? I hope it's not heavy enough to put me to sleep. I have to work afterward."

Dylan glanced up. "Keeping that in mind, I thought we'd try their cold butternut squash bisque, then have roasted root veggie and goat cheese sandwiches on their homemade fourteen-grain bread."

"Sounds yummy. What's the occasion?"

Dylan gave me a wistful smile. "I miss you. We've both been so busy lately, we haven't had a chance to really talk."

"Talk about what?"

He shrugged. "Whatever's been going on in our lives."

I sighed, relieved that Dylan hadn't come to discuss our future. When we'd gotten engaged in July, he'd promised not to rush me into making wedding plans. I knew without a doubt that I wanted to marry Dylan and live the rest of our lives together, but growing up in a dysfunctional family had left its mark on me, and I needed more time to get used to the idea of marriage before we set a date.

"I can tell you what's happening here," I said. "Sally and I met with the construction people this morning. It seems unexpected problems have cropped up that will cost more money. Translated, the auditorium will be smaller than planned. Forty seats smaller."

"Oh, babe, I'm sorry." Dylan leaned over and rubbed my back.

Tears welled up in my eyes. "Or we can forgo having stadium seating, which I refuse to do."

"There's no way of getting around this?"

"Not that I can see. But let's not talk about that now." I tasted my soup and smiled at Dylan. "This is delicious."

"It sure is," he said after he tasted his.

I finished off my soup, making a mental note to buy more soon, then unwrapped my sandwich. "And I'm sure you've heard they've discovered Charlie's identity."

"Of course. Julie Theron's coup was on the radio, TV, and the internet. Did you tell Charlie? How did he react to the news?"

"When I told him his name is Alec Dunmore, he said it sounded familiar."

"I wonder if he'll regain his memory when he finds out more about himself," Dylan mused.

"I sure hope the police find his murderer," I said. "And learn what he was doing here in Clover Ridge when he lived in or near Chicago. He can't continue to hover around the library."

"Poor Alec," Dylan said. "He deserves to rest in peace."

I bit into my sandwich, savoring the tangy, sweet, and pungent flavors simultaneously. When I could speak again, I asked, "And what's happened recently that you want to talk about?"

"We can get into that after we eat."

My anxiety, which had been simmering since Trish had told me Dylan was bringing me dinner, came to a boil. "Is it my dad? Are you going to tell me he's had a heart attack or something worse?"

"I promise you, Jim's fine."

"Okay," I said, then realized how blind and insensitive I'd been. "It's about you!"

Dylan squirmed. "Indirectly. Carrie, sweetheart. I'm in good health. I'm not in trouble with the law. I don't have to work a job out of the area. And I promise to tell you everything as soon as we've finished eating."

"Okay," I said. "I'll stop playing Twenty Questions."

Reassured that Dylan wasn't facing a life-threatening problem, I devoured the rest of my sandwich. I was very hungry and willing to leave whatever was troubling him for the next few minutes.

When I came up for air, I noticed that Dylan had hardly touched his sandwich.

"Do you want to take this home?"

He shrugged. I wrapped it and put it to one side, then gathered up our trash and stuffed it in the bag our food had come in. I stood to brush the crumbs from my skirt.

"Would you like me to get you something to drink from the coffee shop?" I asked as I dropped the debris in my wastepaper basket.

"I don't think so." Dylan put his hand on my arm. "Please sit down, Carrie."

His demeanor was so solemn, my anxiety rose again. *He's lying about being sick. Or about my father.* "What's wrong?"

"I've been in a muddle ever since I heard the news. All day I've been trying to piece together what must have happened. But too many parts are missing for me to figure it out. I wanted to get your take on the situation but hated disturbing you at work. And I couldn't wait until you got home, figuring it would be late and you'd be too tired to focus. So I decided to come here during your dinner hour, which would be long enough to explain. And maybe . . . maybe . . ."

I pressed my lips together to keep from screaming. Instead, I grabbed his hand. "Say it, Dylan, right now. What did you come to tell me?"

Dylan made a sound between a groan and a gasp. "Alec Dunmore is my uncle."

I blinked, not sure I'd heard correctly. "He's . . . your uncle?" He nodded.

"You had no idea until you heard the news this morning that the body found next door was that of your uncle?"

"Of course not. Why would I?"

"I don't know. Maybe because he'd been missing all those years? Because you hadn't heard from him since—I don't know when."

Dylan glanced at me, then off in the distance. Back to the past.

"Uncle Alec was my mother's baby brother. He was thirteen years younger than her. She adored him, and so did everyone else. He grew up thinking the world was his for the asking. Or the taking. Alec got expelled from high school a few times. Never for anything really bad. The usual stuff wilder kids get into. And he never made it through college. He had the brains but not the discipline to attend classes and sit for tests like the rest of us."

"Did you know him well?"

"Not really, since he didn't live near us. But he came to stay with us for a few days every couple of years." Dylan smiled. "And each time he made it seem like an adventure. Once he took me to the circus on a school day. Another time we took the train into Manhattan and went to the top of the Empire State Building. I never forgot those visits.

"Of course my father had no use for Uncle Alec. 'He's a grown man,' he'd gripe to my mother. 'He should be earning real money and raising a family like the rest of the world.' But my mother, who usually went along with everything my father proclaimed, only laughed and said that Alec wasn't like everyone else. He made enough money to live life the way he wanted to. He wasn't hurting anyone. At which point my father would stare pointedly at me and say that Alec set a poor example."

Dylan drew a deep breath, then went on. "As much as I loved our outings, it was Uncle Alec's stories that stayed with me long past his visits. He was fascinated by real-life murders and robberies that had made the news and would tell me about them in the most exciting way. It was almost like being at the theater."

He gave a little chuckle. "I suppose that's how I ended up becoming an investigator. I wanted to live some of those adventures myself."

The more Dylan told me, the more questions I had. "It sounds like you haven't seen Alec in some time. Did something happen that changed your relationship?"

"As I got older, I began to see what my father meant about Alec. He was fun to be with but he wasn't reliable—saying he'd call or we'd get together but never following through. One summer when I was in college, I got a job working in Chicago, where he lived. Twice we made plans to meet for dinner and twice he didn't show. Each time he apologized profusely a day or two later, saying something really important had come up and he'd make it up to me.

"I stopped trying to connect after that." Dylan grimaced. "Especially after I overheard my parents talking about the kind of things he was doing to make money."

"But if he lived in Chicago, how do you think he ended up being murdered in Clover Ridge?"

"That's what I've been trying to figure out ever since I found out that the corpse was Uncle Alec."

"Do you think he came to see your mother?"

"It's the only thing that makes sense. I had no idea he came here. He certainly never got in touch with me. I was twenty when we last spoke. If Alec came here six years ago and my parents knew, they wouldn't have told me, since we were estranged."

Dylan scrunched up his face, looking puzzled. "Still, I can't figure out why he came to Clover Ridge. As I remember, my mother finally got good and disgusted with her brother and swore she'd have nothing more to do with him. It seemed the older he got, the less he earned and the more he wanted a comfortable life. So he'd taken to scamming people. Doing stuff like passing bad checks. He even spent a stint or two in jail."

I thought a moment. "Alec is right here in the building. I mean his ghost is. You can talk to him. Ask him why he came to Clover Ridge. Maybe he'll recognize you. But only if you want to."

Dylan didn't answer.

"Alec's really confused. Maybe if you talk to him, he'll start remembering things."

Dylan gnawed at his lower lip. "Carrie, I do and I don't want to see him. I feel I should because maybe seeing me will jar his memory so he'll remember who murdered him. I owe him that much. Still, I don't want to because the thought of talking to the ghost of Uncle Alec blows my mind. And given that someone offed him and left him in that basement tells me what happened to him is one ugly story."

I nodded, factoring in everything Dylan just told me. Alec, his childhood idol, had proven to be an unscrupulous con artist. Alec was one more adult who had let him down.

"I don't suppose you'd like me to bring him to you now so you can meet him?"

"Not today, Carrie. I'll let you know if and when I'm ready."

"Okay."

We both stood. Dylan took me in his arms and held me tight. "I'm so glad I have you to share my life. I don't know how I managed to get along without you until a year ago."

"I'm the lucky one," I said. "And I'm so happy we'll be together for the rest of our lives."

Chapter Fifteen

Dylan left and I climbed the stairs to the attic to check on Alec. Hardly anyone ever came up here, and for good reason. The attic was the most neglected area of the library. It wasn't very large, and every inch was chock full of pieces of old, discarded furniture. A year ago, following a clue that Evelyn had given me, I'd discovered a journal that had helped solve a fifteen-year-old murder case.

Unused and abandoned, the attic was the perfect place for Alec—to relax and perhaps make use of the reading material I'd brought up earlier. It occurred to me that if we weren't setting up a Teen Scene section in the new addition, this would be a fun place where teenagers could gather to chat and play video games and maybe watch a movie—with a librarian on hand to supervise, of course.

I found Alec sprawled out on a worn leather couch reading a book. He seemed to have calmed down. Perhaps learning his real name had given him hope that he'd soon discover what he was doing in Clover Ridge and why someone had murdered him.

"Hi, Carrie. Any news?" he asked.

As much as I wanted to help Alec regain his memory, my first allegiance was to Dylan. His reluctance to connect with his uncle had rubbed off on me, and I wasn't ready to tell Alec that I'd found a close relative.

So instead of answering, I asked him a question. "Does the name Avery mean anything to you?"

He stretched his arms overhead. "I don't know. Why? Should it?"

"Estelle and Cal Avery? Dylan Avery?"

Alec cocked his head as he thought. "Those names do sound familiar. Why? Did they say they know me?"

"Someone remembered Estelle Avery's maiden name was Dunmore."

"She's my sister?"

"I think so," I said

"Then ask her!" Alec exclaimed. "What are you waiting for?"

"She, er, isn't around."

Evelyn suddenly materialized. "Hello. Sorry I couldn't get here sooner."

Alec turned to her. "Carrie just told me my sister lives in this town. Her name is Estelle Avery."

Evelyn fixed her gaze on me. "Is that so?"

"My apologies, but I have to go." I turned to Alec. "I promise to fill you in as soon as I have more information."

"Carrie, come back! You can't leave me like this," Alec called after me.

I returned to my office and found Susan humming as she created more Halloween decorations to place around the library. I decided that now was as good a time as any to contact a few librarians in nearby towns to ask their opinions regarding a few presenters I was considering hiring. A proposal might sound wonderful on paper, but it gave no indication of how charismatic or boring the person was in front of a live audience.

Sally came by to ask Susan to put in an hour at the hospitality desk. When we were alone, she said, "I'm sorry you found out about the auditorium the way you did."

"I'm sorry, too." *You could have given me a heads-up earlier. Not that it would have made much of a difference.*

"Have you decided which way you want to go with it?"

"Can I tell you tomorrow?"

"You have the weekend to think it over. I'm meeting with Rafe and Sean on Monday afternoon, so let me know before then."

When Sally left, it dawned on me that the real purpose of her visit had been to apologize for dropping the news about the auditorium the way she had. And hoping that I'd made a decision so we could move past the issue. I knew I wouldn't give up the stadium-seating idea, but for some perverse reason I refused to agree to go along with a smaller auditorium until the last possible minute. I was still smarting because they'd chosen to decrease the size of the auditorium instead of making some other adjustment to the plans.

I called Ruth Gonzalez, the head of adult programs at the Merrivale Library, and asked her about a chef I was thinking of signing up to do a food presentation.

"Anton is terrific. His menus are delicious, and he knows how to keep his audience's attention. I book him as often as I can," Ruth said.

"Thanks. Good to know." I then asked about a crafts person who had told me that people who attended her programs absolutely adored her.

Ruth laughed. "Forget Dora. She rambles on about herself, her daughter, her dog, and her daughter's dog. I've never had as many complaints as when Dora came to speak."

We chatted a bit more until someone needed Ruth's attention and we said goodbye. I shot off an email to Anton and was about to send one to Dora Hessler when I felt a chill. I looked up and found Evelyn at my side.

"You told Alec that Estelle Avery is his sister."

"Yes."

Evelyn nodded. "I gather Dylan recognized Alec's name. He must have been shocked to learn the dead man was his uncle."

"Totally, and frankly not eager to have anything to do with Uncle Alec—at least not yet. If I mention Dylan to Alec, he'll nag me to bring him to the library, which I'm not prepared to do."

"So Uncle Alec wasn't such a great guy," Evelyn said. "I was wondering why you acted so cagey and then flew out of room."

"I feel bad about that," I admitted, "but Dylan saw Alec as something of a hero when he was growing up. Then he disappointed Dylan one too many times. I think after Dylan weighs both sides of the situation, he'll come around and talk to him."

Evelyn released an exasperated sigh. "And soon, I hope. Dylan is the one person who might be able to jar Alec's memory. The more Alec remembers what happened to him, the closer we are to finding his killer so he can be on his way."

"If anything, the investigator in Dylan will want to find out who killed his uncle."

"I think you're right, Carrie." She eyed me carefully. "But something else is bothering you." It was disconcerting how well Evelyn had learned to read me.

"This morning I attended a meeting with Sally; Sean Powell; Rafe Torres, the architect; and Buzz Coleman, Sean's foreman. They informed me that due to unforeseen expenses, the auditorium will be short forty seats of what we'd planned. That, or I'll have to settle for an ordinary auditorium."

"Quite a disappointment for you."

"It sure is."

Evelyn rapped her fingers against my assistants' desk as she thought. "I'm wondering . . ."

"Yes?"

"From what I remember, the seats you chose were the top of the line. What if the order was changed to less expensive seats? And they cut back on a few frills? It's called value engineering. I imagine that would make a difference in the cost."

I thought a minute. "It would! But can we make a big change like that so late in the day?"

"I think so, especially since Sean may have already notified the factory there's a problem under discussion."

"Thanks, Evelyn. I'll mention it to Sally."

"And tell her you'd like to join the meeting on Monday."

"Great idea!" I shot her a puzzled look. "I wonder why Rafe or Sean didn't suggest this value engineering possibility."

"Because they took the easy way out."

I stared at her. "How on earth do you know about value engineering?"

Evelyn smiled her enigmatic smile. "You'd be surprised to learn what other tricks I have up my sleeve."

* * *

I decided that Cornish hens, wild rice with mushrooms, a pasta dish with broccoli cheese sauce, and a beet salad would be a nice menu for Saturday night. The hens were sure to turn into a hands-on event, so I placed a package of hand wipes close to the side table in the dining room. Dylan picked up a six-pack of Belgian beer and brought over a bottle of Chardonnay from his stash at the manor house.

I felt a bit nervous as seven o'clock drew near. We'd been to Julia and Randy's house a few times, and they had been here for my birthday party last December, but we'd never spent time together as couples. I suddenly remembered bursting into tears when Randy had said my sunburn made me look like a cooked lobster. *Come on, Carrie*, I told myself. You were nine and Randy was eleven or twelve. Now you're thirty years old, for God's sake, and you know how to deal with Randy's teasing.

Once they stepped inside the cottage, my misgivings faded away. Julia and I exchanged kisses and Randy grabbed me into a fierce bear hug. "Thanks so much for inviting us over," he said.

Everyone opted for beer, so Dylan brought a tray of bottles and glasses into the living room and I carried in another tray of finger foods and set it on the coffee table. We chatted about the council meeting on Thursday, Mark and Tacey, Aunt Harriet and Uncle Bosco (who were babysitting), and other topics that continued as we moved into the dining room.

I served the beet salad and Dylan opened the bottle of Chardonnay.

Randy held up his glass. "To my kid cousin Carrie and her betrothed. A great couple."

I was touched as we all clinked glasses, then sipped my wine.

"This is really good," Randy said as we ate our salad.

I noticed that he'd finished off his plate. "Would you like some more?" I gestured to the salad bowl. "Take what's left."

"Are you sure?"

"Go for it," Dylan said.

Julia laughed. "Well, that's a surprise. At home the only salad he'll eat is iceberg lettuce."

"Why change when you got a good thing going?" Randy said.

Julia helped me clear the salad dishes and bring out the main course. For a while, we were too busy eating and drinking to speak.

"I love Cornish hen," Julia said, "despite the many small bones."

"Yeah, you have to watch those small bones," Randy said.

They looked at each other. I sensed sadness. Julia looked at me. "Mark almost choked on a small bone when he was about Tacey's age."

Randy nodded. "We rushed him to the hospital. Thank God a young resident there knew exactly what to do."

"That's good," I said.

"I don't mean to scare you guys, but raising kids, keeping them safe, is a full-time job."

"We're not scared, are we, babe?" Dylan leaned over and rubbed my arm.

"I'm not scared, exactly," I said. "Just a little nervous about the ways my life is going to change once we get married."

Randy chortled. "And they say men are the nervous ones." I thought he was talking about me, but he was staring at Julia, a broad grin on his face. "Two weeks before our wedding, Julia almost called it off."

"Really?" I stared at her.

Julia shrugged. "Why wouldn't I be nervous? Randy didn't have a job."

"I was laid off temporarily," Randy said. "You knew that."

"Whatever. I was teaching and didn't know if I wanted to teach for the rest of my life. I didn't know if I wanted kids."

"But you're a wonderful mother," I said.

"Thank you." Julia smiled.

"And so you see, folks, it all worked out," Randy said giving his wife a smooch on the cheek.

Dylan and I exchanged glances. *So, other people have their doubts. Couples have their issues. And Julia and Randy are real and not the perfect couple I imagined them to be.* I felt a loosening in my chest I hadn't known was there.

Over coffee and dessert, we got on the subject of work, and Julia admitted she was worried she'd taken on too much responsibility when she'd agreed to work full-time.

"I told her to tell them she wants to cut back a day," Randy said, "but Julia's afraid they'll fire her."

"No, I don't want to let them down," Julia said. "And the money's good."

"Your well-being is more important," Randy said. "And how it affects the rest of us."

"We'll discuss it at home," Julia said, "and not bore Carrie and Dylan with our problems."

I chuckled. "Don't mind us. We're getting an education."

We all laughed and moved on to another subject.

Julia and Randy left shortly after, amid hugs and promises to get together soon. The evening had been meaningful to all of us, and I knew Dylan and I would grow even closer to Julia and Randy in the years ahead.

* * *

By Sunday evening, Dylan decided he wanted to meet with the ghost of his uncle, after all.

"I suppose I owe it to Alec to find his killer," he said while we were eating the pizza we'd brought home for our dinner. "And I'm curious to find out what he was doing in Clover Ridge. For all I know, he and my mother were back on good terms, though I can't imagine what he could have said or done to heal their relationship."

"Maybe Alec gave up his cheating and scamming."

Dylan rolled his eyes. "Let's not go overboard. I said I'll talk to him."

I got up and hugged him. "You're doing the right thing."

Dylan agreed to come to the library the following day, which was Monday. I was glad it was finally happening because every time I saw Alec he bombarded me with questions. He sensed I was holding back information, which made him more agitated. And when he was agitated, whole shelves of books went crashing to the ground. I knew he didn't mean to do it, but his heightened distress sent out an energy force that was beginning to frighten patrons. Finally, I could tell him he'd soon be meeting someone from his past.

I'd asked Evelyn to bring Alec to a small room downstairs that I knew would be free from eleven to one. Dylan had a few early morning appointments at his office in New Haven and would then drive back to Clover Ridge in time for our get-together. I felt nervous as I cleared away some paperwork, then wondered what I had to be nervous about. *I* wasn't about to meet the ghost of my dead uncle I no longer held in high regard. But of course I wanted the encounter to go smoothly—for Dylan's sake and for Alec's.

Dylan took my hand as we entered the small room, and I could feel his racing pulse. He must have been experiencing so many emotions. Encountering two ghosts for the very first time had to be daunting, even for a seasoned investigator. It felt kind of surreal even to me. I'd gotten used to spending time with the two ghosts. In fact, one of them was one of my closest friends. How had I become the ghost whisperer?

Evelyn perched calmly on the edge of the table, much as she did when she visited me in my office, while Alec paced along the side of the room. At least he wasn't pacing in the air as he sometimes liked to do.

The moment he saw us, he whizzed over, causing quite a stir. "At last! You finally got here! I was beginning to think you weren't coming."

Dylan flinched at the draught of cold air, then stared at the ghost of his Uncle Alec. "Yes, I'm here." He was able to see and hear Alec, but not Evelyn. I couldn't explain why this was, but I imagined it had something to do with the different stages they were in.

I held out my hand, gesturing to Evelyn. "Dylan, I'd like you to meet my dear friend Evelyn Havers."

I was proud of Dylan. He smiled as he nodded in her direction. Only the white knuckles of his clenched hands were proof of the ordeal he was going through. "Nice to meet you, Evelyn. Carrie talks about you often."

I repeated what Evelyn said: "And I see you recognize Alec. He has a bad case of amnesia and, until recently, didn't even know his name. But once you heard his name you realized he was your mother's brother, Alec Dunmore."

"I did," Dylan said, not sounding at all happy about it.

"Alec, do you recognize your nephew, Dylan Avery? Does he seem familiar to you?" Evelyn asked.

Alec shrugged. I could tell he was disappointed not to recognize Dylan. "I don't know. The names Estelle and Dylan seem familiar, but that's about it."

Dylan pressed his lips together. "Do you remember visiting us when I was a kid? You used to tell me stories. Homicides and robberies fascinated you. I think that's partly why I became an investigator."

"You're an investigator?"

Dylan nodded. "I am. Until recently, I was recovering high-end art and gems, though now I investigate pretty much anything I'm asked to look into. I leave the homicides to Carrie."

Alec looked at me. "You're an investigator too?"

"Not really."

Evelyn cleared her throat. "I think we're getting off topic."

"So we are," I agreed. "Alec, would you like to ask Dylan something? Anything that comes to mind?"

He made a scoffing sound. "For some reason, I'm suddenly thinking about being at a circus. That sounds crazy, doesn't it?"

"You took me to the circus when I was about twelve," Dylan said. "You were crazy about the elephants. You told me you once rode an elephant when you were in India."

"I don't remember riding an elephant or liking them especially."

Dylan mentioned their trip to the top of the Empire State Building when he was fifteen, but Alec didn't remember that, either.

"That was a long time ago. Didn't we do anything more recently?" Alec asked.

"We hadn't spent time together in quite some time," Dylan said.

"What can you tell me about my sister?" Alec asked.

"My parents are gone now. My mother was very fond of you. But then you—" Dylan stopped, not wanting to insult his uncle.

"I what?"

"You were rather carefree and somewhat irresponsible. So my father always said. And then something happened—I'm not sure what exactly—my parents, even my mother, stopped talking to you."

"Stopped talking," Alec said. He was sitting in one of the chairs, staring down at his hands. I wondered if he was remembering and pretending he couldn't. At any rate, he shook his head and looked at us. "Sorry, but I have no idea what that was about."

Evelyn, who hadn't said much so far, said, "I don't think there's any point in trying to press Alec to remember specific events. I'm no neurologist, but I think it would be best to leave it for now. Maybe bringing up some of these past experiences will jar his memory and they'll start coming back to him in a day or two."

I told Dylan what Evelyn had said.

"I sure hope so," he said, clearly eager to leave. "I'm glad we gave it a shot. I'm willing to try again, but right now I have to get back to the office."

He started for the door when Alec said, "I'm sorry, Dylan."

Dylan stopped in his tracks.

"I may not remember much, but from what you've told me and what you're not telling me, I get the definite feeling that things between your family and me haven't been great."

"That about sums it up."

"Talk to you later," I said to Evelyn and Alec and left the room with Dylan.

"Well, that had to be the creepiest experience of my life," Dylan said.

"I can understand."

He looked searchingly at me. "I could see Alec all right, a kind of a transparent, washed out image of himself, but not Evelyn. You really can see her and hear her?"

"I can."

"Amazing."

"How did Alec seem to you?"

"I recognized him, all right, though he's aged. There was none of the charm and charisma I always associated with my uncle. Now he just seems anxious and sad."

"That might be because of his present predicament—stuck in a strange place, a ghost of himself. Or maybe life wore him down. Or this is how he often was when he wasn't performing for his nephew."

We climbed the stairs to the main level in silence.

"I wish I could have helped him recover his memory," Dylan said.

"Maybe you did more good than we know," I said, hoping that was true.

Chapter Sixteen

Dylan left and I answered a few emails until noon, when I drove to the Cozy Corner Café with Angela. After lunch we planned to stop in at the new Pet Warehouse that was a five-minute drive outside of town. I was running low on cat food and kitty litter, and the warehouse had some wonderful sales going to introduce themselves to the community.

Angela was eager to visit the pet store section of the warehouse to check out the dogs. She and Steve had decided they wanted to buy a small designer dog, but they couldn't decide on which new breed to get. They were torn between a Shih-Poo and a Yorkipoo.

"I think you're crazy," I told her as I pulled into the parking lot that was three-quarters filled. "You could save yourself a lot of money if you went to a shelter. There are so many dogs in need of a home. I'm sure you would find one that would make a wonderful pet."

Angela scoffed. "That's what you know about the subject! Choosing a pet requires research. You have to look into the various breeds, then check out breeders. Just because you let the first cat that crossed your path share your life doesn't mean I should do the same thing with a dog."

We exited the car and walked to the back entrance of the warehouse. "How can you say that about Smoky Joe?" I demanded. "He's the sweetest, most lovable cat. And you have to admit he's the perfect library cat." I sniffed. "I thought you liked him."

"Of course I do—I *love* Smoky Joe. All I'm saying is, Steve and I want to choose the breed we feel will suit us best, and pick the best puppy of that breed. A puppy that's playful but not crazy wild, affectionate, and easy to train."

"A designer dog is very expensive," I mumbled, seriously annoyed with my best friend.

She didn't bother to respond.

Inside the warehouse, I snagged a cart and told Angela I'd meet her at the exit in fifteen minutes. I wandered down the food aisle, marveling at all the wonderful brands the warehouse offered. Smoky Joe liked whatever I fed him, but maybe I should upgrade to a healthier brand.

I was reaching for a can of food I'd seen advertised on TV when a woman behind me said, "So this is where the famous Carrie Singleton shops for the Clover Ridge Library cat."

I swung around, into the grinning face of Julie Theron.

"Not really," I managed. "I thought I'd check out the warehouse. Their prices are good."

"Exactly what I'm doing."

I glanced into her cart. It was piled high with cartons of canned cat food and a giant bag of cat kibble. "You have a cat."

"Three."

Was that supposed to make us sisters of some sort? Was I expected to feel inferior because she had three times the number of felines to care for? I started up the aisle.

"Carrie, I'd like us to sit down and have a serious talk," Julie said.

I stared at her. "About what?"

"The fact that the dead man is your fiancé's uncle."

I gaped at her. That was fast, but I should have expected it.

"Yes, Alec Dunmore was Dylan's mother's brother. Surprised I figured that out?"

How I longed to wipe that grin off her face. Instead, I shrugged and said, "Not really. You are an investigative reporter."

"But I'm more interested in the larger picture, which is where you come in."

"Me? I didn't know Dylan's uncle. I had no idea Dylan even had an uncle."

"Dylan Avery is a respected investigator. He won't give me the time of day if I ask him about Alec Dunmore. But you're another story. Now that the murder victim turned out to be a close relative of your fiancé, you'll want to solve the crime, of course."

She grinned. "You can get Dylan to fill you in on his uncle and what he was doing in Clover Ridge—the visit that cost him his life."

I clamped my lips shut, not wanting her to see how close she'd come to accurately assessing the situation—at least about my wanting to solve the crime. "This is a matter best left to the police."

Julie snorted. "Admit it. You have a knack for solving murders, many of them cold cases. There's no way you're going to let this one pass you by."

I knew better than to protest, so I remained silent, wondering where Julie was going with this.

"I've analyzed your previous cases," she said. "You're going to figure out what Alec Dunmore was doing in Clover Ridge the day he was murdered, who murdered him, and why."

She analyzed my cases? It was unnerving to hear that Julie Theron had studied me like a bug under a microscope. But judging by the way she gripped the handle of her cart full of cat food, this was an emotional time for her too.

"What exactly are you after?" I asked.

"I plan to tag along as your Watson and report the biggest story of my life!"

* * *

"That woman has some nerve!" Angela said as I gunned the car out of the parking lot.

"I told her to stay out of my life. That I had no plans to solve a murder or be part of her story. She smirked and told me to have a good day. I know this isn't the end of it, Ange. She's going to hound me."

Angela laughed. "Can you imagine the story Julie Theron would write if she knew that Alec Dunmore is haunting the Clover Ridge Library and has no idea who killed him?"

I grimaced. "Yeah. That would be a disaster."

Angie spent the rest of our ride back to the library telling me how cute the little Maltipoo she'd seen was.

"That's a . . ."

"Combination of a Maltese and a poodle," she said glibly. "An adorable new breed. They come in three sizes—teacup, toy, and mini, depending on the size of the poodle parent. The woman I spoke to said the tan puppy I was playing with is a miniature. She said Maltipoos can be barkers, but they're easy to potty train."

"Train?" I said. "They're so little. You mean train them to make outside? Where you walk them in the rain and the snow?"

Angela made a face. "First they go on puppy pads in the house, then outside."

"I'm glad I don't have to walk Smoky Joe. Ever."

"Well, he's a cat. What do you expect?"

I wasn't quite sure how to take that.

Back in my office, I found myself wondering if Julie Theron had somehow found out I was planning to visit the new Pet Warehouse and had made it her business to waylay me in her latest attempt to join me in solving the mystery surrounding Alec Dunmore. Impossible, I decided. I was just being paranoid. It *had* to be a coincidence. But the woman was persistent. She was determined to investigate the case with me despite my denials and protestations.

I shut Julie out of my thoughts and focused on what I planned to say at the three o'clock meeting regarding the auditorium situation, which was a far cry from the recommended changes. I had told Sally that going with less expensive seats would allow us to keep the original number of seats as well as the stadium-seating plan. I wasn't sure what she thought of my suggestion or how the others would respond. While I expected opposition to my plan, being on the town council had taught me how to deflect contrary opinions and to stand up for my own.

We were meeting in the conference room because Sally had asked members of the library board as well as the town council to join us. I walked over to the conference room a few minutes before three and greeted Uncle Bosco and Al Tripp. Being in their company helped soothe my nerves. I said hello to the two women on the library board as they arrived and waved to Sally and Rafael Torres, who were laughing at a story he'd just related. Dressed elegantly as usual, today Rafe wore gray trousers, a deep purple blazer, a pale gray shirt, and a gray-and-purple tie.

Sean and Buzz, dressed in workman's attire, joined us minutes later. They ended their animated discussion as they entered the room. Again, I was surprised to see Buzz.

"Thank you all for making this meeting," Sally said when we were all seated. "We've encountered unexpected issues which have accrued new expenses that we hadn't figured on. Rafe thought the easiest solution would be to eliminate forty seats in the stadium-seating auditorium. Or create an auditorium with a shallow slanting rise that would allow for the original number of seats."

So that was Rafe's idea.

"But a new idea has presented itself." Sally turned to me. "Carrie would love to see our original plans go forward—a stadium-seating auditorium with three hundred and twenty seats. With this in mind, she suggests we go with less expensive seats. I agree with her. Now let's work to make this happen."

Sally was with me! I pressed my arm to my side to keep from thrusting it in the air in triumph. Then I glanced at Rafe, Sean, and Buzz and nearly burst into tears. They hated my idea.

"We have the order in for the more expensive seats," Rafe said. "I don't think the company we deal with is going to be happy when we tell them we no longer want them."

"Why is that a problem?" I asked. "I'm sure they're used to changes in orders all the time."

Buzz glowered at me. "This late? Changing the seats can set the whole schedule out of whack."

"Are you sure?" I asked. "Why not call them and find out?"

The discussion went on for some time. Rafe and Buzz both tried to make me "see reason" and go with one of the two recommended alternatives while Sean was clearly considering my idea. Finally, at Sally's suggestion, Sean called the company that manufactured the seats. Whomever he spoke to said he had to run it by his higher-up, but he thought the change was possible and to be prepared for a delivery delay of a week or two. Sally and I exchanged grins and the meeting came to an end.

"Buzz Coleman sure had plenty to say," I told Sally when the others had gone. "And why was he at the meeting, anyway? He's the foreman, but Sean's the contractor."

She looked at me in surprise. "Didn't you know? Sean's selling his business to Buzz. It goes into effect in October."

"Next month?" I stared at her. "I heard he was retiring, but doing it in the middle of a job?"

"Sean's gotten some bad news from his oncologist." Sally lowered her voice. "Seems he only has a few months, and he wants to spend them at home with his wife."

* * *

I made my way back to my office dazed by what Sally had just told me. Sean Powell was dying of cancer. I thought he'd looked frailer, less robust than he'd been just a month ago, but I had no inkling of what he was going through. And Buzz was buying his company. That must have been decided very recently since Trish hadn't mentioned it when we'd discussed Sean's plans to retire.

"Carrie! Carrie! Who are those people I saw leaving a meeting?"

I shivered as a cold gust of wind warned me that Alec was about to manifest. "Why are you wandering around the library?" I demanded. "You can't be out and about scaring the patrons."

"Sorry. I couldn't stay trapped in that room one minute longer. But who are those people who left the room you just came from?"

"Why do you ask?"

"After meeting with Dylan, bits of memories started to come back. Flashes of people and places, but in no particular order. I came up here to tell you and nearly collided with that group."

"And?" I cocked my head, wondering where this was going.

"One or two of the men looked familiar."

I felt a surge of excitement. "Really? Which ones?"

Now he looked uncertain. "I'm not sure. But who are they? Why were they here?"

"They came to discuss changes in the renovations. The older man is my great-uncle Bosco. He's on the library board. The man in the blue suit is our mayor. The others are the architect, the contractor, and the construction crew's foreman."

Alec's brow furrowed as he thought. "Could be I met a few of them when I came to Clover Ridge."

"Which ones, Alec? Can you describe them? I wish I had photos of them to show you, but I don't."

He shook his head. "I'm afraid I couldn't say."

Chapter Seventeen

I drove home that evening wondering which men Alec had recognized leaving today's meeting. Of course he'd seen Buzz—he'd given him a good scare the day of the Fall Festival. And he could have seen Sean and Rafe when he was in his ghostly form since they were in and out of the building being renovated.

Or had he met any of them earlier? Just how much time had he spent in Clover Ridge before he got himself killed? Had he come here because of a previous business deal? Were Dylan's parents involved? I seemed to have more questions to ponder over, but one thing was certain—Alec was starting to remember.

I called Dylan to let him know I'd be arriving home in a few minutes. He was on his way home, too, having stopped to pick up Thai food for our dinner. When I got to the cottage, I changed into jeans and a T-shirt, fed Smoky Joe, and set the table.

Over shrimp pad thai, I filled Dylan in about my encounter with Julie in the Pet Warehouse, the results of my meeting regarding the auditorium, and his uncle's bombshell about recognizing a few of the men who had been at the meeting.

"Wow! That's some afternoon you had." He didn't seem as excited about Alec's comments as I thought he'd be. "Do you think he's imagining it? I mean, he and I meet, I tell him about experiences we shared in the past, and right after that he runs into people in the library he thinks he's seen before."

"He couldn't say for sure, but his mind is definitely clearing. I've noticed the change over the past few days. Finding out his name, where he lived, then seeing you must have jolted it even more."

"Carrie, he could have seen Sean, Buzz, and Rafe any number of times when they were working in that building and gotten that confused with his time in Clover Ridge just before he was murdered."

"I know that, but maybe he met them under different circumstances."

"Hopefully Uncle Alec will soon be able to fill us in on some specific information." Dylan glanced at his watch and stood.

"What's the rush?" I asked as he carried his plate to the sink.

"I forgot to tell you. John's stopping by my place to talk. I called him to let him know Alec is my uncle. John wants me to fill him in on everything I can about the man."

I laughed. "John should only know that he could interview your uncle himself."

"Yeah. But that's not going to happen."

"Of course not," I said. "But I'd like to talk to John."

Dylan's eyebrows shot up.

"Not about Alec—directly. But about Julie Theron and the fact that she wants to help me find your uncle's murderer. I want to reassure him that I want no part of her plans or what she's been saying about him."

Dylan nodded. "That's not a bad idea. John certainly isn't thin-skinned. Civilians make negative comments about the police department all the time. But Julie Theron's on TV and in the public eye. The fact that he hasn't made any headway in the case and that she ID'd Alec *and* learned that he's my uncle might have tongues wagging."

* * *

Dylan texted John, and he agreed to stop by the cottage so he could talk to both of us. He expected to be there very soon. I cleared the table and put on a pot of coffee for the three of us.

John was exhausted as he usually was when he met us in the evening after putting in a long day's work. I thought I saw new lines creasing his craggy face as he sank into a kitchen chair. I placed a mug of coffee and a turkey sandwich in front of him.

"You didn't have to go to this trouble, Carrie," he said. "I managed to grab something to eat earlier."

I rolled my eyes as he bit into the sandwich with relish.

"Have you found out anything new about Dylan's uncle Alec?" I asked when he'd finished eating and was on his second mug of coffee.

"You mean, something that Ms. Theron didn't already manage to uncover?"

I grimaced at the bitterness in his voice. "She's really something, isn't she? She told me she wants to help *me* solve the murder—like I'm Holmes and she's my Watson."

"I'd keep far away from her if I were you," John said.

"Believe me, I try, but she's persistent. I even ran into her at the Pet Warehouse today. She couldn't have known I was planning to go there, could she?"

"Maybe she was tailing you and followed you there."

I shuddered at the thought.

"Have you found out anything new about my uncle?" Dylan asked, bringing us back on track.

John leaned back in his chair and stretched out his legs. "It doesn't appear as if he had any regular employment for some time before he died, but he was involved in a few shady deals. Nothing major or anything that brought in much money." He fixed his gaze on Dylan. "The one solid piece of information we uncovered that might lead us somewhere is your uncle and your mother inherited a piece of property out west. A great-uncle left it to them. Do you know anything about it?"

Dylan shook his head. "Nope. I haven't spoken to Uncle Alec since I was in college. And I wasn't in close contact with my parents the last few years before they died. I wouldn't know anything about their finances except that they lost a good deal of money at one point and were trying to make it back."

"I see," John said, nodding as he took all this in. "According to records faxed to us, your mother gave her brother the power of attorney to handle the sale of the property. He sold the land for two hundred and ten thousand dollars and put two-thirds of the amount in his bank account. He held onto seventy thousand dollars—in cash."

"What on earth did he want with all that cash?" Dylan shook his head "Don't tell me Uncle Alec brought seventy thousand dollars in cash to Clover Ridge?"

"That's a possibility, minus the air fare and any expenses he incurred the week before he arrived in Clover Ridge," John said.

"But that's crazy!"

"One hundred and forty thousand dollars are still in your uncle's bank account," John said.

Dylan laughed, but there was no humor in it. "Why doesn't that surprise me?"

"Is there a chance he'd come to Clover Ridge to give your mother her half of the money?" I asked.

Dylan scoffed. "In dollar bills? And it's thirty-five thousand less than she was entitled to. No, I think he planned to use the money for a deal of some kind and kept back thirty-five thou just in case things didn't work out."

"When Alec Dunmore's body was discovered, there was no wallet. The only money found on his person was a hundred-dollar bill."

Dylan whistled. "It looks like he was robbed and murdered."

John leaned forward. "The question is—if your uncle never gave your mother her share of the money, what was he was doing here in Clover Ridge?"

It was a rhetorical question neither Dylan nor I tried to answer.

After telling Dylan he was free to claim his uncle's body and arrange the burial, John took off, leaving us more puzzled than before.

"So Uncle Alec was up to his old tricks, this time stealing from his own sister," Dylan said glumly as we got ready to go to bed.

"We don't know that for certain," I said. "I'll talk to Alec, try to help him remember why he came to Clover Ridge."

"And what he was doing in that abandoned building."

"Maybe Alec was thinking of buying it."

"Could be, but why? As far as I know, my uncle never owned property in his life. And we can't ask James Whitehead because he's dead."

"True, but maybe he had it listed with a real estate agent," I said. "There are three in town."

"Good point," Dylan said. "I'll call them tomorrow and get started arranging Uncle Alec's funeral."

"And I'll talk to him first thing Wednesday morning."

"That's right. You're off tomorrow and spending part of it at the preserve."

"It's time I visited the preserve and got a definite idea of what I think should be done with that special piece of land."

* * *

It felt delicious waking up knowing I could doze a while longer because I didn't have to get ready for work. Dylan told me to go back to sleep but Smoky Joe kept on butting his head against my forehead, a sign that I should feed him. Dylan called to him, but Smoky Joe was determined that I should be the one to serve him his breakfast. I gave up and joined Dylan in the kitchen where I fed Smoky Joe and ate a light breakfast. Then, after kissing Dylan goodbye, I spent an hour at the gym, came home to shower and change, then got back in my car, ready to spend a few hours at the Seabrook Preserve.

It was a lovely late September day. Despite the bright sun above, there was a slight chill in the air—an advent of the colder weather coming soon. I felt refreshed and invigorated after exercising and showering, and sang along with the radio as I drove. As I pulled into the preserve's dirt-covered parking area, I was surprised to see a few vehicles. Not that I had reason to be surprised, I told myself. The world wasn't made up solely of people who worked Monday through Friday, nine to five. There were retirees, people who worked at home and created their own work schedule, stay-at-home parents caring for young children. And many people like me who occasionally worked weekends and had days off during the week.

I walked over to the small wooden shed open on three sides to study the map. There were two main trails: one that circled the preserve and another that ran along the Sound. The two were joined in places by secondary paths. Since I had plenty of time, I decided to walk the length of each trail. I glanced at the photos explaining what wildlife I might come across—birds, small mammals, insects—as well as various species of trees and bushes. Though the trails and paths were marked, I took one of the brochures that included a map of the property.

I started out on the trail that ran parallel to the Sound. What a glorious sight! On the horizon, a few small boats skimmed the water while a colony of gulls flew about, squawking as some came to perch on a narrow outcrop of land. A dense growth of trees and bushes bordered the land on my left.

I exchanged greetings with a couple my age who were out with their small child. As I walked I had two thoughts: why hadn't I come here before? And no way did I want condos or even a busy park replacing this beautiful treasure!

When I reached the end of the trail, I consulted my map and saw that I was standing near a path that led to the trail circling the preserve. Within minutes I found myself in the midst of a forest. I stopped to gaze at a small pond that had algae growing on its surface. Around me, trees were in various stages of health. A few had fallen to the ground. Others leaned against the limbs of other trees. Care had been taken to clear the trail of downed branches.

I must come back here with Dylan, I thought as I continued along the circular path. A black Lab ran up to me, eager for my attention, followed by his owner, an older man in awesome physical condition. On impulse I stepped on a barely discernable path that, according to my map, led to the center of the preserve.

I had come to another secondary path and had to decide if I wanted to return to the circular path or continue to wander around the center when I heard voices. One sounded familiar. I stopped in my tracks to peer through the undergrowth at the two men a few feet ahead. The older one sat on a fallen tree trunk and the younger man stood beside him. I recognized them both— Sean Powell and his son, Kevin.

Chapter Eighteen

"Are you all right, Dad?" Kevin asked.

"Yeah. I just need to rest a minute or two."

"Here, have some water."

"I don't—oh, all right."

Sean drank deeply from the water bottle Kevin handed him.

"I told you we should've met at a diner or some place you could sit down."

"And I told you I needed to breathe fresh air."

"Where no one would see us talking."

"That, too," Sean said. "We don't need tongues wagging about our business."

Father and son both chuckled, but it wasn't a happy sound.

"I still can't get over how Tim Fisk stiffed me," Kevin said. "Telling me I'd be in charge of the condo project if we snagged the job, then handing it over to his son-in-law."

"I'm not surprised," Sean said. "Even back when we were in business together, Fisk thought nothing of promising an employee a plum job to get him to work his butt off and then giving the job to someone else. It was one of the reasons I ended the partnership."

"Yeah, well, I told him what he could do with his company." Kevin gave a little laugh. "I saw Rafe Torres leaving Tim's office the other day, both of them grinning like idiots. I suppose Tim's hired himself another architect. Do you think I should give Rafe a heads up? Fill him in on how Tim screws over his people?"

Sean let out a snort. "Don't bother. The two of them deserve each other. But on second thought, Rafe's done enough damage. He has to be stopped."

"You mean because he never saw that body in the building you're renovating?"

There was a long pause. Finally Sean said, "He's careless, Kev. His measurements are off in too many places, enough to give Buzz and me serious headaches. But don't worry. We keep coming up with alternate plans."

Shocked, I covered my mouth to keep from making a sound.

Sean got to his feet with effort. "I think we can move on."

"You're sure, Dad?"

"Yeah, I'm sure. Are you sure you want to take over my company?"

"I want to be my own boss, grow the business the way I see fit, not follow someone else's orders."

They continued on their way as I retraced my steps and set off in the opposite direction, pondering all that I'd just learned. Father and son had ended their estrangement and Kevin was going to take over Sean's contracting business. The business I'd been told he was selling to his foreman, Buzz Coleman. And Sean had found problems with Rafe's designs. Which kind of surprised me, since he was the person who had recommended Rafe for the library expansion job in the first place.

I treated myself to lunch at one of the casual seafood restaurants on the Sound, then drove home. I'd visited the preserve and liked what I'd seen, but to be even-handed, I read over the material on the two alternate proposals for the property. When I was done, I came to the same conclusion I'd reached earlier that day: I was strongly in favor of keeping the property a preserve.

I jotted down a list of repairs that needed serious attention. The amenities needed a facelift, the parking lot required repaving, new maps and photos of wildlife. I felt a wave of excitement as I envisioned adding a small building housing a café and a gift shop to encourage visitors—from school groups to birdwatchers. And we had to publicize the updates and renovations so that more residents became aware of the preserve and all it had to offer.

It would be interesting to see how everything played out Thursday evening when the town council met to discuss and vote on the future of the property. Al and I wanted to keep the preserve, Babette was the for park, and Reggie for building condos.

The outcome depended on Sean.

* * *

I'd been home for less than an hour when someone knocked on the front door of my cottage. Surprised because I wasn't expecting any visitors, I went to see who it was. There stood Julie Theron, that infuriating grin on her face.

"You're home! Lucky me."

Unlucky me. "What are you doing here?" I asked.

"I want to talk to you. Don't you check your cell phone?"

I shrugged. I'd noticed she'd called earlier and hadn't bothered to answer.

"Anyway, when I called you at the library, they told me you weren't working today, so I thought I'd try you at home. May I come inside?"

"Do I have a choice?"

I opened the door wide and she stepped inside. Smoky Joe chose that moment to see who our visitor was. Julie bent down to pet him.

"Sweet kitty," she said, standing up. "And this is one sweet cottage!" she gushed as she bounced from room to room.

"Do you mind!" I snapped, as she was about to set foot in my bedroom. "That's private. Off limits. Have a seat in the living room. I'll be right with you."

Instead she followed me into the kitchen, chattering on about the cottage as I fed Smoky Joe some treats. I pointed to a kitchen chair. She sat. So did I.

"Why are you here?" I asked again.

"I'd like us to find out who murdered your fiancé's uncle."

Us? "That's a matter best left to the police," I said, hating how prim I sounded.

Julie laughed. "Are you sure about that? So far they've done squat. If you'll remember, I was the one who ID'd Alec Dunmore."

I nodded. "You did, and you can trust Lieutenant Mathers to take it from there."

"Come on, Carrie. We're talking about your fiancé's uncle. Hey, I know they weren't close at the time of Mr. Dunmore's demise, but I'm sure you want to find his murderer."

How does she know all that? "I'm not investigating the murder."

Julia frowned. "Well, you should be. What was he doing here in Clover Ridge? Was he involved in a business deal gone south?"

I stood. "I have no idea."

"Could be he wanted to buy the building where his body was discovered. The building the library ended up acquiring."

"Maybe," I agreed. "You're an investigative reporter. What do you want with me?"

"You, Carrie Singleton, have the knack. You solve murders." Julie pointed to herself. "And no one tops me in sniffing out information. We'd make a formidable team."

When I didn't answer, she added, "I know John Mathers is your good buddy, but I bet he doesn't play fair when it comes to quid pro quo."

"What do you expect? He's the police. He can't go sharing information on a homicide case."

But something must have given away my true feelings on the subject, because Julie suddenly grinned. "Admit it! It pisses you off."

I shrugged.

"And one more thing, Miss Nancy Drew. You know more about this homicide than you're letting on."

* * *

Julie took off shortly after that, saying she'd be in touch after her sources dug up more information. She left me wondering what it would be like to work on a case with her. I felt guilty for even considering it. Where was my sense of loyalty to John? Julie Theron might be an investigative reporter but she was also a TV personality. I could never trust her not to go running her mouth on the air about an ongoing investigation.

I spent the rest of the afternoon answering personal emails and reading. Dylan called to say he'd be getting to the cottage close to six so I started dinner at five thirty—baked salmon, a salad, couscous, and some fresh veggies. Over dinner I told him about my trip to the preserve and Julie Theron's visit.

Dylan laughed. "You've had quite a day. Much more exciting than mine, which amounted to checking out a few leads on a case and trailing someone, all of which turned out to be duds."

"The preserve is a beautiful place. I'd hate to see it turned into another condo community. Or even a park, since that would mean cutting down most of the trees and clearing the land."

"I've been wanting to go there for some time. Maybe we'll go this weekend."

I smiled. "That would be lovely. As for Ms. Julie Theron, I've no intention of calling her any time soon."

"Our best hope is for Uncle Alec to regain his lost memory."

* * *

The next morning I arrived at the library a few minutes before nine o'clock. I was eager to talk to Alec to find out if he'd managed to recall any details surrounding his death. The sound of men shouting caught my attention. It was coming from the parking lot next door where Sean's crew was working.

"Be right back," I told Smoky Joe. I squeezed past vehicles and pieces of equipment parked helter-skelter in both lots and paused behind a large truck to find out what was going on. Sean and Buzz stood facing Rafe, their faces red with anger as they yelled, often at the same time, so that it took me a minute make out what they were saying.

"It's your fault we ran into these problems," Sean was shouting, "and we're the ones stuck with fixing 'em."

I couldn't hear what Rafe said in return because Buzz began to yell and blocked out his words. I stayed a few minutes more, but learned nothing because they continued to shout at the same time. When there was a lull, Rafe tried to explain once again. Sean turned his back and took Buzz aside. They huddled together, speaking in low voices, then Sean stalked off, a frown on his face.

I didn't wait to see what happened next, but returned to my car to get Smoky Joe. The dispute must have ended, because all was silent as I entered the library.

I released Smoky Joe from his carrier and dropped it off in my office. Then I went in search of Sally to tell her about the altercation I'd just witnessed. She wasn't in her office, so I walked down to the circulation desk and told Angela and Fran instead.

"I heard them too as I walked into the library," Fran said. "Sean and Buzz are blaming Rafe for problems causing delays and added expense."

"No reason to carry on like that," Angela said. "There are always unexpected snags, especially when the renovations are in an old run-down building like the one next door."

I remembered what Sean had told Kevin in the preserve. "Still, they're working from the architect's plans that Rafe drew up after bringing in an engineer to inspect the building."

"Some inspection that was!" Angela said. "Not noticing a body wrapped in a blanket in the basement."

We exchanged worried glances.

"Time to get to work," Fran said.

Sure enough, a few patrons had entered the library through the front door facing the Green.

"See you at noon," Angela said as I left them to look for Alec. I found him waiting for me in my office.

"Carrie, I hope you don't mind that I came here. The other rooms will soon be occupied and I hate staying in that attic. The dust makes me sneeze."

I made a scoffing sound. "Ghosts don't sneeze from dust."

Alec turned up his hands and shrugged. "Sorry. It was worth a try."

I nodded, wondering if fibbing had been Alec's usual way of dealing with whatever he'd found unpleasant in his life. At least he no longer seemed frantic. Why the change? I cringed, hoping it was because he'd remembered something important and not because he was adjusting to becoming a permanent fixture in the Clover Ridge Library.

"You're in luck," I said. "My assistant Trish won't be in for a while so we've got plenty of time to discuss a few things. I'd like to start by asking you some questions."

Alec plopped down on my assistants' desk. "Okay, I guess."

I sat down and spun my chair around to face him. "How was it, seeing Dylan again after all those years?"

"Nice to see he's all grown up and made something of himself." He grinned suddenly. "And that he has a wonderful fiancée. You."

"So you do remember him."

Alec nodded slowly. "I didn't at first. But as Dylan spoke, memories flooded my mind. Like bits and pieces of a movie. I knew he was my nephew."

"Do you remember your sister, Dylan's mother?"

"Yes."

"You don't look very happy about it," I said. "Did you and your sister get into an argument?"

"After you and Dylan left, it all came back. What I had done."

I felt a sense of foreboding. "What did you do, Alec?"

Chapter Nineteen

"Essie and I got word from a lawyer that Uncle Humphrey, our grandfather's brother, left us the parcel of land he'd always planned to develop. There was a small cabin on the property but not much else. Anyway, she said to go ahead and sell it, and sent me a letter giving me power of attorney to handle the sale. I was thrilled beyond belief. My bank account was at an all-time low, and I owed a few bucks to some not-so-savory characters."

I stared at the ghost of Alec Dunmore, seeing the man Dylan had finally figured out when he'd reached college age: a wheeler-dealer with one foot in the criminal world. For whom scamming and lying were all part of a day's work.

"And your sister let you handle the sale?" I asked, not bothering to hide my disbelief.

"Well, yeah. She was my sister. Why shouldn't she?"

"Maybe because she knew the kind of deals you used to pull."

Alec squirmed. "Oh, you know about that?"

I pursed my lips instead of answering.

"All right. I swore I'd do everything by the book. Essie and her hubby were up to their ears in several business ventures and had no time to handle this too. She told me to sell the property for a good price and send her half."

He stopped.

"Go on."

"Well, I found a buyer pretty quickly willing to pay top dollar for the property—two hundred ten thousand dollars, believe it or not—and I put it in the bank."

"And sent your sister a check for half the amount?" I asked, curious to hear his response.

"You know I didn't," Alec said.

I nodded, glad he hadn't lied, though he probably could tell from my expression that I knew the truth. "Why didn't you?"

"That's where it gets hazy."

I laughed. "How convenient."

"No, really. I'm telling you what I remember."

Evelyn suddenly appeared and remained near the closed door. She had her finger to her lips, meaning I wasn't to let Alec know of her presence.

"Okay, please tell me everything you remember."

Alec glanced down at his hands as if they were a source of inspiration. "I hadn't had that kind of money for as long as I could remember. Somehow I kinda forgot that it wasn't all mine and that I owed a good part of my half to people who were getting antsy about me paying it back. I thought—what if I invested the money in something solid? Something that brought me closer to my only living relatives—Essie and Dylan."

"So you came to Clover Ridge."

Alec nodded. "I flew here and didn't tell them I was coming. I wanted to check out the land, so to speak. See what was available before I let them know I was in their hometown."

I waited for him to continue. When he didn't, I said, "Go on."

He shrugged. "I don't remember much more. I caught a taxi at the airport and came to Clover Ridge."

"Do you remember entering the building next to the library where your body was found?" I asked.

"I remember meeting with a real estate agent. She drove me to see a few places in the area." Alec thought a minute. "That night a man called me at my motel. Asked if I wanted access to the best deal in town. I said sure."

"What was his name?"

"Couldn't tell you."

"James Whitehead?" I asked.

"Yeah! That was it." Alec's eyes lit up. "Was that who I saw leaving the meeting the other day?"

"Don't you remember I told you James Whitehead is dead?" I said impatiently.

"Oh. Right," Alec said, but he sounded uncertain.

"The other day I told you James Whitehead thought he had a buyer for the building six years ago. That was you. You even thought you recognized him when I showed you his photo in a newspaper item."

"Yeah."

He started blinking, a nervous tic, and it was obvious that he didn't remember. I was sorry I'd snapped at him. The poor guy was having trouble keeping everything straight in his mind. It was frustrating that he couldn't even remember things he'd already told me.

In a gentle voice, I said, "It doesn't matter. Just tell me what you remember after James Whitehead called you."

"I suppose it was the following day he showed me the building next to the library. It was obvious it had been neglected and would need lots of moolah to get it into shape. But it was structurally sound. And I liked that it was situated on the Green. I remembered that whenever Essie mentioned living in Clover Ridge it was the Green she seemed most proud of. Anyway this fellow— Whitehead, I suppose—said another buyer was interested in the property, but if I gave him five thousand dollars I'd have first dibs on the sale. So I gave it to him."

"You handed the money over just like that?"

"Yeah. He must have given me a receipt. I know I would have insisted on it."

"No receipt was ever found. By the way, what did you do with the rest of the money?" I asked.

"I—I can't remember. Why can't I remember?" He sounded close to tears.

"Let's not worry about that now," I said. "We'll figure that out later."

"All right."

It was my turn now to draw a deep breath. The last thing I needed was a ghost having a meltdown in my office. "What happened after you gave James Whitehead five thousand dollars?"

Alec squinted as though trying to see into the past. "That night or the next I met him and two other men for drinks in a bar. They showed me preliminary plans to turn the building into office suites. The two men said they were interested in putting some money into the project for a percentage of the returns, claiming they knew of at least four companies willing to pay big bucks to have office space on the Green. In just a couple of years the rent would return what we paid for the building and renovations and then I'd be making money hand over fist."

"Interesting, since office buildings aren't allowed on the Green," Evelyn said drily.

Alec turned around. "Really? I should have checked out what they told me. But for the first time in years I was being offered an investment I really liked. It was like a dream come true."

The scammer getting scammed, I thought.

He looked embarrassed when he said, "I shouldn't have, I know, but I mentioned I'd come into some money and wanted in on the plan. Whitehead was asking half a mil for the property, half of it in cash. He said he was willing to take fifty thousand up front and the rest later.

"The two men offered to put in twenty-five thousand dollars each for a share of the profits. I said sure, especially when they said they knew a contractor who would give them the best deal on the renovations."

My mouth fell open. "And you went along with it?"

"It all made sense that evening as we drank and talked. Carrie, I felt like we'd known each other forever. I liked the idea of settling down in Clover Ridge. Being part of the community. Having minor business partners with me on top.

"Of course I'd have to take out a loan for the rest, but I figured my brother-in-law would do that for me at the best possible rate. I figured Essie would see what a great deal this was and want to put money into the project. And so, when the two men both gave Whitehead several thousand dollars, promising to hand over the rest by the end of the week, I thought, why not?" Alec grimaced. "I ended up handing over forty-five thousand dollars.

With the five thou I'd given him earlier, that added up to fifty thousand total."

He paused, waiting for my reaction. When I said nothing, he continued.

"The next morning I woke up with the worst hangover, appalled by what I'd done. I'd given a pile of money to a man I hardly knew. I still owed money back in Chicago. At least Essie's money was safe."

"So what did you do?"

"I called Whitehead and told him I was having second thoughts about the deal and I wanted my money back."

My heart was pounding. I knew how this was ending. "What did he say?"

"He told me not to worry. Of course I could back out of the plan if I didn't want to go through with it. We agreed to meet and he'd return the money."

"Did he tell you to meet him at the building you'd visited the day before—the one you were thinking of buying?" I asked.

"I think so, but I can't say for sure."

Frustrated, I asked, "And then what happened?"

Alec bit his lip. "I wish I knew."

* * *

"How could he have been so stupid?" Evelyn asked me when Alec left. "Handing over all that money to a stranger?"

"I suppose suddenly having a huge wad of cash in his possession made him euphoric. He got caught up in the deal they were spinning until the next day when reality sank in."

"What he did was totally irresponsible."

We shook our heads at Alec's foolish behavior. Sharing his story with us must have exhausted him because as soon as he'd finished he went up to the attic to take a nap.

"And we still don't know who murdered him," Evelyn said.

"He said a few of the men at the meeting on Friday looked familiar. Let's see—my uncle Bosco was there, along with Al Tripp, Sean Powell, Rafe Torres, and Buzz Coleman. I hate to think any one of them murdered Alec."

"Alec might have seen Sean, Buzz, and Rafe at the site while they were working, then thought they looked familiar when he saw them again," Evelyn said. "We can't trust his memory."

"There's a good chance James Whitehead killed him when he reneged on the deal," I pointed out.

"I wouldn't be surprised," Evelyn said. "No one ever had anything nice to say about the man."

"I think whoever murdered Alec robbed him of the rest of his money."

"You're probably right. There was no sign of it or his wallet."

We batted the subject back and forth, but we couldn't come up with any definite conclusion. So far, it looked like the chances of finding out who had murdered Alec Dunmore were very slim indeed.

I decided to call Uncle Bosco to ask who had shown interest in buying the building around the time Alec was murdered. As usual, he was happy to hear from me.

"Carrie, dear, I hope the auditorium problem was resolved and you'll be getting the number of seats you were counting on."

"There's a good chance it will if the company's powers-that-be let us change our order to less expensive seats. I have a question about the building we're renovating. Do you know if anyone seriously considered buying it five to seven years ago?"

Uncle Bosco chuckled. "Lots of people did. Me, for one. Al Tripp, for another. We both had the same idea—renovate it as an office building—but the town council was dead set against having office buildings on the Green, along with dry cleaners, laundromats, gas stations, and a whole lot of other business establishments."

"I see."

"That ruling still stands. One of the reasons why we were able to get the building at a reasonable price for the library."

"Anyone else you know who was interested?"

"Are you sleuthing again, Carrie?"

"Kinda."

"Let me think. Oh, yes, Babette Fisher wanted to open an art gallery and was trying to convince a few friends and neighbors to go in on it with her, but I don't think she got very far."

"Really? Babette?"

"It's the kind of property that looks good on paper until you venture inside. And James Whitehead was asking a lot for it. You had to figure on paying that amount plus for costly renovations."

I thanked Uncle Bosco and mulled over what he'd told me. While I was surprised by the number of people who had considered buying the building and had probably been inside it at one time or another, there was no reason to think any one of them had ever met Alec.

I wondered about the men he'd been drinking with in a bar who claimed they wanted to be his business partners. It sounded pretty fishy to me. Still, from what Alec remembered, James Whitehead remained the number one murder suspect. He'd told

Alec he could get his money back. Instead, Alec was murdered and there was no sign of the money.

I was back to square one.

* * *

Dylan came over at six thirty. I handed him a beer and sat him down in the living room to tell him what I'd learned from his uncle earlier in the day. By the time I'd finished, he was shaking his head.

"What an idiot, falling for something like that."

"And we still don't know who murdered him," I said.

Dylan sighed. "Let's eat."

I'd made pasta and turkey meatballs in tomato sauce for dinner, along with a red lettuce salad and my own dressing.

"This was delicious, babe," he said after finishing a second helping of everything. He patted his stomach. "I'll start gaining weight if you keep on feeding me like this."

"No worries. Tomorrow night I have a council meeting so you'll have to fend for yourself."

"That's right. I'll probably stop for a burger or a couple of slices of pizza on the way home."

"A salad would be healthy," I murmured.

"Hmmm," Dylan said noncommittally. But when I asked what he'd like for dessert, he said just coffee would be fine.

We discussed the private cremation to be followed by a small memorial service that he'd arranged for Alec on Sunday.

"We have to let people know about the service ASAP," Dylan said.

"I'll mention it at the council meeting tomorrow and at the library."

"Thanks, babe."

"I wonder if Alec's ghostly presence will disappear after he's . . . gone."

"Your friend Evelyn seems to think he'll hang around until John solves his murder."

"Kind of difficult with no money trail to follow."

Dylan sighed. "And no clues left at the scene of the crime."

He put his coffee mug in the sink and went into the living room to watch TV while I loaded the dishwasher. I wished there was something I could do to make him feel better, but nothing came to mind.

My cell phone sounded its jingle as I was about to join Dylan in the living room. It was Babette Fisher.

"Hello, Carrie. I hope I'm not interrupting anything important."

"Not really. I was just about to sit down and relax. What's up?"

"Are you ready for the meeting tomorrow night?"

"Sure. As ready as I'll ever be."

"I mean, have you decided how you're going to vote on the Seabrook property?" She sounded exasperated, which annoyed me.

"Why do you ask?"

"Why?" she echoed, now on the defensive. "Because tomorrow night's meeting is uber important. We're voting on the future of a piece of prime Clover Ridge property."

"I know that, Babette. I'm asking, why are you calling me?"

"Oh!" She gave a nervous laugh. "I'm just wondering if you'd like to discuss the various options. You're new to the council, and I've been on it for eight years now."

"Eight years," I mused.

This time her laughter was genuine. "You have no idea how many issues I've voted on."

"And did other council members guide you when it came to voting?"

"Sometimes. Knowing they were more experienced, I listened to what they had to say."

"I see." Though I knew where Babette was headed, I decided to hear her out. "Okay. That sounds reasonable. I am new at this."

"I'm sure you've given the three proposals some thought. Which do you favor?" she asked.

"I like the idea of keeping the Seabrook Preserve a preserve—and adding a few face-lifting projects and programs that won't cost big bucks but will attract more visitors."

"Ah."

"Your preference is the park, and you'd love to see your cousin's group designing it."

"You're right, because the Waterford Group is the best and most innovative group that designs outdoor spaces. A park would make the best use of the property. It would draw in many more people than the preserve, people of all ages. And if we charge an entrance fee, that will go a long way to cover the engineering, architectural, and construction costs."

"Which run pretty high, according to the Waterford Group's prospectus."

"People would love to come to a well-designed park situated on the Sound. It would be a feather in our cap."

"And perhaps too expensive for some Clover Ridge residents," I said. "Not everyone in town has big bucks."

"Face facts, Carrie. Figures show that Clover Ridge is considered an affluent town with a wonderful school system and excellent library. And in order to remain in the forefront—a place where up-and-coming people want to live—we need to come up with new attractions."

"I never thought of Clover Ridge that way," I said. "My father's family owned a farm outside of town."

"Many years ago, Carrie," Babette said. "Your old farmstead is now a successful B and B."

Who was this business-minded woman telling me to get with the times? What happened to the flighty Babette Fisher I knew? Or thought I knew.

"I understand this is a lot for you to take in," Babette said, as if she'd been reading my mind, "and I get the feeling you're leaning toward the preserve. But there's one more aspect I need to mention, a really important one, if not the most important."

"Yes?" I said, wondering what else she was going to hit me with tonight.

"The council consists of five members. We need a majority of three to come to a decision. I figure Sean and I are for the park project, Reggie desperately wants the condo deal, and Al plays his cards close to his chest. If you go along with the park deal, we'll have a majority and won't have to bat this topic among ourselves for the next month or two. Things can get ugly."

"Sean likes the park idea?" I asked.

"He won't vote for the condo deal, and he considers the park a better use of that beautiful piece of waterfront property than a preserve no one visits," she scoffed.

"He told you that?"

"Look, I get it. You like having a spot of nature close by that all residents can enjoy. I'm all for that, too. I'm sure we can find a way to leave part of the preserve intact. Call it a nature trail. That would trim costs. It's doable. Win-win all around."

I nodded. What she said made sense.

"The trick is to muster enough people behind our project so we can start it with enthusiasm and good will. Will you think about it? Consider joining us?"

"Sure, I'll think about it," I said to put an end to her hard sell.

"That's all I'm asking, Carrie. Nothing more."

Chapter Twenty

Thursday morning I informed my colleagues that Dylan would be holding a memorial ceremony for his uncle after the cremation on Sunday. Sally, Angela, and Marion said they would attend with their husbands or partners. When Alec showed up at my office, I found myself in the awkward position of having to inform him as well.

"If that's what Dylan's decided. I suppose my remains have to be taken care of one way or another," was his glum reply.

"It won't hurt," I said.

"That's good, but will the cremation get me where I need to go? Or will I still be here, flitting about your library?"

"You know what Evelyn told you. You'll move on when they find your murderer."

"That's what I thought."

Alec vanished without telling me where he was going. I understood his frustration. If only there were some clues pointing to the person or people who had murdered him. Then he could leave this plane, as Evelyn called it, and leave us in peace.

I looked in on the programs in progress, then made a few calls to potential presenters. I managed to catch one at home and left messages for the other two. Trish arrived just as I received a text from Cynthia Post, the woman scheduled to do a food presentation called Pumpkin Pleasures the first week in October. Cynthia's original plan was to demonstrate how to make pumpkin soup, roasted pumpkin as a vegetable, and pumpkin bread. We always asked presenters to send us the recipes at least a week in advance so we had time to print out copies for the patrons attending the class.

Cynthia wanted to change the soup to pumpkin butter. I told her I didn't think that was a good idea. After some hemming and hawing, she agreed to stick to our original plan and said she'd send me the recipes by Monday.

At noon, Angela and I walked over to the Cozy Corner Café for lunch. I brought her up to date on what Alec said he remembered—putting down a chunk of money to buy the building next to the library, then changing his mind. Angela asked a few questions but I could tell her mind was elsewhere. She and Steve were going over to the Pet Warehouse after work so he could see the dog she liked so much.

I wanted to talk to her about the decision I had to make regarding the Seabrook Preserve, but felt it was something I ought to only discuss with the other members of the council. The upcoming meeting was making me nervous.

I'd been back in my office all of fifteen minutes when someone knocked on the door.

"Come in," I called and was surprised when Sean Powell walked through the doorway.

"Hello," I said.

"Am I disturbing you?"

"Not at all." I turned to Trish. "Trish Templeton, my assistant. Sean Powell. But then you know each other."

Trish laughed as she got to her feet. "Sean and I go way back."

"Right. I remember the day she was born."

"I'll leave you to it," Trish said and closed the door behind her.

"So, what brings you here?" I asked, gesturing to the seat Trish had just vacated.

Sean sank heavily into the chair and brought out a handkerchief to wipe his brow. "I wanted to let you know we heard back from the company that's selling us the seats for the auditorium. They gave us the go-ahead to change our order to the cheaper seats. They have plenty in stock so the delay shouldn't be more than a week. It will be built exactly as you wanted—stadium seating with the number of seats as requested, though they won't be quite as comfy."

"Thanks, Sean. I appreciate your coming in to tell me."

He shook his head in disgust. "We can always expect a few changes as we progress, but that area wasn't planned right. Now we have to make the room next to the auditorium two feet narrower. Sally wasn't thrilled, but she gave the okay."

I remembered his argument with Rafe the other day. "Are things moving along now?"

"Yeah. We're only a few days behind schedule, and the renovations look really great, if I do say so myself." He added glumly, "Now that we've gotten past some unforeseen issues."

"Like discovering a body in the basement," I said.

"Exactly. I don't know how the engineer missed it. Or Buzz. It was his job to look over the entire building before we started ripping out interior walls."

Buzz? How interesting. "And the body turned out to be Dylan's uncle," I said. "Dylan still has no idea what his uncle was doing here at the time of his murder since he never called anyone in the family." That wasn't quite true, but I was curious to see how Sean reacted since he was one of the men Alec might have recognized.

Sean shrugged. "And we may never find out, either. Or how he ended up where he did."

"I know. Dylan's holding a small memorial service for his uncle on Sunday shortly after the cremation. We were wondering if you'd care to attend."

"I would very much like to attend," Sean said, surprising me. "The poor man deserves a respectful send-off after lying there all those years."

"It's just a few blocks from here." I wrote down the address.

"Pat and I will be there. We knew Dylan's parents quite well." Sean stood to leave.

"There is something I'd like to ask you, but I wonder if I'm treading where I ought not to," I said.

"I'll answer if I can."

"It's about tonight's meeting."

Sean rolled his eyes. "Right. Your first council vote. A big one, too. Expect fireworks. The meeting could go on till midnight."

"I know we're supposed to vote for the good of the community, but some people seem to have a personal agenda."

"Care to share what you mean exactly?"

Sean's tone had stopped just short of hostile, but my need for his advice was too pressing to ignore. "Last night Babette called practically urging me to go along with the park option. She said you were in on it, and with me on board that made it a sure thing."

Sean chuckled. "She did, did she?"

"What's so funny?"

"She asked me the same thing a few days ago, implying you were in favor of the park project. Actually, I was leaning toward voting for the park, but now I'm not so sure."

"Why?" I asked.

"Because I like the preserve. I happened to go there the other day and it occurred to me I'd hate to see those woods torn down to be replaced by a park or condos."

"Me, too!" I agreed. "I mean, I'm leaning in that direction."

"There's no harm in trying to convince other council members to see things your way. We'll have plenty of that tonight. The park was Babette's idea."

"That's pretty obvious."

Sean grinned. There was a twinkle in his eye. "And wouldn't she just love to see the architectural company her cousin works for get the bid. As if they'd let him anywhere near designing the project if they did. Babette loves to scheme, but she can be short-sighted and forget to consider the big picture."

I decided not to go anywhere near *that* comment. "And Reggie loves the condo project."

"He does," Sean said. "He'd like to sink some money into it and probably move into one of the units. In fact, he tried to convince me to do the same."

"It gets rather complicated, doesn't it?"

"Only if you let it," Sean said. "You vote the way you see fit." He winked. "See you tonight."

I sat quietly, absorbing everything Sean had just told me. Though I'd heard him express opinions in meetings regarding the new library addition and during town council discussions, I'd never examined my feelings about the man. Now I realized I liked Sean Powell, and not just because he cared enough to let me know

I'd be getting the auditorium I'd dreamed of, although with a few alterations.

He was a man of action rather than reflection, partly because his keen intelligence enabled him to size up a situation quickly and accurately. He may have done some shady dealing earlier on, but he'd made it his business to act honestly and fairly these past few years. From what I'd learned about Sean's earlier relationship with his son, I gathered he could be stubborn. But after seeing him and Kevin together the other day, it was also true that Sean could be flexible and caring. And when it came to deciding the future of the Seabrook Preserve, he was more impartial than Reggie and Babette.

"Who is that man that just left your office?"

I gave a start and reared back in my chair, away from the chill that Alec had caused as he loomed over me.

"Sorry," he mumbled as he stepped backward.

"That's Sean Powell. His company is doing the renovations next door."

"What was he doing here?"

"He came to update me on their progress—why do you ask?"

I'd seen Alec confused, contrite, conniving, but this was the first time I'd seen him angry.

"He's one of the men I met with that night in the bar."

"Sean? Are you sure?"

"Oh, yeah. Real sure."

My thoughts whirled around in my head. "Was he there the night you asked for your money back?"

"I don't remember, but he was in the bar urging me to buy the building, touting all the wonderful things we could do with it. He handed over a few thou to Whitehead, said he'd get the rest to him the next day. He was in on the scam, Carrie."

I tried to help Alec recall specific details—what Sean had done and said when they were convincing Alec to buy the building next to the library—but Alec couldn't add to what he'd already told me. And no matter how I phrased my questions, he couldn't recall if Sean had been present the fateful night that he'd been murdered.

"Enough with the questions, Carrie," he finally said and took off in a huff.

Trish returned to the office, and shortly after that I left to put in an hour at the hospitality desk. I'd just helped a patron sign up for a crafts class when my cell phone jingled. It was Reggie Williams.

"Hello, Reggie. What can I do for you?"

His laugh was forced. "Hi there, Carrie. What makes you think you can do something for me?"

When I didn't answer, he cleared his throat. "Since we're meeting tonight to discuss and vote on the future of the Seabrook property, I thought I'd share with you my thoughts on the matter—being this is your first vote and all."

"Sure. I'd like to hear them."

"Would you?" he sounded surprised.

"Of course," I said. "I want to be as informed as I can be when I cast my vote. You're in favor of selling the land to build a condo community, right?"

"I sure am." This time his laugh was easy and real. "I think it's the best use of the property—upscale condos will do Clover Ridge proud and bring in a good amount of tax revenue we sure can use."

"You don't mind handing over a beautiful nature preserve that's available to all Clover Ridge residents for a project that will benefit only a handful of people?"

"The way you put it sounds cold, but have you seen the figures?" Reggie proceeded to quote numbers indicating that few people, let alone Clover Ridge residents, took advantage of the beautiful preserve.

"But are those figures accurate?" I asked. "I stopped by the preserve the other day. No one was there to count me as a visitor."

"That may be, Carrie, but the few times I've been to the preserve with my family, we passed three, maybe four people the entire time we were there."

"It does sound like it's underused," I said. "And that should be addressed if we decide to keep the property a preserve. Encourage group visits and guided tours."

"Sounds like a good idea if you're after keeping the property as a preserve. I think it would get better use as a condo community. The money we'd make from the sale alone could be used to improve other recreational sites."

I stopped pushing the preserve and listened as Reggie extoled the virtues of building a condo community. He finished by saying, "It might be the very place where you and your future husband might consider living if you didn't already have a beautiful manor house."

A house I have no intention of ever inhabiting. "Thanks for calling, Reggie. I have to get back to work. I'll see you tonight."

"See you tonight, Carrie. Thanks for hearing me out."

* * *

At five o'clock I put Smoky Joe in his carrier and drove to my aunt and uncle's for an early dinner. Aunt Harriet served a delicious array of roasted veggies, salmon, and a tricolor salad. Dessert was a new recipe of lemon squares that I asked her to email to me.

Uncle Bosco was happy to hear that the stadium-seating auditorium, so important to me, was going ahead almost as planned and that Sean had stopped by the library to give me the good news.

"I'm glad, Carrie. Sean's a good man, now that he's cleaned up his act."

"What do you mean 'cleaned up his act'?" I asked, hoping to learn more of what Sean had been capable of when he was younger.

My aunt and uncle exchanged glances. Finally, my uncle said, "Just that for so many years, Sean was set on making it big. People thought he cut corners to save on costs. Using materials that weren't up to snuff.

"Though this certainly hasn't been the case for some time now. We checked very carefully before hiring his company to do the revisions for the library addition. His references going back five years are all glowing recommendations. The irony is, now that he's about to retire, he's finally raking it in. I hear he can't keep up with the jobs they want him for."

My heart twinged with distress. What Uncle Bosco was saying about Sean made Alec's story all the more plausible. Sean might have been involved in whatever scheme had been hatched to scam Alec and sadly ended in his murder.

"Sean's not in the best of health," Aunt Harriet said.

"So I've heard," I said.

"He's selling his business to Buzz Coleman," Uncle Bosco said.

I decided not to mention the conversation I'd overheard between Sean and his son Kevin. "What do you think of Buzz?" I asked.

Uncle Bosco shrugged. "He knows the contracting business. Buzz is a good worker, but a little rough around the edges. I can't see him working smoothly with Rafe Torres like Sean has these past few years."

"Why? Is Rafe a problem?"

"He can be temperamental," Uncle Bosco said, "and he has a reputation for not always anticipating certain problems, like the one involving the auditorium. But he's creative, and builders like him. I've heard he's been asked to join the Lighthouse Builders to work on designing the unit layouts *if* the council votes to go with the condo deal and *if* they win the bid."

Which segued into a discussion about the future of the Seabrook Preserve. Finally, after helping Aunt Harriet clear the table and giving Smoky Joe a quick hug, I headed out to my car and drove to Town Hall.

Al and Reggie were already in our meeting room when I arrived. Since they were chatting in a relaxed manner, I knew that whatever they were talking about had nothing to do with the preserve or any other controversial subject. They both greeted me warmly. Sean joined us at seven thirty when our meeting was scheduled to start. I noticed his halting gait, which reminded me that he was very ill and got me wondering why he hadn't resigned his seat on the council.

Babette showed up a quarter of an hour later, panting and disheveled, as Reggie was reading the minutes from our last meeting. She took advantage of his pause between sentences to spew out apologies for her tardiness. I felt a stab of annoyance for her behavior, then scolded myself for bothering to react. We had to work together in the foreseeable future, and I didn't want to find myself irritated every time she spoke.

190

Al introduced a few issues regarding municipal services that had to be resolved ASAP. I was surprised that my four colleagues were very much in sync as to how to deal with them. Since I wasn't familiar with the matters under discussion, I went along with their decisions, which struck me as sound and fair.

And then it was time to discuss the Seabrook Preserve. Al gave a concise summary of the three options we were to vote on. I was glad that he'd mentioned updates and improvements regarding the preserve if it were to remain a preserve.

I commented that keeping the preserve would benefit every Clover Ridge resident at little cost. Reggie and Babette added facts and figures to bolster their favorites. Again, I was impressed by the way Al handled the situation. He corrected both Reggie and Babette at least once regarding facts they'd used to bolster their argument. I could only imagine the many hours it had taken him to study all three options from every possible angle.

"I think we've heard the advantages of the three options. Now let's discuss the problems or negatives of each."

I gritted my teeth as I waited in dread for criticisms and rebuttals and I wasn't disappointed. Reggie was quick to say that keeping the preserve was a losing proposition since it was underused and not a source of income for the town. Sean attacked Timothy Fisk and his Lighthouse Builders as shoddy workers. To which Reggie responded that Sean was pissed at Timothy because his son worked for them. When Sean said Kevin no longer worked there, Reggie roared with laughter, insisting that was even more of a reason why Sean didn't like the condo deal.

Reggie went on to criticize the park project as not being cost effective. To which Babette responded that Reggie was partial to the condo deal because he planned to put money in the project and move there himself. Infuriated, Reggie pointed out that Babette was all for the park project so her cousin could cut his teeth on his first big job.

Now Babette, Reggie, and Sean were all shouting at the same time.

"That's enough!" Al yelled.

Silence.

"I think we all have a good idea of what we consider to be the best use of the preserve property and how it would best serve Clover Ridge. I'd like to remind you that the companies that made presentations at our last meeting are not necessarily the companies that will be chosen to construct a park or condo community, if that's the chosen project. Please keep that in mind when you make your selection. As you know, three votes are required to decide the future of the Seabrook Preserve property. If, after voting, we do not have enough votes to declare a winner, we will continue to vote until we do."

It took one round to resolve the matter. There were three votes to keep the Seabrook Preserve. Al declared the decision and made it official. As he spoke, Babette and Reggie kept their eyes on Sean. Babette had a wounded expression and Reggie looked angry. "You owe me," he mouthed when Sean caught his glance.

What was that all about? I wondered.

Minutes later, Al brought the meeting to a close. Sean, Babette, and Reggie took off. I turned to Al for his reaction to the evening. He sank back in his chair and wiped his brow.

"Thank God that's over. And with as little fuss as I could hope."

"Sean was the big question," I said.

"I had no idea how he planned to vote. I knew Kevin had left Lighthouse Builders, but that wouldn't make Sean suddenly in favor of the condo project."

"I'm glad he went along with keeping the preserve. Do you think there will there be . . . repercussions?" I asked.

"You mean from Reggie and Babette? I doubt it."

Al put his papers in order and we exited Town Hall together. As I walked to my car, I noticed Sean standing near his truck speaking to someone. Was it Reggie or Babette rehashing the vote? I was too far away to catch the gist of their conversation and for once my curiosity was asleep. I was glad the evening had gone more smoothly than I'd expected, and I was eager to pick up Smoky Joe and drive home. It had been a long day.

Chapter
Twenty-One

T he jingle of my cell phone woke me the following morning, rousing me from a deep sleep.

"Sean Powell's dead."

I blinked, barely able to make sense of the words, let alone figure out why Al Tripp was calling me at six thirty. To tell me . . . The full force of his message hit me.

"I'm so sorry," I managed to get out. "I know he was sick, but—"

"Carrie, Sean didn't die of cancer. Somebody murdered him."

I bolted upright. "Oh, no! Are you sure?"

"Oh, yeah." Al exhaled loudly. "John Mathers just paid me a visit. Don't be surprised if he's on his way to interview you."

I thought a minute. "Last night Sean was talking to someone when we left Town Hall. Did you happen to see who it was?"

"No. I didn't realize he was still in the parking lot when we left the building. Are you sure it was Sean?"

"Yes. Besides, I know his truck."

"Be sure to tell that to John Mathers."

"Of course. Al, how did they figure it was murder so quickly?"

"Someone cut the brake line. The truck was pretty much totaled after Sean drove into some trees, but they were able to see what caused the crash right away."

Smoky Joe nudged me to get up and feed him, so I gave him his breakfast, then decided to have mine as well. I had intended to sleep in since today was a late day for me, but it was clear that the universe had other plans.

I waited until I knew Dylan would be in his office to tell him the news about Sean.

"That's too bad. I wonder who wanted him dead."

"Me, too. The poor guy was really ill. He only had a few more months to live anyway."

"Do you think it had anything to do with last night's vote regarding the preserve?" Dylan asked.

"Babette and Reggie weren't happy with the outcome. I saw Reggie mouth 'You owe me' to Sean, but Sean just shrugged it off. Anyway, the property will remain a preserve." I thought a moment. "Unless the vote can be canceled because Sean died so soon after."

"I doubt it, but it depends on the council's bylaws."

"I can't imagine there's a clause that states a decision will be declared null and void if a person who cast one of the deciding votes is murdered soon afterward."

Dylan chuckled. "Put that way, I can't imagine that, either."

"I'm wondering if Sean's murder has something to do with his company or the work on the library's new addition."

"John will figure it out," Dylan said.

It was a quarter to nine when John called me on my cell phone. "Carrie, Sean Powell's been murdered."

"So I've heard."

"News travels fast."

"Al called me earlier. It's hard to believe. We were with Sean last night at the council meeting."

"Which is why I'd like to talk to you ASAP."

"I'm going into work late today so stop by the cottage any time before noon."

"How about now?" he asked.

"I'll put the coffee on."

Fifteen minutes later, John was digging into a plate of scrambled eggs and munching on a toasted bagel. I refilled his empty mug with coffee and sat back, waiting for him to finish refueling. Most likely he'd been up the previous night without eating anything.

"That hit the spot," he said when he was done. He moved his chair away from the table so he could stretch out his long legs.

"When did you find out Sean had crashed his truck?" I asked.

"Not till two in the morning," John said. "I figured he was on his way home after your meeting. He lost control on a stretch of road that's rather secluded. The truck veered into the woods for several feet. It's only by chance that someone noticed it in the dark."

"Al said someone cut his brake line."

"Not an easy thing to do. From what we can tell, he tried to slow down on a curve. Another few feet, and he would have crashed into the ravine. As it is, the truck sustained considerable damage." John took out his notepad. "But enough about Sean's truck. I want you to tell me about the council meeting last night."

I ran through our agenda, paraphrasing what each of us had said the best I could remember.

John made a few notes then looked up. "Did Sean seem agitated about anything? Were any of the others upset by something Sean said? By the way he voted?"

Suddenly I felt like a squealer, which was totally ridiculous because I wanted Sean's murderer caught. "Well, Babette thought he was with her on the park idea. She knew he wouldn't vote for the condo project."

"And why was that?"

"Because his son was working for Lighthouse Builders when they gave their condo presentation last week. The word was Sean and Kevin weren't getting along." I paused. "But I know that's no longer the case."

"Really?" John cocked his head. "Do tell."

"I was at the preserve on Tuesday and happened to overhear them talking in a friendly manner."

John made a scoffing sound. "You just happened to be there."

"That's right. Since I had the responsibility of voting on the future of the preserve, I felt I ought to go there and check it out."

"Did you *happen* to hear what father and son were talking about?"

I ignored John's sarcastic tone. I knew it bothered him when I managed to acquire information about an ongoing case he'd been investigating. And while he valued what I contributed, it was difficult for him to admit that an amateur's assistance had played a major part in catching the killer and so he had trouble showing his appreciation.

"I got the definite impression they'd recently made up," I said. "It seems Kevin left Lighthouse Builders where he'd been working because after his boss had Kevin do the condo presentation at the open council meeting, he later took Kevin off the project."

"But the way I understood it, even if the council voted to build a condo community, it was far from a sure thing that Lighthouse Builders would get the job."

"True," I agreed, "but Al said Lighthouse Builders is smart when it comes to placing bids and they have a reputation for doing good work, so there was a good chance they'd get the job."

"They're not building condos in Clover Ridge any time soon, so it's a moot point. Anything else I should know?"

"Sean said Kevin could take over his construction company, which surprised me," I said.

John nodded. "Yeah, since Buzz Coleman was in the process of buying it. Did Sean seem upset when he left the meeting last night?"

"No. He seemed tired. Frail. Which I hadn't noticed when he stopped by my office earlier in the day."

"What about?"

"He came to tell me I'd be getting the number of seats I wanted for the new stadium-seating auditorium. There had been some last-minute problems."

"Getting back to Babette, was she angry with the way the vote went last night?"

"She'd called me earlier in the day to urge me to vote for the park idea. She tried to give me the impression Sean was all for it, then admitted his vote was far from certain. I can't see her killing Sean for not voting the way she wanted him to. I mean, I didn't either." I laughed. "Can you picture Babette cutting a brake line on a truck? I don't think so."

John pursed his lips and shook his head. "Why, Ms. Singleton, I believe that's a sexist comment if I ever heard one."

"I stand rightfully chastised," I said meekly. "But I don't think Babette would murder Sean over the vote. And neither would Reggie, for that matter. Even though . . ." I stopped.

"Even though?"

"Reggie was angry at Sean." I told John what Reggie did after we voted. "But he didn't have time to cut the brake line. Someone did that before the meeting and before the vote."

"Or during the meeting," John said.

"Babette arrived late to the meeting."

"Interesting," John said, as he made a notation in his notepad.

I suddenly remembered. "Something else. Al and I were the last to leave Town Hall last night. Sean was talking to someone. It was too far away to see who it was."

"Did you get any sense of the person's size? Age? Gender?"

I shook my head. "No. The other person was standing on the passenger side of the truck."

"Did you catch any words of their conversation?"

"No. Sorry."

John frowned. "Did you see the other person's car? The color? The make?"

"Sorry. He or she must have parked on the far side of the truck."

"Anything else you can tell me about Sean?"

"A few days ago he and Buzz had words with Rafael Torres, the architect, at the construction site. They blamed him for added expenses and delays."

"Anyone else Sean had words with?"

"I don't think so. His men all seemed to like him, and he and Buzz seemed to get along well, though Buzz must have been pretty angry when Sean told him he'd changed his mind about selling him his business."

John ran me through the same set of questions again, something he always did, then finally left saying he and his wife, Sylvia, would see Dylan and me at the memorial ceremony for Alec.

"Anything new on that homicide?" I asked.

"Nothing. A real cold case if ever there was one. No physical evidence to be found, no money trail. Just the decedent's fingerprints on that folded-up C-note. At least we discovered who the poor guy was, only I'm sorry he turned out to be Dylan's uncle."

"Did you ever meet Alec when he came to Clover Ridge?" I asked.

"Not that I remember."

"Did you know Dylan's parents?"

John's expression turned wary. "I knew who they were, but Sylvia and I didn't travel in their circles."

"So you never went to their parties."

"Nope. Never were invited."

"You didn't like them," I said.

John pursed his lips. "I didn't know them well enough to dislike them. They weren't our kind of people—big investors, big spenders, until they got sloppy and started losing money."

"Dylan's not like them at all," I said.

John grinned. "Not a bit, thank God."

He left and I had the sudden urge to call my father. Jim Singleton, former thief and felon, now worked for the investigating company that Dylan and Mac owned, using his former skills to help catch big-time thieves.

He picked up on the second ring. "Hi, Caro. I was just thinking about you."

"You were?" Hearing my father's voice made my heart swell with love.

"Yep. In fact, I was about to call you yesterday when I got a lead on this case I'm working. It's been keeping me busy ever since. What's up?"

I sighed. "Someone I know was just murdered."

"Oh, no! A friend? Someone at the library?"

"No. More of an acquaintance, I suppose, but I liked Sean Powell. His construction company is doing the renovations on the library extension. Sean was also a member of the town council. He was killed on his way home from our meeting last night."

"Sorry about that. Knowing you, you intend to find out who killed him."

"I do."

"Be careful, Caro." After a pause, he asked, "How's Dylan?"

"Still shaken that the body the construction crew discovered turned out to be his uncle Alec. He's arranged to have his remains cremated on Sunday. There will be a memorial ceremony afterward."

"Yeah, he told me. Sorry Merry and I can't be there for him."

I experienced one of those twinges of jealousy I still occasionally got when I found out Dylan and Jim had talked, and mentally scolded myself for being petty. I was possessive of Jim, probably because he'd been absent from my life for so many of my growing-up years, and we'd only gotten close again this past year. I was truly happy that my fiancé and my father got along so well, and that Dylan, who had been so hurt and disappointed by his own parents, considered my father family.

"Dylan would have liked that," I said.

My father sighed. "That's one strange case. Did John ever find out what Alec Dunmore was doing in that abandoned building?"

"No."

"Unfortunately, Dylan's parents are gone and can't shed any light on the situation. I'm afraid this may turn out to be one cold case that doesn't get solved."

"I know. How's Merry?" I asked to change the subject. I would have loved to tell my father that Alec's ghost was hanging around the library and not very helpful with his murder investigation because he was suffering from amnesia, but I couldn't deal with his shocked reaction right now.

Jim chuckled. "She's fine. In Chicago, checking the provenance of a few paintings a museum is considering buying."

"And you miss her," I teased.

"I sure do. Remember, we're newlyweds."

"How can I forget when I watched you both say 'I do' a month ago?"

Dylan and I had flown to Atlanta in late August to attend their small wedding, where we met Merry's son and daughter and their families.

"Any news on another upcoming wedding?" my father asked meaningfully.

"Nothing to report."

"Take your sweet time, my darling daughter. But not too much time."

"I'll keep that in mind."

Chapter
Twenty-Two

When I arrived at work, the library was abuzz with the news of Sean's murder. Patrons stopped me to express their shock over this latest calamity. One woman lowered her voice and asked if I thought the old curse on the building had spread to the library. I assured her that wasn't the case, but I couldn't come up with a reason why anyone would want to see Sean Powell dead.

The noise level in the library was blessedly silent. No sounds of hammering or sawing or men's booming voices came from the work area because, as Trish had informed me when I entered my office, Buzz had given the men the afternoon off in recognition of their boss's demise.

"Sally's fit to be tied, wondering if he plans to let them all attend the funeral and cause further delays."

"When is the funeral?" I asked.

"Wednesday morning. The wake is Tuesday afternoon and evening."

I went through my email, made a few calls, then left to check on the programs in progress. Evelyn joined me as I started downstairs to look in on a jewelry bead craft program and the movie in the meeting room.

"I heard the news about Sean Powell," she said. "I'm sorry. I liked Sean. He was a good soul."

"He was murdered right after our council meeting last night."

"Do you think someone on the council had it in for him?"

I stared at her. "Of course not! Why would you think that?"

Evelyn shrugged. "My Robert sat on the town council for a few years. I know how contentious those meetings can get."

"Well, last night's meeting wasn't contentious."

"I thought you were scheduled to vote on the future of the Seabrook Preserve."

"Yes, that's exactly what we did. I had no idea you were so well informed about town events," I said.

"I try my best."

We had reached the bottom level. Evelyn waited while I peered into the meeting room. The movie was running and the sound was fine. I closed the door.

"Interested parties had their say. Then we voted and it was decided to keep the preserve," I told her. "There were no fireworks. No angry arguments. The vote was accepted."

"Then who do you think killed Sean?" Evelyn asked

"I have no idea. But I'll tell you this much—Alec saw Sean yesterday afternoon when he stopped by my office. He recognized him as one of the men who scammed him."

"Really. Now that's interesting."

I nodded. "I thought so, but I have no way of moving forward on this. Not that it proves that Sean killed Alec. Which makes me wonder—where is Alec?"

"Upstairs in the attic room, reading."

"He seems to have calmed down quite a bit."

"So I've noticed," Evelyn said. "I wonder why."

*   *   *

Who murdered Sean? I asked myself when I was back in my office. Certainly not his son with whom he'd recently reconciled. Could Buzz have gotten angry enough to kill Sean because he'd changed his mind about selling him the company? I suddenly remembered that John hadn't commented when I mentioned Sean's decision to hand over his company to his son instead of selling it to Buzz. Could be Sean had never found the right time to tell Buzz about his change of plans.

Who had Sean been speaking to when Al and I left Town Hall? Such an odd time and place for a chat. Had the person situated himself or herself on the far side of the truck to intentionally avoid being seen? Not knowing the person's gender or height meant I couldn't exclude Babette and Reggie from the lineup. Though even if one of them had stayed behind to chat with Sean, it didn't mean he or she had murdered him.

My thoughts spun around in circles, churning out more questions than answers. I told myself it was high time I buckled down to library business. Future programs and events required my attention.

I skimmed through the list of people wanting to present programs in the near future. They were varied and sundry—from proposed lectures on nutrition to talks about art history. Since I'd soon have more rooms available for more programs, I decided it was time to expand my horizons.

So much of what we offered was for our patrons' enjoyment. Maybe it was time to include more programs that were helpful in a practical way. Discussions about aging, nutrition, travel, health, and financial assistance were a few areas to explore. Feeling a burst of excitement, I began researching what other libraries were offering their patrons along these lines.

I was reading about a program that offered conversation classes to immigrants who wished to improve their English language skills when someone knocked on my door.

"Come in," I called out.

The door flung open and Julie Theron appeared, panting and red-faced as if she'd been running.

"Carrie, we need to talk." She made a beeline for my assistants' empty chair and plopped down.

"We do?"

She leaned forward, elbows on knees, and gazed into my eyes. "Yes, there's been another murder, and the police are doing nothing to solve this one either. If we work together we'll catch the—"

"Julie, Lieutenant Mathers is hard at work going after Sean Powell's killer. He's already interviewed me since I was at the council meeting with Sean last night."

"Do you have any suspects in mind?" she demanded.

"Not really," I admitted. But even if I did there was no way I'd mention it to this newshound for fear of hearing my suspicions broadcast on the evening news.

"Well, I've done some thinking and I've come up with a theory," she said smugly.

"Is that so?"

She nodded. "I think the two murders are connected."

I stared at Julie. "You're saying the same person murdered Alec Dunmore and Sean Powell."

She nodded. "I did some research. Dunmore and Powell were involved in a business deal that went sour."

My heart began to pound. "How do you know?"

Julie giggled. "A little birdie told me."

"A birdie?"

"All right. A man. An elderly gentleman who wasn't there but has it on good authority."

"What elderly man?" I was growing exasperated.

"Albert Whitehead, James's cousin. It turns out that James met with Sean, Alec Dunmore, and a few others. Alec was in the process of buying the building next door to *your* library. Which might explain how his body ended up there."

"Wow!" I exclaimed. This fitted in with what Alec remembered.

"You're surprised," Julie said, pleased with herself.

She had no idea what I was surprised about, and I meant to keep it that way. "Yeah, I'm surprised Albert failed to mention it to me when I spoke to him and his cousin Marcella."

Julia shot me a look of pure glee. "Albert told me you'd paid them a visit. But he felt uncomfortable mentioning details of the possible sale since he'd never told Marcella that James had confided in him about the sale. James told Albert not to say a word to Marcella until the sale went through. And since it never did, Albert stayed mum. He didn't want to hurt Marcella's feelings and let her know she'd been left out."

"I see." Now I was reeling from the fact that Julie had managed to learn something very important that I'd missed because I'd never thought to speak to Marcella and Albert separately.

"So why do you need me to help solve these murders?" I asked, a bit ungraciously. "You seem to be doing pretty well on your own."

Julie blew off my comment with a wave of her hand. "Are you kidding? You know everyone in Clover Ridge—Alec Dunmore was your fiancé's uncle. You were on the town council with Sean Powell. His company is doing the renovations for the library's new addition. You know people connected to the victims. You *know* Clover Ridge."

I nodded, seeing the logic in her theory.

"So, are you in?" she demanded.

When I didn't answer, she said, "Are you willing to admit that two heads are better than one when it comes to solving these homicides? You have the experience of working cases and I've got sources and access to all sorts of information."

I nodded, acknowledging the logic of her argument.

"Great!"

Julie had taken my nod to mean I was agreeing to her proposal. But could I even consider it? She held up her hand for a high five. Reluctantly, I tapped my palm against hers.

"I'm in, but I have two conditions," I heard myself say. "One, you never do anything rash that puts us in danger, and two, you never mention my name on TV or tell anyone we're working on this together."

"Sure. Whatever you say." Julie swung out of the chair and headed for the door. "Gotta go. I'll be in touch."

I've signed a pact with the devil! I stared at the closed door, wondering why I'd agreed to work with Julie to solve the two murders. Dylan would be upset. John would be angry and hurt because I was his friend and Julie was a thorn in his side.

But the truth was, I'd already made up my mind to investigate both murders. I'd never really considered that they might be connected. And Julie did have sources and resources. Much as I hated to admit it, I had to admire the way she'd wheedled information out of Albert that he hadn't shared with me. *Well, she is an investigative reporter*, I reminded myself as I settled back down to work.

"Finally! I thought that woman would never leave."

I glanced up as Alec materialized. "Hello, Alec. And how are you today?"

"Fine. Or as fine as I can be, given the circumstances." He seemed to have something on his mind, something he was having difficulty expressing.

"Are you nervous about the—er, ceremony on Sunday? I told you, you won't feel a thing."

"I know that. I left my shell of a body some time ago." He cleared his throat. "But just in case the experience moves me someplace else, I'd like to see Dylan. Do you think he'll be willing to see me?"

"I'll ask him," I said. "If he says okay, it will have to be tomorrow."

"Thank you, Carrie. That means a great deal to me. By the way, who was that young woman that made a mad dash to your office then flew out like a demon was chasing her?"

I chuckled at his description. "That's Julie Theron. She's a TV investigative reporter. I don't know if you're aware that Sean Powell, the man you thought you'd recognized yesterday, was murdered last night."

Alec shook his head. "I had no idea. His construction company is doing the renovations on the building next door."

"That's right."

He cocked his head as he thought. "I know it's a stretch, but do you think the person who killed me also killed him?"

"Julie thinks the two murders are connected. She managed to convince me to join her in looking into the possibility."

"That's great!" Alec reached out to touch my arm. I lurched back, just in time.

"Sorry, Carrie. I want to thank you for all you've been doing to help me. I know I'm not the easiest person to deal with. We'll both be glad when this is over."

He faded away, and I decided I had one more thing to do before getting back to work. I looked up the phone number of the Clover Ridge Home for Seniors and asked to be connected to Albert Whitehead. I smiled when his croaky voice answered.

"Hello, Albert, this is Carrie Singleton. How are you?"

"Fine, thank you."

"How would you like to join me for breakfast tomorrow morning—say eight thirty?"

"Sure. As long as the place serves French toast. I love French toast."

"The diner I'm thinking of makes terrific French toast," I said.

"Will Marcella be joining us?" he asked.

"Not this time," I said carefully. "And please don't mention it to her."

He laughed. "It will be our little secret then. Just like old times."

"Just like old times." I wasn't sure what that meant, but I intended to find out.

Chapter
Twenty-Three

It was close to ten o'clock when Smoky Joe and I arrived home that evening. I found Dylan half-asleep on the living room sofa, the TV on mute. He looked up, groggy but grinning and happy to see me. I bent down and gave him a hug.

"Did you find something to eat in the fridge?" I asked.

"Yep. Leftover chicken, guacamole, and salad."

"I had a bowl of chili at the Cozy Corner Café for dinner," I said. "Dessert would be nice."

"Ice cream!" we said at the same time.

Minutes later, as we sat at the kitchen table downing spoonfuls of pistachio ice cream topped with dried cranberries and chocolate syrup, I told Dylan about my various visitors during the day.

"So," he said when I was done, "you're joining forces with Julie Theron, our local Lois Lane, to solve the two murders she believes are connected. And Uncle Alec wants to chat with me before going up in flames on Sunday."

I nodded. "Which would mean you coming into the library tomorrow."

Dylan's face remained impassive as he considered his uncle's request. I was hoping he'd agree because he and Alec had been close at one time and this might be their last chance to communicate with one another.

"I suppose I can do it. I have to go into the office tomorrow morning, but I could get to the library around two."

"I'm glad. It seemed important to Alec."

"After all, he is my uncle, and I feel I owe it to him. But babe, teaming up with Julie Theron might not be a good idea."

I nodded. "John will be furious when he finds out. If he finds out."

"I don't suppose you caught her latest TV appearance. The one that aired tonight."

"No, I've been working."

"She announced she was on the track of the person who murdered Sean Powell and Alec Dunmore and plans to reveal his identity very soon."

I stared at Dylan. "The idiot! She's asking for trouble."

Dylan grimaced. "She's a loose cannon, Carrie. You know I never tell you what you should or shouldn't do, but I'm worried about you associating with Julie Theron. I'm relieved she's never said you're involved in the investigation."

"She has instructions not to," I said grimly.

"Thank God she's followed through . . . so far."

* * *

Saturday morning I drank my mug of coffee while Dylan scrambled a few eggs, which he ate with peanut butter on toast. I knew he was apprehensive about my arrangement with Julie Theron, but I wasn't about to call it off. Her announcement about outing the murderer was foolhardy, but her investigative instincts were solid. She was spot-on thinking the two of us, with our particular skills, made an awesome duo. If only she were less pushy and in-your-face.

I stroked Smoky Joe, kissed Dylan goodbye, and climbed into my car heading for the Clover Ridge Home for Seniors. I was worried that Albert might have forgotten or changed his mind, but no, there he was waiting for me outside the entrance to the senior residence. I drove slowly around the circular drive and he hobbled up to the car on his cane, grinning as he climbed into the passenger seat.

"This is such fun!" he declared. "I never get to eat breakfast out with a stunner like you."

"Thank you, Albert. Did Marcella wonder why you weren't at breakfast this morning?"

"Last night at dinner I told her I planned to stay up late to watch a favorite old movie on TV and sleep in this morning. It's something I do from time to time, so I doubt she'll be suspicious."

"That's good."

He shot me a shrewd glance. "We're cousins, Marcella and me, and I love her dearly, but we're not joined at the hip."

"Got it," I said.

We made light conversation as I drove to the diner. Albert was fun to chat with, and we got on the subject of how Clover Ridge used to be when he was young.

"There were many more farms around like the one your family owned, and the elementary school went from K through nine. Marcella, James, and I attended high school in Merrivale," Albert said. "I made plenty of good friends there, though many of them have since died."

"I suppose you knew my grandfather and Uncle Bosco."

"Of course, though they were a decade or so younger than me. And I remember your dad." Albert chuckled as he shook his head. "Jim Singleton was one funny kid. Had an angle to everything he did. One summer he sold strawberries for a crazy low price. He set up a stand close to the two or three inns where tourists came to stay. It was an especially good season, and he was raking in money hand over fist. Until his father and your uncle got wind of it. They'd been planning to sell the strawberries at the market for more money."

I winced, figuring Albert also knew that my father had done a few stints in prison for theft. "Well, my father has a great job now, and he's remarried—to the nicest woman."

"Good for Jim," Albert said as I pulled into a spot in the diner's parking lot.

At a quarter to nine, the diner was crowded, mostly with families. Albert and I managed to snag one of the last tables. When our waitress appeared, we both ordered French toast.

As she left to get our coffee, Albert said, "I was sorry to hear that Sean Powell died. Murdered, that young reporter announced on TV."

I nodded. "According to Julie Theron, your cousin James told you that Sean and Alec Dunmore were interested in buying the building next to the library."

Albert had the grace to look ashamed. "Julie told you that?"

I nodded.

"Sorry. I couldn't say anything in front of Marcella. Actually, it was Alec Dunmore who was interested in buying the building, only he balked at the large down payment James insisted on getting up front. So James got the brilliant idea to have Sean Powell and a few others join him and Dunmore in a local bar and pretend they wanted in on the deal too—at a smaller percentage. Meanwhile, James made sure Dunmore got good and drunk until he forked over the money."

Albert laughed. "Sean said his company would renovate the place, saving Dunmore a bundle of money, and since it was well situated on the Green it couldn't help but turn into a moneymaker."

I frowned as I followed what he was telling me. "But why would Sean do that?"

Albert shrugged. "My guess is he owed James a lot of money. This was one way he could wipe the slate clean. So Sean asked a few of his friends to play along. Or maybe they also owed my cousin. Jamie Boy had a way of getting his claws into people and draining them dry. It's amazing no one offed him and he died of natural causes."

I felt my pulse speed up. "Do you remember who else was involved in this scam?"

Albert closed his eyes and thought. "Buzz Coleman. He worked for Sean."

"Yes, I know Buzz. Anyone else you can think of?"

"There was an architect, too. Roger, no, Rafael Torres."

"Did James ever say what Alec wanted to do with the building?"

Albert laughed. "He didn't care as long as we got top dollar for the place. One of them—I think Sean—threw out the idea of a boutique B and B. Or was it an office building? Not that it mattered. The deal never went through."

"Is that what James told you?"

"Sort of. When I ran into him a few days later, I asked what was happening. 'Nothing. Absolutely nothing,' he said and rushed past me. The deal was dead. I knew better than to press the issue."

The deal was dead, Alec was dead. "Did your cousin ever say whether or not he gave Alec Dunmore back his money?" I asked.

Albert scoffed. "James hand back money? You gotta be kidding. Not that Marcella or I ever saw a penny of it."

Our French toast arrived. I poured maple syrup on mine while Albert opened tiny containers of blueberry and strawberry jam to smear on his. For a minute we were too busy eating to talk. I barely managed to finish half of my portion and marveled that Albert was scarfing his down to the very last bite.

"That was delicious," he said, pushing the plate away. "Too bad they don't serve food like this at the Home."

Our waitress came by to refill our coffee mugs. I looked at Albert. "Would you like something to go with your second cup of coffee?"

He grinned. "I wouldn't mind a blueberry muffin." He glanced up at our waitress. "Very lightly toasted, with plenty of butter. And I'll need more jam."

When she left, Albert looked at me. "I thought I'd bring back half the muffin for Marcella."

"That's very nice of you, but I'd be happy to get her her own muffin."

"No need. Marcella and I are used to sharing."

I nodded. "Except you never told her about the one time James let you know the building had a good chance of being sold."

"Nope. Interestingly enough, James mentioned it in passing when the three of us were together. It must have been a month or two after the deal fell through. He wasn't angry anymore, just resigned, so I figured there was no need to tell Marcella that he'd confided in me earlier. Why hurt her feelings?"

"Good point," I said.

When his muffin arrived, Albert cut it in half and asked our waitress for a bag to bring half of it home with him. I asked for a container for my French toast. As soon as she left, I asked, "And you really think your cousin was capable of murdering Alec Dunmore for changing his mind about the sale?"

Albert nodded, his mouth too full of blueberry muffin to speak. "Sure, if he was in a fit of anger. James had difficulty controlling his temper. And losing that sale would have sent him over the edge."

"Then six years later someone murders Sean," I mused.

"Makes you wonder," Albert said.

We chatted easily as I drove him back to the Home for Seniors. Albert was surprisingly up on current events and took great interest in everything concerning Clover Ridge. He was delighted when I told him that we'd voted to keep the Seabrook property a preserve.

"Good move! People need a bit of nature in their lives. You can't go around building houses and shops on every parcel of land." He turned to stare at me. "Did Sean vote for the preserve?"

Though we weren't supposed to divulge who voted for what, I nodded.

Albert pursed his lips. "That could be why someone killed him."

I laughed. "I hope that's not the case, since it would mean Al Tripp and I are next."

Minutes later I pulled into the driveway of the Clover Ridge Home for Seniors. I got out of the car and walked around to the passenger side to help Albert out of the car. "Don't forget Marcella's muffin," I said, reaching for the paper bag.

"Thank you so much for a delightful outing," Albert said as he steadied his cane on the ground. He winked. "Feel free to call on me any time you want a breakfast companion. I'm sorry I couldn't be of more help."

I was about to step back into my car when Marcella came striding toward us, walking faster than I'd imagined a woman her age could move.

"Did you have a pleasant outing?" she demanded, glaring at her cousin, then at me. The words "without me" hung in the air as if she'd shouted them aloud.

"For you," Albert managed to say. He held out the bag containing the half muffin.

"Thank you!" Marcella swiped it from his hand. "And what did you have to tell Carrie that you couldn't say in front of me?"

"Er—why don't we go inside and discuss it?" Albert said.

Marcella glowered at me. "Coming, Carrie?"

Do I have a choice? "Of course."

They both assured me that despite the No Parking sign it was fine to leave my car in the circular driveway as I'd only be a few minutes, and we headed for the entrance. Marcella walked briskly ahead, chest out, a bantam of a woman spoiling for a fight. Albert and I followed meekly at a slower pace and caught up with Marcella in the far corner of the large social room. As soon as we were seated—the two cousins in chairs, me facing them on a loveseat—Albert began his explanation.

"Carrie asked for my assistance with her investigation into two local murders. Alas, I wasn't much help—"

"Clearly it concerns that poor man found dead in that dratted building. What can you possibly know that I don't, Albert Whitehead?" It occurred to me that the timid, shy Marcella had inherited some of her brother's personality.

Albert hunched his shoulders as though to protect himself from her onslaught. "James told me he was in the process of selling the building to that Alec Dunmore fellow. Estelle Avery's brother. Only it turned out he never did buy it."

Marcella shrugged. "We know that."

"Only I knew about it a bit earlier than you did. I didn't tell you at the time because James said not to mention it to you, and then I forgot about it because he told us the sale never went through a few months later when the three of us were together. I didn't want to hurt your feelings."

Marcella scoffed. "So kind of you."

"Then you're not hurt," Albert said.

"Hurt? No, I'm angry. Angry at my brother for his bossy ways and at you, Albert, for being so touched that he'd confided in you that you followed his instructions like a good puppy dog."

"Sorry," Albert mumbled. "You're right."

Marcella grinned suddenly. "Did it ever occur to you that I might have known something about the goings-on at the time?"

"No!" Albert said.

We both stared at Marcella, awaiting her next words.

"At the time James thought he had a prospective buyer, I knew something was up. How could I not, living in the same house with him? He'd get phone calls, jot down notes, then get back on the phone. He was careful to throw most of his notes away, but I saw

219

one or two showing the times of day or night when he was meeting someone at the building we all owned."

She jutted her face toward Albert. "And we had every right to know about it."

"You're right," Albert said, swallowing. "James should have kept us in the loop."

"But I knew my dear brother wouldn't tell me anything, so I decided to follow him one night."

Good girl! I stared at her in admiration.

"I watched from the shadows to see who James was meeting. A few men showed up. The only ones I recognized were Sean Powell and Buzz Coleman."

I nodded, certain I wasn't about to learn anything new. At least Albert knew that Alec and Rafe had also been present.

Marcella must have read the disappointment in my face because she said, "Hold on. There's more."

"Okay," I said, mostly to be polite.

"I waited outside for at least half an hour. Good thing it was warm. I considered going into the building but was afraid someone would catch sight of me. A breeze started up. I felt chilled so I had decided to leave when the whole bunch of them, including James, traipsed outside. *Okay*, I thought, *show's over*, when my brother went back inside the building.

"This time I followed him. He'd locked the door, but I had my own key. I slipped into the small front hall and tried to figure out where James had gone and why he was back in that ruin of a building."

Marcella paused.

"And?" I said, caught up in the story.

"For about twenty minutes nothing happened. I was about to take off when someone knocked on the door. I had just enough time to hide in the kitchen. James went to let in whoever he was expecting. There were two people—a man and a woman."

"Who were they?" Albert asked.

"Babette Fisher and Reggie Williams."

Chapter
Twenty-Four

*B*abette and Reggie. As I drove to work I thought it curious that they'd met with James Whitehead in that dilapidated building around the same time Alec Dunmore was murdered. I knew from Uncle Bosco that Babette had been interested in buying the building at one time. But why had she gone there with Reggie?

Though I didn't know either of them very well, I'd never heard that they'd ever considered going into a joint business enterprise. From my time on the town council, I knew Babette and Reggie were both in favor of turning the Seabrook Preserve property into a money-making venture. Both of them had expected Sean to vote for their pet project.

Is that why one of them had killed Sean?

No, no, no! As I pulled into the library parking lot, I scolded myself for jumping to conclusions. Time to stop speculating about Reggie and Babette, about the two murders, and focus on the work day ahead.

I was in my office, having just listened to Trish's report of the morning's activities—she was working today, Saturday, in lieu of taking off a day next week—when Sally stopped by, excited about an idea she had.

"Why don't we start a Summer Reading Book Club? Two, actually—one for kids, another for adults. Patrons can sign up in early June and the program would run from the middle of June until the middle of August. Everyone who signs up has to read and report on six books. We do giveaways at the midpoint and hold a party—two separate parties—in late August."

"Sounds like a fun idea," I agreed. "We could have a theme. Like faraway places. And do some programs on different countries during the two months."

Sally grinned. "I like that!"

"Susan could make posters for the library and drawings for the newsletter," Trish said.

"During the party, a musical group could play songs from countries around the world," I said.

"And let's not forget foreign films," Sally added.

"And maybe serve international food," Trish suggested. "Mini tacos. Pierogi. Baklava."

"Let's not go crazy," Sally, ever aware of the bottom line, chided.

The three of us burst out laughing.

I glanced at the clock, suddenly remembering that Dylan would be arriving soon and why. "Trish and I will start setting up tentative dates for some of these events," I said.

"I'm off to the children's section to see what Marion thinks about our idea."

"I'm sure she'll love it," I said to Sally, who was already halfway out the door.

"Time for me to take over the hospitality desk," Trish said, getting up from her desk.

She'd no sooner left than Dylan called to say he'd be arriving very soon.

"Great. Now to find your uncle so you can have your little chat."

I headed for the staircase leading to the downstairs rooms. I was pretty sure I'd find Alec in the small room that was currently unoccupied. Now that he was feeling calmer, he made a conscious effort to keep out of the patrons' way. I figured if he wasn't in the room, I'd find him upstairs in the attic.

As I stepped onto the lower level, I sensed Evelyn's presence even before she materialized at my side.

"Alec and I had a serious talk this morning. With all this free time on his hands he's been looking back on his life." She pursed her lips. "He admits he's made a sorry mess of things."

"That's probably why he wants to talk to Dylan," I said.

I was surprised when Evelyn took off without saying another word, but I supposed she wanted to allow Alec and Dylan some privacy. I entered the small room and found Alec nervously pacing a few feet above the ground, a most disconcerting sight.

"Dylan will be here shortly," I said.

"Oh, good!" he said fervently as he dropped to ground level.

I called Dylan to tell him where we were. When he joined us, I left the two of them and went upstairs to work on the Summer Reading Book Club. I thought it was a great idea, but then I was in favor of any idea that encouraged people to read.

Dylan was gone for forty-five minutes, considerably longer than I thought he'd be. He seemed subdued when he entered my office.

"So how did it go?" I asked.

"Not quite as I expected."

"Oh?" I shot him an inquiring glance.

"I had no idea he and my mother grew up in such a dysfunctional household. I only remember visiting my mother's parents a few times. When I asked why we never saw them more often, she always gave some reason—they lived far from us; they led busy lives. But the way Alec tells it, they were distant. Strange—something he never realized until he was in high school and saw how warm his friends' parents were when he came over.

"They were strict and demanding of my mother—that she get good grades and always dress nicely—and were more lenient with him. Too lenient, Alec supposed. When my mother started dating my father, their parents urged her to end the relationship, insisting he wouldn't amount to anything. They all but cut my mother out of their lives when she got married."

"How awful," I said.

"Alec said he and my mother were close when they were growing up, but she changed after she married my father. He was intent on making money as a way of earning respect, and his values rubbed off on her."

"Did he say anything about you?" I asked.

We both looked up when Trish came in. "Sorry to interrupt. Just getting my things." She gathered up her pocketbook and sweater. "See you Monday morning."

"Goodbye," Dylan and I called after her.

The door closed behind Trish and we resumed our conversation.

"Alec said he sensed I wasn't getting the attention I needed from my parents. He meant to come to Clover Ridge more often, but his business deals swallowed up most of his time so his trips here were few and far between." Dylan laughed. "He said he tried to be as entertaining as he could. Coming up with stories and taking me on outings when we were together. Until he fell upon hard times and had serious money problems. So he drank more and got into debt."

"What did he have to say about the scams and rip-offs you heard your parents talk about?"

Dylan chuckled. "Nothing, and I certainly didn't bring them up. He apologized for letting me down when I was in college and said he didn't blame me for cutting him off. That he deserved it."

I waited, knowing there was more.

"And then he talked about you, saying what a terrific person you are and that I'm so lucky to have you in my life. He told me to forgive my parents for being callous and to concentrate on our future together." Dylan sniffed. "He said he wished he could share that, but it wasn't to be. He had a feeling that very soon he'd be going where he was supposed to be."

I hugged Dylan close and felt his racing heart. His final talk with his uncle had left him emotionally wrung out. Finally, he kissed the tip of my nose and pulled away.

"Lots for me to think about. And now I'll let you get back to work." Dylan consulted his watch. "I'll see you at home."

* * *

Choosing something to wear to Alec's memorial service that said "serious" but not "somber" was proving to be harder than I'd expected. In my Goth Girl days, before I became head of programs and events, I would have put on something black or deep purple for the occasion. But those days were gone forever. This memorial service was meant to celebrate Alec's life, not his death. At least, that was how I viewed it. Finally, after poring through my closet, I decided on a beige silk blouse, a beige-and-black patterned midi skirt, and black sling-back heels.

Alec's remains would be dealt with at one o'clock at a nearby crematorium with Dylan and me in attendance. The memorial would follow shortly after. Dylan had rented a hall a block from Town Hall for the occasion. We expected about thirty people to attend and had arranged for a local caterer to set out cheese and crackers, fruit, cookies, cake, and coffee and tea and a waitress to serve hot hors d'oeuvres.

Though the circumstances were strange if not downright weird, I was glad I'd gotten to know Alec, especially since he was Dylan's only relative I was likely to meet. Except for Dylan and me and the men he'd met briefly years ago—perhaps his killer among them—no one attending the memorial had known Alec. Our guests were coming to show their respect to Dylan, out of friendship to us both, or because they were working on the renovations of the building where Alec's body had been discovered.

The event was scheduled from two to four. I had asked everyone to arrive by two thirty, at which time Dylan planned to say a few words. The first to appear were Gary Winton, the young detective Dylan had recently hired, and Rosalind Feratti, Dylan's gal Friday, followed by my aunt and uncle, my cousins Julia and Randy, and my library pals and their menfolk. I greeted Rafe Torres, the architect, and several construction workers, all looking sad because of their boss's recent demise.

At two twenty-five Al Tripp and his wife, Dolores, arrived with Babette, Reggie, and Reggie's wife close behind. I was thanking them for coming when Julie Theron stormed through the door sporting a bruise on her cheek.

"What happened to you?" I asked.

"No biggie. Some idiot was waiting for me when I got home last night. Shouted 'Stop playing Sherlock Holmes,' pulled back his arm and socked me, then took off."

"Aren't you terrified?" I shook my head in disbelief. "That must have been the killer warning you to stop investigating. Challenging him on TV wasn't very smart."

She shrugged. "Maybe, but I got his attention."

I rolled my eyes. "Julie, you were reckless. You're lucky he didn't kill you."

She scoffed. "Hah! Like you've never been reckless when hunting down a killer?"

I opened my mouth to dispute that, then, remembering my last adventure, shut it quickly. Before I could stop myself, I asked, "Did you get a good look at him?"

"Unfortunately, no. It was dark out and he made sure to stand in the shadows."

"You're certain it was a man?"

"Pretty sure, though he wore a mask and a hoodie. Now if you'll excuse me, I'm off to swipe a cookie. I'm about to faint from hunger since I haven't eaten since early this morning."

She's pretty sure it was a man. Does that mean I can cross Babette off my list of suspects?

Conversation died down as Dylan went to stand at the front of the room and picked up the mic.

"Thank you all for coming here today to celebrate Alexander Dunmore's life. Uncle Alec was my mother's younger brother and, for many years, my hero. Sadly, he took many unfortunate turns in life, the last being his visit to Clover Ridge six years ago. So far, we don't know why he came here or why someone killed him. Only that his life was cut short and his body left in the basement of the unoccupied building next to the library. I have full confidence that the police will find the person who murdered Uncle Alec."

As if on cue, all heads turned to the door as John and Sylvia Mathers entered the room. "Sorry for our late arrival," John said. "Police business delay."

Had John finally gotten a solid lead on Sean's murderer? Or Alec's? The whispers around me told me that others were wondering the same thing.

Dylan shared a few childhood memories of Alec, then invited everyone to have something to eat. On cue, a waitress appeared bearing a tray of hot appetizers.

I knew everyone present and felt comfortable moving from group to group, chatting with our guests and thanking them for taking the time to honor Alec's memory. I kept my eye on Julie in case she zoomed in on John and berated him for not having found Alec's murderer yet, but so far she'd kept her distance. Not that John needed protection. Besides, Sylvia, John's beautiful redheaded wife, was one tough lady and more than a match for a novice like Julie Theron.

I finally joined John and Sylvia, who were conversing with my aunt and uncle. Sylvia embraced me warmly, but I got a cool reception from John. Uh-oh. He was pissed at me. But why? There was no way he could have found out I'd agreed to investigate the murders with Julie.

Or was there?

"Do you have any new leads on either homicide?" I asked John when there was a lull in the conversation.

He grimaced. "As if I'd tell you." He ignored the frowns coming from Sylvia and my uncle. John jerked his chin in Julie's direction. "You'd probably rush over to our TV Wonder Girl so she could announce it to the world."

We all turned to look at Julie, who was deep in conversation with Gary and Dylan. I felt a stab of jealousy, which I quelched almost as quickly as it had risen. Julie was after a story, not my fiancé. Still, all three seemed totally engrossed in whatever they were discussing.

"I'd never tell Julie anything that would jeopardize your investigation," I said as my aunt and uncle made a quick departure.

"I can't take a chance, Carrie, knowing how buddy-buddy the two of you have become."

I was afraid to ask where he'd heard this for fear I'd learn that Julie had tipped him off herself. Instead, I decided to try a new tack.

"I talked to Albert and Marcella Whitehead again and learned a few things."

"I'm sure whatever they had to say was very interesting. Now if you'll excuse us, I'd like to have a few words with your fiancé. After all, we're here for his sake." John slipped his arm around Sylvia's waist and led her to where Dylan now stood munching on an appetizer.

I didn't like being dismissed so abruptly. Nor did I like John's assumption that I'd gone over to the enemy. A glance around the room verified what had been lurking in the back of my mind. I stormed after John and Sylvia and tugged on his arm. He paused in midsentence and glanced down at me.

"Would you have told me you arrested Buzz Coleman for killing Sean if you weren't pissed at me?"

Though trained not to show his emotions, John couldn't stop his eyes from widening. "How—what makes you think that?"

I shrugged. "He's not here, is he? While many of his workers are."

John burst out laughing and I found myself laughing too, relieved he was no longer angry. But how could he stay angry when he'd just arrested Sean's killer—or so he thought.

Chapter
Twenty-Five

B uzz, it turned out, was the person Sean had been talking to in the Town Hall parking lot after the council meeting. The reason John had questioned him so extensively was because his fingerprints were found on the underside of Sean's truck. That was because, Buzz insisted, he had fixed various mechanical problems on that vehicle.

"He also has a record and was very belligerent during his interview," John told me the following day when he came to the library to question me once again about the town council meeting. "He didn't want a lawyer because he insisted he didn't need a lawyer. 'Why on earth would I kill one of my best friends who was in the process of selling me his business?'

"He was so obnoxious, I decided to let him cool his heels while Sylvia and I attended the memorial. Of course I couldn't keep him indefinitely, so I arranged to have Danny Brower release him around dinnertime."

"Did Buzz tell you Sean changed his mind about selling him the business?" I asked.

"Nope, and I don't think he's a good enough liar to pretend they never had that conversation."

"So maybe Sean never found the right moment to bring up the subject," I said. "I wonder if Kevin knew."

"That's something I intend to find out," John said, stretching out his long legs. "Now, please tell me once again exactly what you recall of the discussion regarding the Seabrook Preserve property."

* * *

Tuesday evening, I ate a burger at the Cozy Corner Café, then drove over to the Ryan Funeral Home to attend Sean's wake. I'd been there a few months ago, after Angela's cousin's husband had been murdered. I felt a bit nervous because I had only known Sean a short while and didn't know his family, though I'd once met his wife, Pat.

But I needn't have worried. As soon as I entered the large room filled with Clover Ridge residents who had come to pay their respects, I spotted several people I knew. Al and Dolotes were there. So were Reggie and his wife and Rafe. I recognized a trio of workers and greeted them, then stood on line to offer my condolences to Sean's family.

Pat Powell was a small blonde woman in her mid-seventies with a good sense of style, judging by her chic haircut and the navy blue dress that flattered her stocky figure. She was still attractive and must have been a beauty in her youth. I'd been told by several people that she and Sean had had a happy marriage, and I knew she must have been devastated by this sudden loss.

When I finally reached Pat, I extended my hand but she pulled me in tight for a hug and thanked me for coming.

"Of course," I said. "I was very fond of Sean, though I hadn't known him long."

"My husband had a special fondness for you, Carrie," she said. "He thought you'd make a great mayor one day."

I smiled. "I'm touched, but right now I'm happy if I manage to keep up with my council duties." I remembered why I was here and quickly moved to solemn mode. "I'm so sorry for your loss, Pat."

"Thank you, Carrie." She held out her hand to her son and a pretty teenager who stood at her side. "This is my son, Kevin. I don't think you two know each other. And his daughter, Felice."

I murmured my condolences. Pat gestured with her chin to the young attractive woman chatting with a couple a few feet away. "And that's my daughter, Lianne. My other grandchildren are around somewhere."

"Again, my deepest condolences," I said to Kevin, Felice, and Pat.

I was about to move on and let the people in line behind me have their moment with the bereaved family when Kevin beckoned me to follow him. He led me through the throng of mourners to a small adjoining room that was unoccupied.

"Carrie, I know you've solved some homicides here in town, and I'm hoping you'll find my father's killer."

"Well, I . . ."

"Please!" Kevin's expressive face was filled with pain. "He was dying."

"I know."

"For years Dad and I didn't speak. When my mom told me how ill he was, I ended all that nonsense. I figured we had some final time to spend together. And then someone murdered him! Someone he knew well." He blinked back tears.

"Do you have anyone in mind?"

"Of course!" Kevin scoffed. "Buzz Coleman. My father's right-hand man. The police arrested him, then stupidly set him free."

"Why do you think Buzz killed your father?" I asked.

"Isn't it obvious? Buzz was always jealous of Dad. And he must have blown a gasket when Dad told him he wasn't selling him the business after all because I'd be taking it over."

While I felt sympathy for Kevin for having lost his father, his in-your-face aggressive attitude was unappealing. "Do you know for a fact your father told Buzz he'd changed his mind about the sale?"

Kevin shrugged. "He promised me he would."

Something kept me silent. Sure enough, when Kevin spoke again, it was with some reluctance. "I'd just gotten stiffed by my boss, and Dad asked if I'd like to take over his business. I said yes, and only found out later that he'd arranged for Buzz to buy it. I hate to say it, but I told Dad he could shove his offer. He insisted he wanted me to have it and he'd make it right with Buzz."

"Do you know how he meant to make it right?" I asked.

Kevin shook his head. "Haven't the foggiest. But let me tell you, Buzz has a ferocious temper. He physically attacked Dad one time when they had a disagreement. Mom barred him from the house. And from coming to the wake."

Highly volatile emotions made Kevin insist Buzz must have killed his father. Kevin claimed he didn't know if his father ever told Buzz he'd changed his mind about selling him the business. Kevin and Buzz were two hotheads with a reason to lie. Frankly, I didn't know whose story to believe.

"So you'll investigate my father's murder, starting with Coleman." It was a statement, not a question.

"I'll try to find out what I can," I said. After all, I was already looking into the two murders.

"Thanks, Carrie!" Kevin shot me a quick smile and took my hand in both of his. "Now I better get back to the receiving line or my mother will have a fit."

I watched him walk away and decided it was time to leave. I'd only gone a few steps when I found myself face-to-face with Rafe Torres.

"Having a tête-à-tête with Kevin?"

I felt my ears grow warm. "He wanted to talk to me about Sean."

"No doubt to ask you to find his father's killer."

"Well . . ." I gave a nervous laugh. "I wish people had more faith in the police department. I'm sure they'll find the person who murdered Sean without my help."

"First time you're meeting Kevin?"

"Yes."

"What do you make of him?"

I tried to be tactful. "He's not like Sean. Or Pat, though I hardly know her."

"He's a hothead. Always shooting off his mouth," Rafe said.

"I gather you're not a fan."

"Soon as he could walk, he gave his father nothing but grief."

"Kevin said he patched things up with his father. Sean told him he could have the business, then Kevin found out his father was in the process of selling it to Buzz."

Rafe laughed. "That must have pissed him off."

"Kevin claims his father told Buzz about the change of plans. Do you know anything about this?"

"I don't," Rafe said. He exhaled a puff of exasperation. "But I wouldn't believe one word that comes out of his mouth."

Chapter
Twenty-Six

I considered telling John about my conversation with Kevin, then decided not to bother since Kevin must have told John exactly what he'd told me. Besides, most of what he'd said was no more than a rant against Buzz Coleman. Kevin sure had it in for his father's foreman. And, according to Rafe, Kevin had no compunction about lying.

But he sounded sincere about wanting me to find his father's killer. Unless he was a member of Actors' Equity, I took him at his word about that.

Sean's funeral was scheduled for eleven the following morning at St. Stephen's, where Angela and Steve were married three months ago. I left early enough to have time to find a parking spot on the street in case the church's lot had already filled up. Sean was a popular figure in the community, and many people would be in attendance to say their final farewell.

I managed to park in the lot after all and took a seat in a row halfway down the nave. I greeted Al and Reggie, who were sitting a few rows behind me, and waved to my uncle, who was with two other library board members.

The church filled up quickly. I glanced around, spotting many Clover Ridge residents and Sean's workers. John Mathers stood leaning against the back wall, his usual place when he attended a homicide victim's funeral. There was no sign of Julie, which surprised me.

At eleven sharp, the organist played a few notes. The pallbearers were poised to escort the casket to the front of the church when Babette came dashing down the aisle. She sank into the empty seat beside me.

"Made it!" she whispered triumphantly.

I supposed for Babette, cutting it this close was arriving on time.

After the rituals and prayers and a few psalms, the priest asked for elegies from members of the congregation. Kevin went up to the podium and gave a long speech about his reconciliation with his father and how he wished they'd had more time to spend together.

"I think he doth protest too much," Babette quoted under her breath.

"Are you saying . . .?" I began, but the murmur of conversation drew my attention to Buzz, who was making his way to the front of the church.

It was odd seeing him dressed in a sports jacket, shirt, and trousers. I wasn't the only person to stare. Kevin glared at Buzz but made no attempt to stop him from speaking.

"Sean Powell was one of the best men I've ever known. I worked side by side with him for many years and know what a genuinely good human being he was."

"Another who doth protest too much," Babette said softly when Buzz sat down and another worker got up to speak.

I stared at her. "It sounds like you knew Sean really well."

She looked at me solemnly through unshed tears. "I knew him *very* well. And I'm so sorry his life ended this way."

There was no mistaking what Babette was telling me. She and Sean had been lovers.

My mouth must have fallen open at the realization because Babette pressed her lips together to keep from laughing. "It happened a long time ago, but we remained good friends," she whispered as one of Sean's tennis buddies stood to say a few words.

He reminisced about his friendship with Sean in a humorous vein and a few chuckles sounded through the room. Kevin's daughter talked about her beloved grandfather, then Al spoke about Sean's wonderful contribution to the town council.

"I thought he and Pat were devoted to one another," I whispered to Babette.

"They were. It happened when they were going through a rough patch." She sighed. "Still, it was a special time for me. And for Sean." She sighed again. "*He* was special. One of a kind."

Time for a hymn. The organ sounded. We opened our prayer books and sang. The priest said a prayer and it was over. Sean's casket was placed in the hearse and his family ushered to a limo as cars lined up to start the procession to the cemetery.

I thought about Sean and Babette as I made my way past the throng of people and walked to my car. She'd told me about their love affair because she'd needed to celebrate the special relationship she'd had with Sean with someone attending his funeral, and that someone turned out to be me. Oddly enough, I was flattered.

Sean *was* special, I decided, remembering how he'd come by the library to tell me I'd be getting the stadium-seating auditorium he knew was so important to me. I stopped at a nearby diner for a quick lunch, then headed back to work.

Trish told me that the daily programs were running smoothly. I read through my emails and answered the ones requiring immediate attention, then went downstairs to the small room where Alec had taken to hanging out when the room wasn't occupied. It seemed that, despite his cremation, Alec would continue to haunt the library until his killer was caught.

"How was the funeral?" he asked.

"Fine. Uneventful."

"Do you think the same person who killed me murdered Sean?"

"I have no idea," I said.

Alec let out a deep sigh of exasperation. "I can't stay cooped up in this tiny room much longer. Or in the attic!" he added fiercely before I could suggest it.

"I'm sorry, Alec. I can imagine how frustrating this must be for you. This afternoon I plan to do a deep dive into the lives of people I suspect might have killed Sean. Hopefully, I'll uncover something crucial."

Alec looked sad when he said, "I sure hope so, Carrie. I'm counting on you."

Evelyn appeared and accompanied me as I climbed the stairs to the main level.

"The guy's in bad shape," she said. "We really need to find out who murdered him so he can go where he belongs."

"I know."

"Did you learn anything at the funeral that might be a clue to Sean's murderer and hopefully Alec's?"

I shook my head. "Kevin gave a speech, portraying himself as the loving son. And Babette told me she and Sean were lovers for a very short period."

"Interesting on both counts, but nothing conclusive."

"Babette had no reason to murder Sean," I said. "But Kevin?"

"You're thinking he might have killed his father. Why?" Evelyn said.

"Because I heard Sean tell Kevin that he could have the business. Yet Sean was in the process of selling it to Buzz. John never mentioned that Buzz was angry about the sudden change of plans. Which leads me to wonder if Sean decided he couldn't do that to Buzz and ended up telling Kevin 'Sorry, I can't leave you my company, after all.'"

"Which would have infuriated Kevin," Evelyn said.

"And let's not forget that Kevin tried to convince me Buzz had killed his father."

"Maybe he did."

I stared at Evelyn. "You're right. Maybe Sean delivered the bad news, Buzz decided to kill Sean, then when John questioned him Buzz simply omitted telling him about the change of plans. If the paperwork for the sale is in place, Buzz simply has to pay Pat whatever he and Sean agreed on."

"We're back to square one," Evelyn said.

"It looks that way. Meanwhile, please go and talk to Alec. It helps him pass the time."

She grimaced. "I will, but I'll be happy when this whole business is resolved. Having to deal with an unhappy ghost is hard work."

* * *

That evening, Dylan and I were finishing dinner when the door-bell rang. Puzzled, we glanced at one another and I went to see who was visiting us on a weekday evening. I felt a sudden chill as I imagined the worst—my aunt or my uncle had taken ill or . . .

Finding John on my doorstep, a somber expression on his face, did nothing to assuage my anxiety. "I'm sorry to be stopping by so late, but I need to speak to Dylan."

Dylan? "Sure, come on in."

I led him into the kitchen.

Dylan looked up from his seat. "Hello, John."

They men shook hands. So serious. Had I ever seen them shake hands before?

"Can we go inside and talk?"

"Sure."

John led the way to the living room. This was strange. Usually he sat down at the kitchen table and I'd serve him coffee. Or food. I hesitated, wondering if John wanted to speak to Dylan in private, but Dylan put his arm around me. We followed John, both of us wondering why he'd come.

John opted for a chair and we sat on the sofa. He removed a packet of papers from a briefcase I hadn't noticed he'd been carrying and placed them on the table between us.

"Dylan, Charles Twining called me this afternoon. He was Sean Powell's lawyer. I don't know if you knew, but Sean was quite ill. He only had a few months to live, and he'd given his lawyer a letter to open upon his death."

"Okay," Dylan said.

John cleared his throat. "The letter turned out to be a confession. In it, Sean claims to have killed your uncle, Alec Dunmore."

Dylan let out a whoosh of air. "Why? Did he explain?"

"He did in some detail. It seems Alec Dunmore came to Clover Ridge and showed an interest in buying the building next to the library." John handed Dylan a sheet of paper. "Here's a copy of the letter. You can see for yourself."

Dylan scanned the page. After a minute, he began reading aloud.

"Upon my death, my attorney, Charles Twining, is to hand this letter over to the police. Since my oncologist has just told me I have two months to live if I'm lucky, that won't be too far off. I wish to bring to a close a sad set of events that never should have happened."

Dylan stopped. "The letter is dated ten days ago."

He continued. "Alec Dunmore had recently come into some money and wanted to invest it in Clover Ridge because he had relatives living in the area. He got real excited when he found out a building on the Green was for sale. Three members of the Whitehead family owned the building. James Whitehead, who was handling the sale for his sister, his cousin, and himself, couldn't wait to unload the property for an outrageous price. Whitehead told Dunmore a few members of the community were willing to invest in the property, providing a backer plunked down a hefty down payment. A few of us agreed to pretend to go along with this, for various reasons I needn't go into here.

"We met with Dunmore and Whitehead in Kenny's Bar. Dunmore turned out to be a sociable fellow and liked the ideas we proposed for the property. He handed over a large chunk of money to Whitehead for the down payment. We handed over bogus checks as well. The next day Whitehead called me to say Dunmore had second thoughts and asked to have his money returned, something he had no intention of doing. Except he told Dunmore no problem. He could have his money back if he liked.

"I wondered why Whitehead was telling me all this. I had played out my part in the scheme like he'd asked me to do. We were even. But he offered me three thousand dollars to try to get Dunmore to change his mind. More if I succeeded. I had Dunmore meet me at the property so I could explain that the condition of the building didn't matter. I was a contractor and knew that the outer structure was sound and we could demolish the entire interior if we liked. Now that we had a down payment we could do anything we wanted with the property. We were in a great position to make a lot of money.

"But Dunmore wasn't interested. He thought I'd called to return the money. When I started my spiel he got more agitated by the minute. He said he needed the money back. Some of it belonged to someone else, and he demanded that I return it there and then. I thought he was bluffing. After all, who walks around with all that cash if he doesn't have lots more in the bank? I tried to reason with him, but he kept on shouting he wanted his money.

"I got annoyed. He got belligerent and took a swing at me. We got into a tussle and I ended up belting him hard. He fell back, hitting his head on a piece of metal jutting out of the wall. When I checked his pulse, there was none. He was gone.

"I panicked and wrapped the body in a blanket that I found in one of the closets. Then I carried it down to the basement, slipped it under a shelf, and left. I took a chance leaving the body in the building, but I figured it wasn't getting sold any time soon. And if someone discovered the corpse, I had no problem leaving Whitehead to explain how it got there since he was the reason I got involved in the business in the first place.

"The next day I made up a story to tell Whitehead—that Dunmore admitted he'd stolen the money from the place where he worked. When I threatened to call the cops he backed down and left town. Whitehead didn't believe me but he was glad to get fifty thousand dollars free and clear so he paid me—not three but two thousand dollars.

"I'm sorry I took a man's life. I'm sorry I didn't own up to what I did. I have regretted it every day of my life since. I haven't much more time to live and I've asked that this letter be made public. I feel the deepest sympathy and regret for the people Alec Dunmore leaves behind.

"And to my darling Pat; my son, Kevin; and my daughter, Lianne: I hope you will forgive me for shaming you this way."

Dylan folded the paper and looked at me. All I could do was shake my head. I knew from his faraway expression he was comparing Sean's confession to what Alec had told us. There were a few discrepancies. And unfortunately Sean had omitted the names of the people who had been at the bar with him getting Alec drunk so he'd hand over all that money. But now at least we had a clear picture of how Alec had died.

"Thanks for sharing this with me," he finally said to John. "It brings some kind of closure. Is this letter enough to consider the case closed regarding my uncle's death?"

"As far as I'm concerned, though the DA may have other thoughts."

"Sean Powell," I said. "I wish he hadn't been the one responsible."

"Why?" John scoffed. "Because you knew him and liked him?"

"I suppose."

"You met him recently, after he'd mellowed. I always liked the guy, found him perceptive. Able to see a side of things others often missed. But Sean had some rough edges."

"What did he do?" Dylan asked.

John cleared his throat. "I hate to tell tales out of school, but I heard from more than one person that Sean sometimes cut corners on jobs to save a few bucks. He had friends on the planning board in town and a few other places, so he got a pass on some inspections. But not the last few years," John was quick to add.

"That's what Uncle Bosco told me," I said.

"Also Sean used to have all kinds of deals going, some of which required money up front. I'm willing to bet that the only reason he agreed to help James Whitehead with the scam was because Sean owed Whitehead big time. Then Whitehead hooked him with the promise of money, so Sean did his darnedest to convince Dunmore not to renege on the sale."

"Interesting that Sean didn't name the other people he was with the night they got my uncle drunk," Dylan said.

"I noticed that, too," John said. "Maybe he left off naming them because they played no part in Alec Dunmore's death. He didn't want to incriminate them."

"How noble of him," Dylan said sarcastically. "And James Whitehead kept the money. A bunch of thieves and lowlifes."

"We'll run a check on the banks in the Chicago area," John said. "Whatever's in your uncle's account is yours, Dylan."

Dylan shrugged. I knew his thoughts were focused on what had happened to his uncle and not on any bank account.

"Sean didn't mean to kill Alec," I said, not to defend Sean but to help Dylan realize that the death wasn't intentional.

"Regardless, he struck the fatal blow and covered it up, then confessed when it suited him," Dylan said.

I put my arm around him.

After a minute, John said, "So now we know how your uncle Alec died. I'm sorry about that. I was so certain that Sean's murder coming right after Alec's body was discovered meant the two murders were connected, but now I'm not so sure."

Chapter
Twenty-Seven

I drove to work the following morning eager to tell Alec the news that we'd discovered who was responsible for his death. Now he could move on to wherever he was supposed to go. I wanted him to know that Sean hadn't meant to kill him—which technically made it involuntary manslaughter, not murder. Of course that wouldn't mean a hill of beans to Alec because regardless of Sean's intentions, he'd ended up dead.

But if Sean hadn't meant to kill Alec, why didn't he report it? Was it because he couldn't afford to come clean regarding what he and the others were up to? Once he mentioned a scam, everything behind it was bound to come to light. And there was always the chance that Sean would have been charged with manslaughter and gone to jail.

I wondered if Sean had ever told anyone that Alec was dead. He might have told his friends that Alec left town after Whitehead had agreed to return some or all of his money. James Whitehead might have suspected what had really happened but decided to keep quiet. Which led me to wonder if Sean killed Whitehead. No, I decided. James Whitehead died a few years after this all went down. Sean wouldn't have waited that long to act.

James Whitehead had died a natural death at a ripe old age. What's more, he'd kept the hefty down payment that Alec had paid that fateful night. The man had been a despicable human being. I could only hope he had received his just desserts somewhere sometime.

Sean had killed Alec. Shortly after Alec's body was discovered, Sean himself had been murdered. John didn't think the two were necessarily connected. Simply a coincidence. Or was there a link, as Julie had suggested? The situation was complicated, and I was surprised to find myself wanting to hear Julie's input regarding the latest developments. I planned to call her after I spoke to Alec.

As soon as I released Smoky Joe from his carrier and entered my office, Evelyn appeared.

"I have news," I told her. "John received a letter from Sean's lawyer to be opened upon his death. He brought it over to Dylan and me last night. Sean killed Alec. They were fighting and Sean knocked him down. Alec struck his head and died."

"Yes," Evelyn said, not looking at all surprised.

I opened my mouth to ask how she'd found out and shut it just as fast. I ought to know better than to expect that she'd tell me. "Now Alec can leave us in peace and go where he's supposed to be. Isn't that good?"

"Yes, it's good that we know how Alec died and who was responsible, but unfortunately the situation is . . . far from simple."

"What do you mean? Sean admitted he and Alec got into a fight. Sean knocked him down and Alec banged his head and died from his injury."

"Yes," Evelyn said, looking decidedly unhappy.

"Do you think Sean was lying?"

"No."

I put my hands on my hips. "So what's the problem?"

"Someone murdered Sean, complicating the situation. We need to find out who killed Sean and why before Alec can go to his rest." She glanced upward, as if I didn't know where this mandate was coming from.

I pursed my lips. "That isn't fair."

"Fair or not, the two murders are linked. We have to find out who murdered Sean and why, then Alec will be on his way."

I quickly scanned through my emails and phone messages, intent on telling Alec the situation ASAP, but seeing him any time soon was not in the cards. Sally called to ask me to accompany her to the work site to check on the progress.

The connecting arch hadn't been created yet, so we walked around and entered the new addition through the front door. Buzz was expecting us and had arranged for a young worker named Jack to take us around.

"Just be careful where you step," he said as he led us from room to room.

"It looks great," Sally said. "So open and airy."

I loved the smell of the new woodwork and how the sun streamed in through so many windows. It was difficult to remember we were inside a centuries-old building.

"I'm sorry I didn't arrange to have my office moved to the new wing," Sally said.

"Me, too," I agreed.

Jack paused in front of the doorless entrance to the auditorium. "They're working here, so we won't be able to go inside."

"I'll be careful," I said, too eager to see how the auditorium was coming along to heed his words.

"Miss, you're not supposed to—Buzz said it will be finished next week."

But I kept walking down the pitched floor. I passed a workman sawing lumber on a cutting table and stopped to watch a pair of workers laying down the floor of the stage. I smiled, thinking of the many shows and concerts I planned to bring to the library patrons just as soon as the new addition was finished.

I waved to Buzz and Rafe across the room. They were too engrossed in conversation to notice me, so I went to join them.

"The acoustics stink," Buzz was saying. "You can hear how the noise of just one saw and a bunch of guys talking fills the room."

Rafe waved his hand. "Don't worry. There won't be a reverberation problem once the seats and the drapes are in place."

"But Sean said—"

"I know what Sean said," Rafe cut in, his tone calm. "And I'm telling you what I told him: the acoustics will be perfectly suited for library performances. And if there are any problems, we can easily add a few acoustic panels. Not to worry."

Buzz sighed. "All right. I don't want any screwups. I want this project to be perfect—for Sean's sake and the future of the company."

They turned to me as I approached, both wearing artificial smiles.

"So, what do you think, Carrie?" Rafe asked, gazing around the unfinished auditorium.

"Looks good to me," I said.

"We're making great progress," Buzz added.

We all turned as Jack waved frantically to us.

"Let's continue this conversation in the hall so we can hear ourselves," Buzz said.

Minutes later, as Sally and I were walking back to the library, I wondered if either Buzz or Rafe had murdered Sean—Buzz to stop Sean from changing or canceling the sale or Rafe because Sean was constantly dissatisfied with his work.

* * *

It was midmorning when I finally climbed the attic stairs where Evelyn said Alec was hanging out. There was no sign of Evelyn, so I figured she was leaving me to deliver the bad news by myself.

I walked gingerly into the dusty room, dreading Alec's reaction when I told him he wouldn't be leaving Clover Ridge just yet. Poor guy. Right now he looked calm, lounging comfortably in an armchair, a book on his lap, but I wouldn't blame him if he starting ranting at me.

"Hi, Carrie. What's up?"

"Sean Powell left a letter with his attorney to be opened when he died." I told him about the contents of Sean's letter. When I finished, I asked, "Do you remember any of this?"

Alec nodded slowly. "Some of it. I remember having a terrible hangover when I went back to that building next door. So Sean was one of the guys I recognized when they were in the library the other day."

"Did you see any of the men from the bar ever again?"

He squinted as he thought. "Maybe. I'm not sure."

I let out an exasperated sigh. "It would help if you remembered things more clearly."

"Believe me, Carrie. I'm doing the best I can."

"I know," I mumbled, regretting my outburst.

Alec grimaced. "So Sean claims he didn't mean to kill me. Only that's exactly what he did— kill me."

"He said the two of you were fighting."

"Because he wouldn't give me back my money. The way I remember it, you have three days to cancel a big sale like buying property."

"Come on, Alec. By now you know you fell for a big con. The people you were dealing with weren't about to hand any money back."

Alec pursed his lips. "Yeah. I let them get me drunk and sweet-talk me into putting down the money." He scoffed. "How many times did I do that myself? It's hard to admit I let those guys make a chump out of me."

"I'm sorry."

"At least now we know who killed me. When can I leave this place?"

Before I could open my mouth, Evelyn joined us. I was never so glad to see her.

"I'm afraid you're going to have to stay here a little while longer," she said.

"Why? We know Sean killed me. You said finding that out would release me from being earthbound."

"The problem is, Sean was murdered," Evelyn said.

"What does the fact that someone bumped him off have to do with me?"

Evelyn leaned against a table. "I just had a meeting with the officials upstairs." She jerked her head upward. "I was hoping to find out more, but all they would tell me was that since there's a link between your death and Sean Powell's, you have to remain here until his homicide has been solved."

"I can't believe it!" Alec scrunched up his face, and I thought he was going to burst into tears.

"I promise to do all I can to find out who murdered Sean so you can move on," I said.

"With my assistance," Evelyn added. "Carrie and I make a formidable detective team."

"We do," I agreed, but right now all I could think of was calling Julie.

Evelyn and I left Alec moping. I'd been hoping to get a start on scheduling programs for the Summer Reading Book Club, but finding out who had murdered Sean was now my top priority.

Trish was in my office going over the repertoire of an acting troupe that had sent us a brochure of the various dramatic and musical works they performed. She had checked off several she liked and was eager to discuss her choices with me. I didn't have the heart to brush her off, so we spent most of an hour discussing her selections. I agreed with many of them but wanted to go over the brochure myself to see if there were any she'd missed that I thought our patrons would like.

It was close to noon when we finished, just enough time to stop by the ladies' room before meeting Angela for lunch. How the morning had flown by. For a short while I'd forgotten about Alec and Sean, but Alec's plight and Sean's unsolved murder suddenly filled my mind like a whirling tornado. I'd promised to investigate the situation, and Trish was a perfect source. She'd lived in Clover Ridge all her life and knew most of the people in Sean's life.

"Trish, who do you think killed Sean Powell?"

"You mean besides his son, Kevin?"

"Well, yes. But first tell me why you like Kevin for his father's murder?"

"Because I've seen Kevin in action—screaming at his wife in the supermarket. His ex-wife, that is. Hearing him mouth off at Sean when Sean's construction company was renovating my parents' kitchen. He said some pretty awful things. That was just before he left the company." Trish thought a moment. "Though I have no idea why Kevin would suddenly be angry enough at his father to want to kill him."

I can think of a reason. "Anyone else come to mind?"

"Not really. Buzz and many of the other guys have worked for Sean for years. Buzz can be gruff, as you've seen for yourself. Sean has always liked being 'the boss in charge,' at least until he got sick, and the two of them have had their share of disagreements. But Buzz never quit, so that answers your question."

"What about Rafe Torres?"

Trish shrugged. "I don't know much about Rafe except that he and Sean have done several home improvement jobs together. Although there was that one time . . ."

"What happened?" I felt my pulse quicken.

"Reggie Williams hired Sean to renovate his house from basement to attic. Sean recommended Rafe Torres as the architect, and Reggie went ahead and had them redo his house. Took the better part of a year. At first Reggie was thrilled, but not when the roof began to leak and a few other structural problems came to light. He blamed Sean for doing shoddy work. Sean said he was just following the architectural plans."

"I had no idea," I said. "And I was on the council with them both."

"Did you ever notice the two of them having a conversation?"

"I never noticed them avoiding one another. In fact, Reggie tried to urge Sean to vote for the condo project he liked so much."

And now I understand what he meant when he told Sean "You owe me." "Thanks, Trish."

"I hope you find Sean's killer, and soon," she said.

Over lunch, I asked Angela who she thought had murdered Sean. She didn't have much more to offer except to add that Kevin's wife had brought charges of domestic abuse against him in their divorce. "Not that it proves he killed his father."

"No," I agreed, "but it does show that he's capable of violence."

The office was empty when I got back because Trish was at the hospitality desk helping patrons with various tasks. I fed Smoky Joe and gave him some attention before releasing him once again to his many admirers. Then I called Julie Theron.

Chapter
Twenty-Eight

Julie's voicemail message told me she was either live on TV, investigating a story, or working feverishly on a deadline and couldn't be disturbed unless this was a life-or-death situation. I'd no sooner disconnected when she called me back.

"Hi, Carrie. What's up?"

"Lots of things. For starters, Sean Powell left a letter with his lawyer saying he was responsible for Alec Dunmore's death."

"Old news. We got notice of it a few hours ago. Anything else?"

"I'd like you to look into the background of a few suspects in Sean's murder."

Julie laughed. "So you don't think his son did it?"

"What do you mean?"

"Kevin Powell was brought in for questioning an hour ago. Turns out he was badmouthing his father to his ex-wife. Said some really awful things about his dad. Kathy Powell got scared and called the police. Turns out a witness also came forward to say he overheard a heated argument between Sean and Kevin the afternoon of the day Sean was murdered."

"Interesting."

Julie went on. "But that doesn't mean we should stop investigating. Who do you want me to look into and why?"

"Buzz Coleman, Sean's foreman. Sean was about to sell his company to Buzz when he had a change of heart and wanted Kevin to have it. But I'm not sure what happened after that since Buzz seems to think the original plan is going through and Kevin had that argument with Sean after being told he could have the business."

"I'll look into it," Julie said. I was relieved that she hadn't asked me how I knew all this. But then, she kept her sources a secret.

"Who else?" she asked.

"Kevin, of course. And Rafael Torres, the architect who often worked with Sean."

"Is that it?"

"Reginald Williams. He and Sean were on the town council together, and I just learned that he was dissatisfied with Sean's work when he had Sean renovate his home."

"Anyone else?"

I thought a moment. "Babette Fisher. She and Sean had a brief affair in the past. They remained on good terms, at least it seemed that way to me. I don't think she had any reason to kill him after all these years, but still."

Julie laughed. "A doomed romance. I love it. I'll look into those suspects and get back to you."

"And I'll do some investigating on my end."

"Figured you would."

So John had brought Kevin Powell in for questioning. He'd been heard badmouthing his father, which led me to believe that either Sean had gone back on his word about giving Kevin his construction company, or he never got around to telling Buzz of his change of heart. Which meant Buzz Coleman was in the clear.

*It most certainly does **not** mean Buzz Coleman's in the clear*, I reminded myself. There were too many unknown factors to be considered. For one thing, Sean was one of the leading figures in the scheme to trick Alec out of his money. There were others, and it seemed logical that Buzz, who was close to Sean, was one of those people. Besides, hadn't Alec recognized *two* people the day Buzz had come to the library for a meeting? There was a good chance Buzz had links to both murder victims.

Julie had her secret sources, and I had Facebook and Google at my disposal. I thought I'd start with Rafe Torres. He had worked with Sean on several projects. I'd heard them arguing, which might or might not mean anything. I turned to his Facebook profile. It had many pictures of beautiful houses and buildings and a few of him with a very pretty woman and a little boy. But that photo was two years old. Did that mean he was divorced? I googled Rafe and saw that this was indeed the case. *Too bad*, I thought. Too many divorces. But it didn't tell me much more except to offer more links to his architectural projects.

I clicked back to Facebook and looked up Babette Fisher. She had many photos of her artwork—some of gloomy landscapes and others of angry-looking women. I was surprised. I had imagined her work would be lighter and more frivolous. But there it was. To mix a metaphor or two: I couldn't judge a book by its cover.

I was also surprised to see that most of her photos were of students in her art classes and exhibits she'd taken a few of them to see. Nothing much to glean about her personal life. Though she often came across as ditzy, Babette was savvy enough to realize her positions as council member and high school art teacher required tact and discretion—much to my disappointment.

I'd just turned to Buzz Coleman's Facebook page when my cell phone rang.

"Hi, Carrie, it's Al." He sounded agitated.

"What's wrong?"

"Reggie just called. He wants us to hold an emergency meeting tonight. To elect a replacement for Sean. And"—he gulped in air—"he thinks that with Sean's untimely death so soon after our vote on the Seabrook Preserve, we should cancel our decision and revisit the future of the property as soon as a fifth council member has been voted in."

"Wow! Can he do that, cancel last night's vote?"

"I've been looking into the council's history and bylaws. Nowhere does it say a decision should be declared null and void because one of the members who voted on it died soon after."

"And Sean's vote carried the decision," I said.

"It did."

"So what do you think we should do?"

"I'd like to hold a meeting tonight and discuss Reggie's proposal." Al sighed. "I don't much like it, but I can't very well ignore it."

"I can make it."

"I've left a message for Babette. She's in class now. If she's free to meet tonight we'll need a meeting place. Every room in Town Hall is spoken for tonight."

"The library's conference room is available."

"You're a lifesaver! I'll get back to you as soon as I hear from Babette."

"And please ask everyone if we can start at seven. We can order in pizza and eat while we talk."

"Will do."

* * *

When Evelyn stopped by a short while later, I filled her in on my phone call with Julie and regarding the latest council business.

"It sounds like Reggie hasn't given up on the condo plan," she said.

"That's what I thought, too," I said, "but it has no hope of going through unless he's convinced Babette to vote for it. Remember, she's dead set on the park idea because of her cousin."

Evelyn raised her eyebrows. "Could be he promised her something that appeals to her even more. Like promising to vote with her on a future project. Another park project, say."

My mouth fell open. "But that's . . ."

"Politics. Exactly." Evelyn grinned. "And if Reggie can recommend someone to take on Sean's seat, there's a good chance the Seabrook Preserve will be replaced by an upscale condo community."

I stared at her. "Which he seems to want very badly. It makes me wonder if he'd go so far as to murder Sean as the first step in his crazy plan."

"Maybe Julie will find something relevant," Evelyn said.

We discussed the other suspects. But while Evelyn agreed we couldn't eliminate any of them at this point, she had nothing to add or suggest.

She left me poring through catalogues, something I enjoyed doing that kept me from mulling over more serious matters. Every month I made lists of upcoming DVDs, audiobooks, and music

CDs I thought our patrons would enjoy. Sally and Norman Tobin, the reference librarian, drew up lists as well. Then Sally checked our selections. If two of us chose a particular title we ordered it. Knowing patrons' tastes were wide and varied, we always included a few offbeat items that one of us liked.

When I was satisfied with my choices, I walked over to Sally's office to hand her my list of selections. I could have emailed it to her, but I'd been sitting for more than an hour and I needed to move. I knocked on her closed door and heard Sally call "Come in." Marion Marshall was sitting in one of the visitors' chairs.

"Oh, sorry. I didn't mean to interrupt. I just wanted to give you the monthly list."

I turned to leave when Sally said, "Have a seat. We finished our business and now we're talking about Sean."

"How shocked we are that he murdered your fiancé's uncle," Marion said.

I stared at her. "When—where did you hear this?"

"Your pal on TV. Julie Theron."

My pal? Of course. How many times had Julie announced that she wanted to solve the crimes with me?

Marion said almost reverently, "When something like this happens, I check in on *Julie Theron Reports* every hour."

Sally shook her head. "Sean's had a few brushes with the law in the past. But killing that poor man and leaving him there . . ." She sighed. "And then someone goes and murders Sean. If that isn't the weirdest."

"Not long after the body was discovered. I wonder who killed him," I said.

"His son, Kevin. Who else?" Marion said without missing a beat. "Those two butted heads as far back as I can remember."

"Kevin claims they were on good terms when he was murdered. At least that's what he said at his father's funeral."

Marion made a scoffing sound. "And you believe him? Kevin has given Sean and Pat nothing but grief since the day he was born."

"Really?" I said, hoping Marion would elaborate.

And elaborate she did, filling me in on Kevin's misdeeds from the time he was fifteen until two month ago.

"What do you know about Rafe Torres?" I asked.

"The architect?" Sally said.

I nodded.

"Only that he made a few miscalculations on our new addition, but nothing that couldn't be fixed."

"Reggie Williams?"

They both stared at me.

"From what hat did you pull that name?" Sally asked.

"Just wondering. What about Buzz Coleman?"

"Buzz and his wife are very active in Kids With Cancer. Their middle child had cancer. Thank God he's in remission," Marion said.

"I had no idea," I said.

"Buzz is a wonderful person," Marion went on. "Sure, he can be gruff and argumentative with the guys, but he's the sweetest man when you get to know him. He plays the guitar, and even though his son's no longer in the hospital, Buzz still goes to the children's ward to play when he has the time."

"A sweetheart of a guy," I said.

"He is," Marion said, ignoring my sarcastic tone.

I returned to my office, thinking about what Marion had just told me about Buzz. Kindhearted or not, that didn't mean he wasn't capable of murdering his friend and his boss if Sean had changed their deal.

Chapter
Twenty-Nine

Al called me back to let me know that Babette and Reggie were able to meet at seven. I said I'd have coffee, tea, and bottles of water available and he said he'd bring two pizzas—his treat. I thanked him and found myself smiling as we ended our conversation. The longer I knew Al, the higher he rose in my estimation. He was kind, ethical, and I liked working with him. As for the others . . .

I called Dylan to let him know I had an unexpected meeting that evening.

He snorted. "Sounds like Reggie hasn't given up on pushing the condo deal through."

"Evelyn thinks he's gotten Babette to go along with it in exchange for some future quid pro quo. I only hope he didn't kill Sean over this."

"Whatever you do, promise me you won't express that thought tonight."

"Don't worry. I won't. But I'm curious to see how it all plays out."

"Me, too. Call me later and fill me in. I think I'll invite Gary to have a bite out with me after we finish up at the office."

"Good idea. Talk to you later."

I went to find Max to tell him the council members would be meeting in the conference room at seven. Without my having to ask, he offered to prepare a pot of fresh coffee and hot water for tea along with cold bottles of water. "And we have a container of those good cookies in the freezer. Shall I defrost them?"

"I think half the container should be enough," I said. "Take a few yourself."

"Oh, I was planning to," he said with a wink.

There was one more thing I wanted to do before getting back to my library duties. I climbed the stairs to the attic. Alec was happy to see me.

"Any news?" he asked.

"No, sorry, but I'm having a meeting with the other members of the town council at seven. I'd like you to be in the room. There's a small alcove near the door where you'll just about fit. If you stand still, no one will know you're there."

"Really?" His eyes lit up. "Why? Do you think I'll recognize someone on the council?"

"There's a possibility. I'm asking you not to get too close to anyone. And once you've taken a good look at everyone in the room, you can leave."

"Don't worry, Carrie. I'll make myself invisible. I can do that when I'm calm."

Is he ever calm? "All right. Just make sure they don't see you or know you're in the room."

Alec's laughter followed me all the way down the stairs.

Evelyn appeared suddenly. "Do you know what you're doing?" she hissed.

I shrugged. "We'll find out."

Susan came in and we worked on plans for the Halloween party. This year we were turning the meeting room into a haunted room with ghostly figures hanging from the walls and the ceiling. The entertainment was a group of five young men and women dressed in creepy Halloween costumes singing scary songs they had composed, accompanied by a guitarist. Following that would be the costume parade and contests that had been so popular last year. Trish, Susan, and I would make and serve spooky-looking refreshments that Trish had discovered in her grandmother's old recipe book. It was a pity that only the patrons lucky enough to have won lottery tickets were able to attend the party. In future years we'd be able to accommodate many more people.

Al and Reggie showed up at five to seven. Babette arrived minutes later, for once on time for a meeting. I waved her over to the four settings I'd arranged at one end of the long conference table. Was it a coincidence that Al and I sat side by side facing Reggie and Babette?

Since we were meeting in the library, I took on the role of hostess and cut up pizza slices and handed them out on paper plates. Pete wheeled in a cart bearing a freshly brewed carafe of coffee, hot water and the necessary accoutrements for tea, bottles of water, and a plate piled high with cookies.

"How kind of you, Carrie," Reggie said. He nodded to Al. "And thanks for treating us to dinner. Where did you get these pies? They are delicious."

Al told us, which led to everyone naming his or her favorite pizza parlor. Then silence reigned as we concentrated on eating. Both Al and Reggie asked for a second slice, which I happily provided.

Just when I began to wonder when the meeting would get under way, Al cleared his throat. "We're here to discuss a few matters that Reggie has brought to my attention."

A sudden movement caught *my* attention and I glanced at the far end of the table. Alec sat atop the back of a chair at the other end of the table. He grinned as he waved to me. I had to stop myself from sending him a hand signal to disappear. After all, I'd invited him to come tonight. Besides, no one could see him but me. But Babette must have sensed his presence. She turned to stare in Alec's direction, a puzzled expression on her face.

". . . I'd like you to tell us why you were so determined that we meet tonight." Al extended his open palm across the table. "Reggie, the floor's all yours."

Reggie cleared his throat. I didn't know if it was in preparation for the spiel he knew wasn't popular with Al or because the formality of Al's presentation was in sharp contrast to the casual scene of the four of us sitting around eating pizza.

Was it Al's intention to mock Reggie's scheme as something Machiavellian as well as ridiculous? Surely Al wasn't *that* calculating?

Or was he?

"I thought it our duty, as members of the Clover Ridge Town Council, to meet as soon as possible after Sean's terrible demise. A very sad event for all of us who have known and loved Sean for years. But we were elected to serve the best interests of the residents of Clover Ridge. With that in mind, I have two proposals. One, that we find a replacement for Sean ASAP, and two, that when we are five members once again, we take a new vote regarding the future of the Seabrook Preserve."

I watched Babette, curious to gauge her reaction. Her lips formed a small smile as she nodded in agreement. Alec, at the other end of the table, was punching a fist in the air as if he were cheering Reggie on. Which he wasn't, of course. Alec was just releasing energy—if ghosts released energy. Unless he was expressing something else. Whatever it was, I glared at him until he calmed down. He *had* to remain invisible!

"Babette, what's your take on Reggie's suggestions?"

"I agree with him."

"On both issues?"

"I do."

"Interesting." Al turned to me. "Carrie, I know the situation under discussion is new to you, but it's new to the rest of us as well. As a board member, please share your thoughts and concerns regarding the issues that Reggie has brought to our attention."

Four pairs of eyes focused on me. Though Alec had no horse in this race, so to speak, he was smiling now in an encouraging way, probably because I was his nephew's fiancée as well as the person who was doing everything she could to help him move on. Emboldened by his support, I decided to be brave and speak my mind.

"I think we should get someone to take Sean's place very soon. I'm not sure of the protocol, but I imagine the procedure is spelled out in the bylaws."

"It is," Reggie said, "but the way it's written, it could take weeks before a new member joins us on the council."

And you're in a rush to push this through, I thought. "As for the Seabrook Preserve property, we voted to keep it a preserve. I don't see how Sean's death changes anything."

"But he died mere hours after the vote," Reggie said.

"I'm aware of that," I said a bit sharply. "Is there anything in the bylaws regarding a decision being rescinded because a council member died—in this case, was murdered—shortly after the meeting ended?"

"Nothing," Al commented, "and believe me, I read and reread them several times. I also reviewed two important votes that were followed soon after—in one case days, in the second case almost a month—by a council member's death. In neither case was the vote declared null and void."

"Which doesn't mean we couldn't do it," Babette said.

"Why would we?" I asked. "Three of us voted in favor of the preserve. Babette, you and Reggie each voted for different projects." I met her gaze, then Reggie's. "Besides, the only way one of your projects would carry is if one of you changed your vote and if the new member joining voted for that project too. I don't see that as a viable option."

Al shot me a glance of concern. I knew I was treading in dangerous waters.

"Sure, it's possible," Reggie said.

"Very possible," Babette agreed.

"I agree that we function best as a body of five," Al said. "With that in mind, I think we should hold an election on the third Tuesday in November as usual."

"But that's two months from now!" Reggie said.

"If you think we need a fifth council member present at our meetings till then, we can ask one of our retired members to fill in." Al smiled. "I spoke to John Runstock and Gil Forrester. Both offered to attend our October and early November meetings." He shrugged. "I'm fine with either of them, but we can put it to a vote if you like."

Reggie grimaced. "I see you've taken care of everything."

Al ignored the sarcasm and said, "As mayor, it's my responsibility to make sure the council runs smoothly and continuously even when we lose a member. The bylaws recommend that we ask a former council member in good standing to act as a substitute fifth until the election. John and Gil are the only two people that fit this description since the others are either too infirm or have moved away. Which former member shall we ask to fill in?"

"Neither!" Babette snorted. "John rambles on about extraneous topics and Gil's losing it."

"John was very coherent when I spoke to him the other day, but there's no question the man likes to hear himself talk. I have no compunction about reminding him to stay on topic when he wanders off."

"You want *him* to vote on the Seabrook Preserve property?" Reggie said.

"No. As far as I'm concerned, that matter was voted on and passed," Al said.

"Not where I'm concerned," Reggie said loudly. "Sean voted and died soon after."

"Voted is the operative word," Al said. "He was coherent and sane when we voted and that's what counts."

"I agree," I said.

Al looked at them. "Unless you have something to share that Carrie and I are unaware of, I believe this matter is closed."

Babette and Reggie exchanged glances. She was the first to shrug. "I suppose not," she finally said.

"Reggie?"

He nodded.

"On to the next subject. John or Gil?" Al said. "I agree with Babette's assessment and vote that we ask John Runstock to attend the next three meetings. All in favor?"

I raised my hand, as did Al and Babette. Finally, Reggie made it unanimous. Al ended the meeting and Reggie and Babette made a quick exit.

"Whew!" Al exhaled. "I'm glad that's over. Not that Reggie had a chance in hell of getting what he was after."

"A second shot at pushing through the condo plan."

Al nodded. "Don't think that's the last you've heard of it. Next time a large parcel of land comes under discussion, he'll be sure to recommend a condo community. But that's another fight for another day."

I closed the box of the nearly untouched second pizza and handed it to him. Then I cleared the table of used paper plates and coffee cups and tossed them in the trash. Pete would take care of the rest. Al and I walked slowly toward the door.

"Coming?" he asked when I halted in the doorway.

"Actually, I have a few things to take care of before I leave tonight."

"Oh." He sounded disappointed. I sensed that he wanted to talk more about the meeting and perhaps fill me in on John Runstock, but I needed to talk to Alec.

I waited until Al turned the corner and headed for the back door leading to the parking lot. Then I stepped back into the conference room and closed the door behind me.

"So," I said to Alec, who now lay stretched out a foot above the table. "That was our Clover Ridge Town Council. Did any of them look familiar? Do you remember meeting with any of them at any time six years ago?"

"Sure, I recognized them," Alec said.

"You did?" I felt a burst of excitement. "Who?"

"All three of them—your mayor, Reggie, and Babette."

Chapter Thirty

I was deep in thought as I left the conference room, Alec's words echoing in my head. I would have questioned him further, except he'd made a quick exit. How many people *had* he met when he came to Clover Ridge six years ago? Surely Al, Reggie, and Babette weren't involved in James Whitehead's con. Of course Alec might have met them in passing during the few days he spent in Clover Ridge. Not that it mattered. Sean had left a letter confessing that he was responsible for Alec's death. Still, it was interesting that Alec had somehow come into contact with all the current board members other than me.

Unless he was mistaken. Or lying. But why would Alec lie about recognizing people? I got a queasy feeling remembering the kind of person he used to be.

My shoulder jammed into the arm of a man who, like me, hadn't been looking where he was going. Our collision forced him to glance up from the papers in his hands and I recognized Rafe Torres.

"I'm so sorry," I said. "I just left a meeting and I was replaying our discussion in my head."

"Was this a meeting about the new addition?" he asked. "I hope Buzz hasn't been complaining about some new problem."

"No, not at all," I said, wondering why Rafe wouldn't be the first to know of a problem regarding the renovations. "It was about—" I stopped. "Nothing to do with the library."

"Glad to hear that." He looked considerably relieved. "You must be happy the library will be able to make use of the new addition in just a few weeks."

"I can't wait," I said. Then, to be polite, I said, "I suppose you're looking forward to starting your next project."

Rafe shrugged. "I've a few things in the fire."

"You and Sean did several jobs together. Do you think you'll be working with Buzz in the future?"

He laughed. "You gotta be kidding. But I'm hoping Kevin will see things differently."

"Kevin Powell?"

"Yeah. Didn't you hear? Turns out Buzz and Kevin agreed to co-own the construction company with plans to expand. Benefits them both." He gave a little laugh. "If they don't kill each other over some stupid argument."

"Oh!" I put my hand to my heart.

"Sorry, Carrie. That was thoughtless of me." Rafe waved the papers in his hand. "Anyway, I have to go. I just found some great photos and info to add to my article."

Smoky Joe came dashing up to us. He rubbed his face against my leg. I bent down to pet him. "There you are! I was just about to go looking for you." I stood. "And it's time I took this little fellow home."

"Take care, Carrie."

"See you." I picked up Smoky Joe and headed for my office.

Smoky Joe began to howl. And for good reason. Alec had placed himself directly in our path. Darn! I set my frantic cat down and watched him scamper away, knowing I was going to have a hard time finding him again. But I had no choice. I glanced around, relieved that no one was within hearing distance, and glared at Alec.

"What are you doing here?" I hissed. "You dropped a bomb-shell on me minutes ago then disappeared. And now you're back again."

"Who was that man you were just talking to?"

"Rafe Torres, the architect that designed the addition where you were found. Why? You're not going to tell me—"

"Yep. Another one."

"So far you claim to have met half the residents of Clover Ridge six years ago," I scoffed. "Either you're hallucinating or making half of it up."

Alec shook his head. "I'm not lying, Carrie. I swear. Once I realized I wanted to buy property in Clover Ridge, I made it my business to talk to as many people as I could those three or four days I was here—in a local bar, in restaurants, in real estate agents' offices. I checked out the building I was considering buying at least three times. I don't remember who I was with or where, or ever getting into a fight with Sean Powell. But I know I saw every single person I told you I saw."

"And you spoke to almost everyone you've seen me with, and all in just three or four days," I sneered, not bothering to hide my disbelief.

He looked beaten down. "Okay, maybe I didn't speak to them all, but I never forget a face, and I saw every person I said I did—Buzz, Sean, Reggie, Babette, Al. This Rafe you were just talking to."

"Oh, yeah. What do you remember about Rafe? He's an architect. Did he offer to draw up plans for the building next door?"

Alec thought a minute. "Maybe. Or could be he was talking about designing some other building. Then one of his friends—Sean, I think it was—laughed and said knowing his past performance, he wouldn't trust Rafe to design an outhouse."

* * *

I drove home on autopilot, my brain barely able to process all that I'd learned in the past few hours. I exhaled loud enough to make poor Smoky Joe meow. "Sorry, boy," I said. "Your mommy's a bit agitated."

If I gave credence to what Alec had told me, he'd met with a long list of Clover Ridge residents, all of whom I knew. Some were in on a deal to scam him; others he'd chatted with or had simply noticed while walking around town. The problem was Alec's faulty memory. He couldn't differentiate between the con men and innocent encounters. When or where. I sighed. He couldn't even remember Sean knocking him down and causing that fatal blow.

I had to shift gears and stop focusing on Alec. The more important question now was who had murdered Sean. And was that murder connected in any way to Alec's death? The fact that Alec recognized all three of my fellow council members might or might not be relevant.

After tonight's meeting, I couldn't help but be suspicious of Reggie. The way he'd tried so hard to cancel our vote to keep the preserve. He wanted that condo built in the worst way. The question was, how far would he go? Did he kill Sean, hoping he'd be able to steamroll through his plan for a new vote? And what had he offered Babette that had persuaded her to go along with his plans?

As for Babette, I couldn't see her involved in a plot to murder her onetime lover. From our short exchange at the wake, she seemed to harbor fond memories of her brief affair with Sean.

And Al? I knew in my heart that Al didn't kill Sean. I'd seen him make enough decisions to know he always kept the good of the community he served in mind. I couldn't be that far off when it came to judging character, could I? As for Alec recognizing him, six years ago Al was a lawyer who lived and practiced locally. Alec might have met him or seen him anywhere or anytime during his visit.

Then there was Rafe. I had trouble making sense of what Alec claimed he'd heard Sean say to the architect, the architect he'd worked with on so many of his recent projects, unless he was joking. I needed to give the subject a rest. At this point, there were too many suspects.

I called Dylan and gave him an abbreviated version of the last-minute council meeting, running into Rafe, and my conversations with his uncle.

"Wow, babe! You've had as much intrigue and excitement this evening as an action film. Too bad Uncle Alec's memory is shot full of holes."

"I want to run everything past you in detail and get your take on the situation. But not tonight. I'm all wound up. My mind's spinning like a hamster on a wheel."

"We'll talk tomorrow evening," Dylan said. "I'll leave work early and we'll have plenty of time to discuss things over dinner."

"I'd really like that." I smiled as some of the stress I'd been feeling released. "I want to hear your thoughts about everything."

"You mean because I'm a real investigator?" Dylan teased.

"Exactly."

The jingle from my phone let me know I was getting another call. "Someone's calling. It's Julie."

"Go find out what she wants. Love you." He made a kissing sound, which I returned.

"Hi, Carrie. Where are you?"

"On my way home. Why?"

"I'm tailing Buzz Coleman. Looks like he's on his way to a house that's not his own."

"Why are you following him?"

"Just following a hunch. I've been busy doing deep dives into a few of the people you asked me to."

"Find out anything interesting?"

"A few things. Did you know Buzz Coleman has a record?"

"No, I had no idea."

"A few B and Es. Breaking and entering. And for breaking a guy's nose. But that last was seven years ago. Nothing since."

I thought about Rafe's comment that if Buzz and Kevin ever got into a fight, there might be serious damage. "Find out anything about Kevin Powell, Sean Powell's son?"

"He was a wild kid in his teens—went joyriding and stuff like that. A bar fight or two in his twenties. Worked for his father, but they didn't get along. Recently he was fired from his job at Lighthouse Builders."

"Fired? I overheard him tell his father he left Lighthouse because Tim Fisk dropped him from the condo deal—if that project ever went through."

"Oh, it will go through one way or another if I know Timothy Fisk." She laughed. "A little birdie told me he was working on getting the Clover Ridge council to reconsider the condo deal. Know anything about that?"

My God! Does the woman have spies everywhere? "Nope. Those condos won't be built here any time soon. But getting back to Kevin—"

"Can't talk now. Gotta go. Coleman's about to pull into a driveway. Call you in a few."

Julie disconnected. I drove home, my thoughts more jumbled than ever. Why on earth was she following Buzz? And why had Kevin been fired from his job at Lighthouse Builders? Unless Julie's source had gotten it wrong. I'd heard Kevin telling his father that he left because Timothy Fisk had put his nephew in charge of that project. Of course Kevin might have lied to his father to save face.

And if Sean found out that Kevin had lied . . .

Julie was well informed about the goings-on in Clover Ridge—about business matters most people knew nothing about. She even knew that Fisk hadn't given up on his plan to build a condo community in Clover Ridge. I chuckled. It sounded like she had an investigating team chasing down clues like Sherlock Holmes's Baker Street Irregulars.

Finally, I turned onto the Avery private road that led to my cottage and let out a deep sigh of relief. Five minutes more and I was home. Snug in my own private cocoon. I smiled as I drove past Dylan's manor home that he would be putting on the market just as soon as we firmed up our future plans regarding our wedding. I was going to miss his company tonight, but I looked forward to a shower, watching some silly TV shows, and Julie's next phone call. She had sounded excited, so she must have had a good reason why she was following Buzz.

* * *

"Carrie, are you asleep?"

"No," I lied. I blinked at the TV and noticed the program wasn't the one I'd been watching previously. I must have conked out. "Just resting. Why?"

"We have to go somewhere."

I looked at my watch. It was ten to eleven. "Now? And why are you whispering?"

"I'm not whispering." In her normal voice she said, "I got a tip Kevin Powell is meeting someone. Coming or not?"

"At this time of night? Who told you? And what about Buzz?"

"Oh, Coleman." Julie dismissed him as her sense of urgency faded away. "That turned out to be nothing. A false alarm. A member of my street team thought he was having an affair, but he was wrong. He was visiting a couple to talk about a fundraiser for Kids With Cancer."

"Your street team?" I said. "What's a street team?"

Julie laughed. "That's what I call the young cub reporters eager for their own bylines. I promised they could have 'em as soon as they brought me some worthwhile info. The tip on Buzz Coleman sounded promising but ended up being a dud. Still, I couldn't know that, could I, unless I followed it up."

I felt a pang of jealousy. Julie really had her own group of Irregulars—a slew of young reporters, hungry for recognition, chasing down facts and clues. But then, I had my own street team, didn't I? Evelyn was a fount of Clover Ridge information, and no one did research like Dylan's gal Friday, Rosalind, who had helped me track down a missing person. And there was Dylan, of course—a real, bona fide investigator.

Not that I was in competition with Julie Theron.

"Carrie, did you fall asleep again?"

"No, I was just thinking. How do you know Kevin's meeting someone tonight?"

"Why don't I come by your place in, say, seven minutes? I'll dash in, use the bathroom, and off we'll go. I'll explain everything in the car."

"All right," I said after a moment. After all, what choice did I have?

Chapter
Thirty-One

"Do you have anything to eat? I'm starving."

I stared at Julie. "I thought you were in a rush to leave and only came in to use the bathroom."

Julie gave me a shamefaced grin. "Maybe I overstated the need to hurry." She bent down to pet Smoky Joe, who was weaving between her legs.

"This way," I said, none too graciously. Not because I resented having to feed her but because Julie was calling the shots while she kept me in the dark.

I led her into the kitchen and had her sit at the table while I studied the contents of the refrigerator.

"I have some roast chicken, egg salad, sliced turkey, cucumber salad."

"Chicken and some cucumber salad would be lovely. Dark meat, if you have it."

I filled a plate with what she'd asked for, along with some chickpea salad.

"Seltzer, water, or orange juice?"

"Hot tea would hit the spot," she said, already chewing.

Julie ate quickly and neatly, and soon finished everything on her plate. Since her mouth was constantly in motion, there was no way she could answer my questions, so I reined in my curiosity until we were on our way to God knew where. Finally, we climbed into her aged Camry. It was filled with plastic bags of debris from takeout meals. A mixture of their telltale scents still lingering in the air. I recognized pizza, hamburger, Indian, and Chinese food. No doubt about it. Julie spent a lot of time in her car.

She made a quick call as we drove off, telling whomever was on the other end that she was now on her way, and then called someone else. She asked a litany of questions regarding our upcoming assignation, then requested an update on two other stories she was tracking. Julie frowned as she disconnected, clearly not pleased with the answers she'd received.

There weren't many cars on the road, which Julie seemed to regard as her right to speed. I didn't ask her to slow down, partly because I didn't want to come off sounding like an old woman and partly because she was an excellent driver.

"Where are we going?" I asked.

"To a town on the other side of Merrivale."

"Is that where Kevin lives?" I asked.

"He lives in Merrivale. His wife and kids live in North Branford. His son had a twilight soccer game. When it ended he was taking the kids out for dinner and a movie."

"That's quite a lot to do on a school night," I said.

Julie shrugged. "What can I tell you?"

"How did you find all this out?"

She turned to me and grinned. "One of my cubs has a sibling that goes to the same school as Kevin's son."

"How did he learn about the meeting we're about to spy on?"

Julie's nose crinkled. She was pissed. I wasn't sure if it was because she objected to the word "spy" or hated to let me in on her investigative methods.

"I asked someone to keep an eye on Kevin," she finally said.

"Ah. This someone is following him."

"I don't know who Kevin's meeting this late or why. Must be something illegal."

"Or the person is desperate and willing to meet when and where Kevin demands."

She shot me a look of admiration. "Spot on, Nancy Drew."

Julie turned on the radio to a rock station and blasted the music. I covered my ears. "Please turn it down."

"Sorry. I like to listen to music when I'm about to go in for the kill."

The kill? What is she expecting to go down?

"Thanks," I said when she lowered the volume, and decided to hold all questions for now.

Fifteen minutes later, we pulled up in front of what looked like a log cabin. It was the only building in sight amid trees and bushes growing wild on both sides of the road. Surprisingly, the parking lot was packed with cars. I glanced at my watch. It was close to midnight.

"Welcome to Tootsie's, famous to those in the know for showcasing up-and-coming music groups and stand-up comics," Julie said as if she were reading my mind.

"But why meet someone here to talk?" I asked.

She shrugged. "Couldn't tell you. Maybe Kevin likes the entertainment. But there's a bar and a few rooms off the main hall that are soundproof and the lights are kept low."

"Where people can meet in between listening to music or watching comedy gigs."

"Whatever. You can see for yourself it's a popular place."

I moved to open the car door when Julie stopped me.

"Just a minute." She turned around and began rummaging through a large carton on the back seat. A minute later she pulled out a wig of long red hair topped by a perky newsboy cap in dark green leather. She fitted it over her blonde hair. The transformation was amazing.

"Let's see what we have for you."

"I don't need a disguise," I said, but she paid me no attention. "Ah!" she declared a minute later, handing me a wig with curly blonde hair with a beret set rakishly to one side.

I shook my head. "No way."

She went back to digging in the box. Up came a wig of long black hair with purple streaks and dangling shoulder-sweeping earrings.

I laughed. "That was me a year ago."

"Put it on."

I did and grinned at myself in the rearview mirror. I missed my eye makeup and dark lipstick, but in the dim lighting I could pass for Goth Girl.

"Last but not least," Julie said as she drew long, dark plastic coats from the flat box next to the carton and handed me one. "Slip this on before we go inside."

We parked and walked to the entrance. I caught my reflection in the side mirror of a parked car and was startled to see a stranger. Hair and hats did wonders to change one's appearance, and the long coat gave my figure a nondescript shape. Neither Kevin nor the person he was meeting would be able to recognize me, especially if the lighting was poor.

Tootsie's was larger than it appeared from the parking lot. A young woman met us in the entranceway. After exchanging words with Julie, she led us past the main room, three-quarters filled with people watching a stand-up comic, to a table in a dimly lit room with a bar that ran the length of one wall. I was surprised to find my chair well upholstered and very comfortable.

We hadn't been there two minutes when an emaciated-looking boy who couldn't have been more than eighteen approached our table. "What can I get you ladies?"

"We'll each have tonight's special drink," Julie said.

I opened my mouth to protest, then shut it again when Julie nodded ever so slightly.

"That'll be two margaritas," our waiter said. "Good choice. They're extra yummy tonight. Be right back with some nibbles."

He hurried away.

"You have to order at least one drink if you want to stay here," Julie explained.

"Okay." I glanced around. It was dim, all right. Our table was a few feet from the bar. Most of the twelve barstools were occupied, but it was too dark to make out anyone's features. I was beginning to think this was a really bad idea.

"Kevin's in the far corner," Julie said when she'd finished stretching her neck in all directions. "At the table surrounded by all those plants."

I had to squint to make out Sean's son sitting at the small table diagonally across the room about thirty feet from us. I wondered if he had requested that table for its privacy. A planter filled with bushes hid the person who was sharing the table with Kevin. I hadn't a clue if was a man or a woman.

"Look! The restrooms are in the alcove just beyond their table," Julie said as if I couldn't see that for myself. "When you go to the ladies' room you'll pass right by their table. You'll see who Kevin's with and catch the gist of their conversation."

"Why me?" I asked automatically, then wished I hadn't bothered. I had no problem checking out the situation. In fact, I had to force myself to remain in my chair and not rush over impetuously. What I didn't like was Julie giving me orders.

Our waiter returned with our drinks and nibbles, and my hand reached out automatically to the dish filled with trail mix. The nuts were delicious, as was the dried fruit, though it was a type I wasn't familiar with. But now wasn't the time to think about nibbles.

"What are they doing?" Julie demanded. She sounded annoyed, probably because the focus of our attention was not in her line of vision but in mine.

"As far as I can tell, they're just talking. Kevin just called the waitress over for something to eat or drink."

"Probably to drink," Julie said. "That's what people do here."

"And not their first," I said when the waitress picked up two glasses and left.

She returned a few minutes later with fresh drinks.

Julie downed the last of her margarita and ordered a second. Her fingers rapped against the table. Clearly she was nervous, while I felt strangely calm. I glanced over at Kevin and his tablemate. They were practically nose to nose over the table. Their conversation had reached its boiling point. I drained the last of my margarita and stood.

"Where are you going?"

I flinched because she'd spoken loud enough to draw attention to us. But one quick look around the room and I realized no one had so much as glanced our way. The other patrons were talking and laughing, some even louder than Julie because of all the drinks they'd imbibed, while the two people in the corner were too busy arguing to give a thought to anyone else.

"I'm going to the bathroom."

I reached for my pocketbook and slipped the long leather strap over my shoulder. I got out my phone and pretended to make a call as I walked across the room. I slowed down as I approached their table. Kevin was ranting.

"I don't care what arrangement you had with my father. Buzz and I have other plans."

He's talking to Rafe! Kevin's face was red with anger. Rafe's emotions seemed tamped down—except for the tic pulsating in his neck.

"You're making a big mistake, Kevin."

"Are you threatening me? Because that's not gonna work."

I continued past them and hovered in the small hall, doing my best to stay out of Rafe's line of vision. I needn't have worried. His complete focus was on Kevin.

"Not a threat, but it would be a courtesy to tell me why you and Buzz are so quick to wash your hands of me. Your father's called me in on several big jobs. We worked well together for years."

Kevin snorted. "Really? You're honestly telling me that you and my father worked well together? That every single job didn't incur costs above and beyond the expected because of your mistakes? I don't know why he kept referring you for the jobs. Neither does Buzz."

Rafe shrugged. "There are always unexpected glitches. I hope you'll be prepared for them in your new role as contractor."

"Yeah, well, my father thought your mistakes were excessive."

"What else did he say?" There was a different tone to Rafe's question. He was no longer goading Kevin. He wanted a genuine answer.

"About what?"

"Mistakes your father claimed were excessive."

Kevin reared back in his seat. "Nothing. What else is there to say?"

The two men stared at each other.

Kevin downed the rest of his drink. "That's it. I told you there was no point in us meeting. I wasn't about to change my mind." He held up his hand to call over the waitress. "I'm tired and I'm going home to bed."

I hurried back to Julie. She'd been watching, but I could tell from her grimace that she had no idea what was going down. Kevin had just told Rafe that he wouldn't reconsider his refusal to work with him on future jobs. There had been a subtext to their discussion that I didn't comprehend, but I'd sensed something ominous was about to erupt.

"They're leaving. We have to go," I said.

Julie heard the urgency in my voice and stood. We each fished a twenty from our wallets and made our way to the exit. The air was cool outside. I shivered, appreciating the warmth that my disguise provided. We walked around the corner of the building and waited for Kevin and Rafe to leave.

Chapter
Thirty-Two

We didn't have long to wait. Kevin came storming out the back door, mumbling to himself. We watched him fumble in his pants pocket for his car fob as he headed to his car. Rafe followed a minute later. He glanced around in a furtive manner. I elbowed Julie behind me, thinking it was a good thing we'd hidden from sight. She stood close enough for me to feel her nod. Good. She knew what I was thinking.

Rafe called out to Kevin. "Wait a minute, Kev. There's just one thing more I need to tell you."

Kevin spun around, clearly pissed. He retraced his steps. "What is it?"

"This." Rafe pulled out a pistol and used it to wave Kevin closer. "I want you right here when I talk to you."

I looked around. No one else was in the parking lot. How could that be? The place was filled with people. We were alone with an armed man who had his sights on Kevin Powell. Was Rafe a murderer? Was he planning to kill Kevin?"

Kevin approached Rafe slowly, his hands up but below shoulder height as if he couldn't believe Rafe was for real. "What's with the gun, Torres? You planning to shoot me?"

"It depends on what you're about to tell me."

"Tell you? I told you everything I had to say inside." Kevin turned around.

Before he could take a step, we heard the click of the gun.

"Don't be stupid, Powell. Get over here and answer my question or I'll shoot you here and now."

Kevin obeyed. The dim light of the tall lamppost a few feet from where he stood revealed the horror that was dawning on his face. "Did you kill my father?"

"What did your father tell you?" Rafe asked. His voice cracked with emotion.

"About what?"

"About me, dammit."

"I told you. You caused too many headaches. Screwed up issues you should have noticed early on. You cost the business big bucks, but he had no choice but to keep working with you." Kevin sneered. "I have no idea why, but you must have been holding something over his head. Is that what you want to know? Is that why you killed him?"

Rafe's gun arm wiggled a bit. "What else?"

Kevin said nothing, but a look passed over his face. He understood what Rafe was after. "There's nothing else. Now can I go home?"

But Rafe had caught his expression. His lips formed a smile that held no mirth. "So you know. He told you."

"I don't know what you're talking about."

Rafe moved closer to Kevin. "Let's go to your car. Start walking."

"Are you crazy? So you can kill me?"

Rafe poked the gun in Kevin's chest. "Or should I shoot you here and now?"

"Please. Why are you doing this?"

"Your father had no right telling you something that was a *secret*!"

Rafe shouted the last word. Kevin turned and slowly headed for his car with Rafe close behind.

I shot Julie a look of anguish. *We can't let him kill Kevin! But how can we stop him? It's too dangerous.*

Julie must have thought I was begging her to do something. And do something she did. She jumped on Rafe's back, yanking up his arm.

Oh, God! What is she doing? Rafe spun around and shook free of her grasp. Julie's wig came flying off.

"Carrie, help! What are you waiting for?"

I hesitated like any normal person would in this situation, but Kevin got in the act. By the time I reached them, he and Julie were wrestling Rafe to the ground. With one great burst of effort he broke away from their grip and lurched to his feet. Which was when I lowered my head and rammed into him, downing him once again.

When Rafe tried to get up again, Julie drew back her arm and punched him right in the face. I cringed as her fist made contact with his nose. Rafe shrieked in pain.

"That's for assaulting me the other night," Julie said.

I guess she figured out who her attacker was. When I was sure that Julie and Kevin had things under control, I reached inside my pocketbook for my cell phone.

"I'm calling Lieutenant Mathers," I announced and speed-dialed John's private cell number. Though it was after midnight, he picked up immediately.

"John, it's me. I'm in the parking lot of a place called Tootsie's."

"Yeah, I know it. What are you doing there at this time of night?"

I told him and asked him to come ASAP.

"Stay there. I'll be there as fast as I can."

* * *

John drove up minutes later, followed by Danny Brower in a patrol car and two state troopers in an unmarked car. His eyes widened when he caught sight of me. I realized I was still wearing that ridiculous wig and yanked it off my head.

He shot out orders to Danny and spoke gruffly to the troopers—not sounding at all like himself. John was in a mood, all right. Learning that Julie and I had solved his homicide and stopped Rafe Torres from killing Kevin had to be humiliating. I was going to have to make it up to him big time.

Though no sirens had sounded, somehow the people inside Tootsie's had realized something was going down and had spilled out into the parking lot. The state troopers kept the crowd at bay.

"Thank God you're here," Kevin said as he climbed off Rafe's back. "I couldn't have held him much longer."

Danny pulled Rafe to his feet. John all but growled at the sight of Julie snapping photos with her phone of Danny handcuffing Rafe and putting him in the back of the patrol car, but he didn't tell her to stop. He couldn't, I supposed. After retrieving Rafe's gun, which he put in a plastic bag, he huddled briefly with the state troopers and they took off shortly after Danny.

Most of the looky-loos went back inside. John questioned the three of us briefly. He asked Kevin if he was up to coming down to the station to make a statement.

"Sure," Kevin said. "Why not get it over with?" He looked dazed as he turned to Julie and me. "Thanks again for saving my life."

"It was Julie," I said.

Julie raised her hand to acknowledge him, but her attention was focused on whatever the person at the other end of her phone was saying. When she disconnected, she was beaming. "Carrie, a crew is on its way to shoot footage of the scene."

"Why? Danny took Rafe to the precinct. John's leaving and so is Kevin. There's nothing here to report."

"We're here, silly! This is your big chance to be on television. We'll let the public know how we took down a murderer."

John looked up from his conversation with Kevin. "Make sure you stick to the facts, Ms. Theron."

"Certainly, Lieutenant Mathers. I'll be sure to mention how quickly you arrived on the scene when Carrie called you."

John frowned. Poor guy. Did she have to rub it in? "I'd like you to come down to the precinct at nine tomorrow morning to make a statement."

"Certainly, Lieutenant. I'll be there!" Julie practically sang.

John waved to Kevin, I supposed to let him know he was leaving and he'd see him at the station, then strode over to his car.

Frantically, I called after him. "John, wait a minute. Please."

He turned. "What is it, Carrie?"

"Do you think you could drop me off home? Julie brought me here and I want to leave."

"Carrie, you can't leave," Julie said. "You're my big story."

"No, you're your big story. I don't want to be part of it."

"But you *are* part of it. We're Rizzoli and Isles."

I ran over to John. "Please. I need to go home."

He studied me for a moment. "Get in the car."

This is going to be the most awkward twenty-minute ride, I thought as we rode out of Tootsie's parking lot and headed for Clover Ridge. But I had no choice. It was after one in the morning and I needed to get home.

"Whose idea was it to come here tonight?"

"Julie's."

"Ah."

"John, I'm sorry."

"What are you sorry about?"

That your male ego is bruised. "That you're annoyed with me."

Silence. "I'm not happy that you put yourself in danger."

"We were never in danger." The image of Julie leaping onto Rafe's back flashed before me. I stifled a giggle. "At least I wasn't. Julie got to him first. I never could have done that."

"Good to know! That was the stupidest, most reckless, dangerous act. The gun could have gone off, killing Kevin."

"It was Kevin's only chance. Rafe was about to kill him."

More silence. Then, "What brought you and Julie to Tootsie's tonight?"

"She has some cub reporters at her beck and call. They're out tailing people and running down leads like Sherlock Holmes's Irregulars. One of them found out Kevin had arranged to meet someone there. We didn't know who until I saw him inside."

"Rafael Torres. Did you suspect he killed Sean?"

I shook my head. "No. I knew that he and Sean had had their share of arguments, but I didn't think Rafe would kill Sean over that." I sighed. "I liked Rafe. He was writing an article about old buildings in our area. He thought it might even lead to a book deal."

When we stopped at a red light, John turned to me. "He should have stuck to writing."

"What do you mean?"

"I did some deep dives into the various suspects. Turns out Rafael Torres only came into existence eight years ago."

My mouth fell open. "Then who is he? Is he an architect?"

"His name is Victor Ramas. Yes, he was an architect, but he lost his license about twelve years ago because a building he designed came crashing down. Five people died."

"Oh, how awful!"

"He could have gotten his license back after a couple of years, but he probably knew he'd never live down that disaster. And so he left Colorado and came east."

"And took on a new identity," I mused.

"Uh huh. He found someone to forge an architect's license and started drumming up business."

"But why did he murder Sean?" I asked.

"I'm hoping both Ramas and Kevin will tell me why. Kevin's grateful he escaped being murdered, so he'll likely come clean about everything his father told him."

I turned to John. "I realized Kevin was holding back about something. The trouble was so did Rafe—I mean, Victor Ramas."

"According to Buzz, Sean was really pissed with the flaws in Rafe's plans, flaws that a good architect would never make. Buzz couldn't understand why Sean kept on working with Rafe, though he did say that Sean told him he was going to take care of the Rafe problem once and for all."

I sighed. "And then he was murdered."

John patted my shoulder. "Sean knew he was dying. The library renovations were to be his last job. He told Buzz he wanted them to be perfect, largely because of you and the great job you've been doing there."

"Really?" I smiled. "I'm touched."

"You should be. Sean was a good man."

I stared at him.

"Yeah, I know. He killed Dylan's uncle, not that he meant to, and he did some other things he shouldn't have, but Sean Powell was my friend and I miss him."

"I had no idea you two were friends," I said.

That struck John's funny bone. He laughed and laughed until a bout of coughing made him stop. "There are plenty of things in Clover Ridge you know nothing about."

"Maybe, but I intend to find out," I said.

"I know you will. That's what scares me."

John grinned, and I knew all was forgiven.

Chapter
Thirty-Three

When I mentioned to John that Dylan was spending the night at the manor house, he insisted on seeing me safely inside the cottage. I couldn't imagine why, since the only killer I knew about had just been apprehended. Smoky Joe must have heard us talking, because he came dashing into the hall, meowing loudly.

I yawned as I picked him up. "Thanks for driving me home."

"You're welcome. Get some sleep. I'll take your statement tomorrow."

John drove off and I fed Smoky Joe a few treats. Now Alec could finally leave. I drew a deep breath when I realized I had to call Dylan. I hated to wake him up but we needed to talk.

He answered immediately, sounding sleepy but alert. "What's up?"

"Julie called me after I spoke to you last. She had a tip that Kevin Powell was meeting someone later tonight."

"Carrie, don't tell me—"

"Let me finish. Turns out he met Rafe Torres, the architect. He was about to kill Kevin in the parking lot when Julie stopped him."

"Julie did?" Dylan sounded skeptical.

"Well, Kevin got into the act, and I helped out. I called John. He came and arrested Rafe for attempted murder." I paused. "We're sure he killed Sean but that has to be proved."

"Ah," Dylan said, seeing where this was going.

"Right. Now Alec can go to his resting place. I don't know when that will happen or if it's happened already, but I think it would be nice if you stopped by to say a final goodbye."

Silence.

"Don't you want to do that?"

"The thing is, I have an early breakfast business meeting. I can't very well change it this late in the game. Though the restaurant's only a fifteen-minute drive from Clover Ridge. When the meeting's over, I'll get to the library soon as I can."

"That's great. I know it will mean a lot to Alec—you coming to say goodbye."

* * *

The following morning I drove into the library parking lot feeling woozy and strung out from too little sleep and too much coffee. It was ten to nine. I had ten minutes to pull myself together. I yanked open the door and was startled to find Angela, Sally, Marion, Fran, and a few others milling around as though they were waiting for me.

They *were* waiting for me.

I set Smoky Joe free of his carrier, and he trotted off. "What's wrong?"

"Nothing's wrong." Sally was beaming. "You're a celebrity!"

Julie and her TV show.

Angela hugged me. "I'm so proud of you! Julie described every detail of how the two of you saved Kevin Powell's life."

"Well, actually Julie—" I started to explain.

"And tackled that architect," Marion broke in. "What did he have against Kevin? She never explained."

Fran, Angela's boss, pursed her lips. "I always thought he looked suspicious. Just like a murderer."

What does a murderer look like? I wondered.

"Sean Powell killed someone," Harvey Kirk, who had just joined the group, pointed out. "Did he look like a murderer?"

And suddenly they were all babbling at the same time. I was relieved when Sally announced it was two minutes to nine and patrons would soon be coming through the doors. The crowd dispersed. I breathed a sigh of relief and headed straight to my office.

Evelyn was waiting for me, calmly perched on the edge of my assistants' desk. I dropped into my chair and closed my eyes.

"I hear you've had a busy night," she said.

"You could say that."

"Shouldn't you be happy you helped catch a killer?"

"Of course I'm pleased. And if Julie and I hadn't been there, Kevin would be another of Rafe's victims. It's just . . ."

"Just?" Evelyn encouraged.

"Julie. She's so pushy and bossy. She acts as though breaking a story is the most important thing in life. Up there with finding a cure for cancer and a solution to global warming."

"From what I've heard, she certainly shared the spotlight with you."

"I'm not interested in being in the spotlight. Or haven't you noticed?"

Evelyn pursed her lips, knowing she'd gone too far.

"I care about these people. Okay, I hardly know Kevin, but I knew and liked his father. I even liked Rafe—I mean, Victor.

But they're not important to Julie. She's only interested in making news. And she doesn't care whose feelings she hurts."

"Like John's," Evelyn said.

"Exactly. I hate the way she talked about him on TV. She made him sound like a bungling idiot. And John Mathers is no bungler."

"I understand how you feel," Evelyn said.

"And no matter what she says or does, I don't intend to get involved in another one of her schemes." I felt a pang of anxiety. "Where's Alec? He hasn't left, has he?"

"No. He's upstairs in the attic."

"Does he know that the man we knew as Rafe Torres killed Sean?"

"I certainly didn't tell him."

"I'd like to tell him now. I don't know how this works or when Alec will be leaving, but Dylan will be stopping by to say goodbye."

"I'll go get him."

Evelyn vanished. She reappeared two minutes later with Alec.

"Hello, Carrie. Any news?" he asked as he often did.

I smiled. "Yes, indeed. We know who murdered Sean Powell. He tried to murder Sean's son last night."

"Who was it?"

"The architect, Rafael Torres."

"The good-looking fellow? Dresses well? Came here to the library a few times?"

I nodded.

"I recognized him. I'd seen him in the building next door and in the bar."

"Really?" I scoffed. "You claim to have met half of Clover Ridge six years ago and all within a couple of days."

Alec exhaled loudly. "What can I say? Whitehead made it his business to introduce me to lots of people—at the bar, over dinner, in the house. In fact . . ." He stared at me. "It just came back. Torres was there when Sean Powell and I got into that scuffle."

"The scuffle that ended your life," Evelyn murmured.

"So that's why Sean kept on using Rafe as the architect for his projects," I said.

Evelyn nodded. "Rafe was essentially blackmailing him."

I thought back, remembering how frantic Rafe had been last night, wanting to know what exactly Sean had told Kevin. "And at some point, Sean learned the truth about Rafe and held it over his head."

Evelyn snorted. "They ended up blackmailing each other."

"What did Sean find out about Rafe?" Alec asked.

"That he'd lost his license because he'd designed a building that collapsed. His real name is Victor Ramas. He changed his name to avoid being associated with the catastrophe and got a fake license."

"But why did he kill Sean?" Alec asked.

"I suspect Sean got fed up with having to deal with an architect who was incompetent or careless—or both—and he let Rafe know he was planning to inform the authorities. Sean was dying and no longer worried about the consequences to himself. A fake architect's license would mean the end of Ramas' career and possibly a prison term."

"So I can leave, right? Go wherever I'm supposed to go?" Alec asked.

"You will be on your way very soon," Evelyn said.

Alec and I stared at her.

"You knew all along," I said.

"Well . . ." Evelyn lifted her palms. "You had a few things to tell Alec so I thought it best to wait till you were done."

"This is wonderful news!" In his delight, Alec rose and floated about the room. Papers on the two desks rustled and blew about. Some spilled to the floor, but I didn't have the heart to reprimand him.

"I can't wait to move on, though I'll miss you, Carrie. Thank you so much for looking after me." He glanced at Evelyn, who was frowning. "And thank you, Evelyn."

"Dylan should be here any—"

The door to my office opened and Dylan entered. Alec dropped down to a standing position.

"Hello, Dylan. Good to see you again," Alec said.

"I stopped in to say goodbye," Dylan said, "and to wish you well, wherever it is you're going."

"Thanks, Dylan. It means a lot. I'm sorry I wasn't a better uncle."

Dylan shrugged. "That's all history."

"Still, I should have been more responsible and at least showed up when I said I would. I've always loved you and . . . you deserved better."

"Thanks." After a minute, Dylan said, "I still have some great memories from the times you visited when I was a kid."

"That's why I came to Clover Ridge six years ago. I had some money and wanted to invest in a property. Eventually move here to be closer to you."

"I would have liked that," Dylan said softly.

I became aware of the seconds ticking by. "Alec, is there anything else you remember about the time you spent here before . . .?"

He shook his head. "Not really. Just meeting all those people and hearing about their various plans and projects. The days and nights seemed to run together."

I exchanged glances with Dylan and Evelyn. The murders had been resolved, and we knew why Rafe had murdered Sean. Of course the story behind it was complicated. Only Alec and Kevin knew that Rafe/Victor had been with Sean when he'd struck that fatal blow. It was up to John's expertise as an interrogator to extract a confession from the murderer.

"One more thing," Alec said.

"Yes?" The three of us said together.

"The period before I came to Clover Ridge is clearer in my mind. This morning I suddenly remembered the one thing I saved when I sold Uncle Humphrey's house."

"What was it?" Dylan asked.

"A painting." Alec laughed. "Brilliant colors. All squiggles and swirls. Not my taste at all. I only kept it because Uncle Humphrey said a childhood friend of his had painted it. He'd become famous, even more so after he died. In fact, many of his paintings are in museums."

"Where is this painting now?" Evelyn asked.

"I stored it in my friend Jack Winslow's place. Jack has a large finished basement and he said I could leave the painting there along with a bunch of other stuff till I decided what to do with it."

"What's the artist's name?" Dylan asked.

"Haggerty. Was it . . . Tom Haggerty?" Alec said.

"Terrance Haggerty?" Dylan asked, his eyes glowing with excitement.

"Yeah, that could be it."

Dylan put his hand to his head. "Terrance Haggerty was one of the most famous abstract artists who lived in the Chicago area. He died about fifteen years ago. His paintings are worth hundreds of thousands of dollars!"

"Maybe not this one," Alec said. "I think he painted it when he was twenty, twenty-one."

"Still," Dylan said, "all of Haggerty's work is valuable. How did Uncle Humphrey come to acquire it?"

"If I remember correctly—he told me the story years ago—it was his twenty-first birthday and they were going out drinking with a bunch of friends. Terry didn't have money to buy Uncle Humphrey a gift, so he painted him a picture."

"Where does this Jack Winslow live?" Dylan asked.

"About a half hour's drive outside of Chicago. In a big, rambling house near a lake."

I sensed the change in the air even before it began to undulate. I blinked as the office was bathed in a dazzling light. Tiny sparks, like hundreds of fireflies, flittered throughout the room.

"It's time," Evelyn said, reaching for Alec's hand.

A moment later they were gone and the office resumed its usual appearance. Dylan wore a dazed expression, no doubt mirroring the way I looked as well.

"He's gone." He sank heavily into my assistants' chair. "So suddenly."

I went over to Dylan and put my arm around his shoulders. Though they hadn't been close in many years, Alec was still his uncle, and his final departure had clearly filled him with deep emotion.

Dylan rubbed his head against my arm. "And now I'll never see him again."

"Despite all the trouble Alec caused, I'm going to miss him."

"And all that talk about a painting just before he took off."

"It's your painting now," I said, "along with the money from the property sale that's still in Alec's account."

Dylan glanced at his watch. "I guess so, but I can't think about that now. I have to get to the office."

He stood up and held me close. "Thanks for encouraging me to say goodbye to Uncle Alec. I'm glad I got to see him one last time."

"Now that he's gone and the murders have been resolved things will settle down. We'll finally have some peace and quiet."

Dylan laughed. "We'll see how that plays out. The excitement never seems to die down when you're involved."

Chapter
Thirty-Four

Dylan had just closed the door to my office when the jingle of my cell phone informed me that I had a caller.

"Carrie, thank God! Are you all right?" It was Jim, my father, sounding unusually agitated.

"Of course. I'm fine."

"What a relief." He had to take a few deep breaths before he could continue. "I saw a clip of your local TV reporter. She said the two of you caught a killer and stopped him from murdering someone else."

I groaned. "That was Julie Theron. The story appeared on TV in Atlanta?"

"Caro, honey, it must be on every station along the East Coast. What made you do something so dangerous? She said the man had a gun. You could have gotten killed."

I leaned back in my chair. "Trust Julie to hype the situation and make it sound riskier than it was. She became obsessed with finding out who killed Dylan's uncle. She maligned John Mathers on TV for not finding the killer fast enough and announced that she wanted to team up with me to solve the case. I agreed, partly to stop her from mentioning me on TV. And since I was doing my own investigating, I figured why not make use of her resources. Last night we followed a tip she'd gotten and ended up witnessing an attempted murder. Julie tackled the guy and stopped it from happening. I only added my bit when he started to get up. Then I called John."

"So it's all over and done with?" Jim asked.

"As far as I'm concerned. John still has to take my statement, and I might have to testify when the case comes to trial, but that won't be for a good long time."

"I wish you wouldn't get involved in every local homicide. One of these days you won't be so lucky."

Who are you and what have you done with my father? "I don't plan it that way, Dad. It just . . . happens."

"I know. I don't mean to come on like a . . . helicopter father."

We both laughed. My father's earlier career as a thief had kept him away from home a good part of my growing-up years.

"Given any thought to what we talked about last time?"

What did we talk about? I suddenly remembered. The wedding. "Nope. Haven't had the chance."

"Don't let it go too long, Caro. I want to have grandkids while I'm young enough to play with them."

"Jim!" I exclaimed. This was so out of character. "What's gotten into you?"

"Nothing. Sorry."

A shiver of fear ran down my spine. "Did you get a bad medical report you're not telling me about?"

"No. Of course not."

"You're telling me the truth?"

"I'm fine, Caro. Really. It's just that Merry's daughter came to spend a few days with us. She brought little Francie, of course. Such an adorable child. It got me thinking."

Someone started thumping on my door.

"Just a minute!" I called out. "Listen, Dad, I have to go. We'll talk soon."

I disconnected as Julie sailed into my office. She closed the door behind me, but not before I caught sight of a TV crew carrying cameras and other equipment.

"Hello, partner," she said gaily.

"Julie, what on earth are you doing here?"

"I've come to inform the good people of Clover Ridge how their own Nancy Drew helped bring down another criminal."

"But you're the one—"

"Shh. Just listen. I'm the reporter; you're the local hero." She looked around. "This room is too damn small. We'll set up in the reading room. Or should we do it outside the new addition? No, I think indoors is better, with a few patrons around for atmosphere and comments. Do you have a mirror in here?"

"I don't think so."

Julie whipped out a good-sized mirror from the duffle bag I suddenly noticed at her feet. She scrutinized my face. "Fix your hair, add some lipstick and blush. And some mascara, if you have any."

"I don't."

"In that case." She opened her large pocketbook.

I frowned but did as she instructed.

"Great!" she declared, eyeing me carefully. Her smile dimmed as she studied my skirt and blouse. "They'll have to do. Ready?"

Ready for what? I shrugged.

She led me out to the reading room, a space I crossed many times during my working day. What were all these people doing, standing back from the center of the room, staring at me? Every patron and employee in the library had to be watching us. As we drew closer to the brightly lit area, Julie held out her palm. I halted and watched her move into the limelight, a glowing smile on her lips. Someone handed her a mic and she began to speak.

"As promised, we're going to chat with Carrie Singleton—head of programs and events at the Clover Ridge Library and member of the town council as well as our own Nancy Drew who takes down criminals. Thank you, Carrie, for inviting us into your workplace."

With the mic in my face and the camera focused on me, I had no choice but to smile and go along with Julie's charade. I had no idea why she'd chosen to make me come across as the hero of this story, but I was tired of following her lead. Ms. Julie Theron was in for some surprises.

"You're so welcome, Julie," I gushed. "It's the least I could do after the brave heroics you showed last night when you tackled Rafael Torres—aka Victor Ramas—and stopped him from shooting Kevin Powell."

Julie's mouth fell open. For a moment she was speechless, but she was too experienced a TV personality to remain nonplussed by my comment.

"I think it's safe to say we worked as a team. You were right behind me, stopping Ramas in his tracks when he tried to escape. And then you had the good sense to call the police and let them take it from there.

"Carrie," she went on, not letting me respond, "you've helped solve many homicides in the short time you've lived in Clover

Ridge. Tell me, were you surprised to see Rafe Torres—er, Victor Ramas—pull a gun on Kevin Powell?"

"Totally. You told me Kevin was meeting someone at Tootsie's last night. How exactly did you know that?"

Julie's smile curdled like sour milk. "You know I can't reveal my sources. But getting back to last night's situation, did you wonder why Ramas kept on asking Kevin Powell questions about his father?"

I shrugged. "Rafe Torres, as everyone knew him, and Sean Powell worked on many projects together."

"Yes, they both worked on the renovations of the new library addition," Julie said. "Are you pleased with the way things are moving along?"

"I certainly am! I can't wait for them to be completed so we can begin to use the new section for new programs. The new auditorium will be perfect for concerts and plays."

"Were you aware of any altercations between Ramas and Sean Powell?"

"They argued occasionally. I've learned that construction and renovation jobs never progress without some unforeseen problems."

Julie's eyes lit up. "One of the problems was discovering a body who unfortunately turned out to be your fiancé's uncle."

I smiled sadly. "Yes, poor Uncle Alec. He's gone to his much-deserved rest."

Julie raised her eyebrows and gave me a searching look. "Don't you think it's interesting that as soon as Alec Dunmore's identity was revealed, his killer was murdered?"

I suddenly knew what she was after: a tie-in of the two murders. Last night John had told her not to make assumptions she couldn't prove. It could have an adverse effect on the case in court.

Julie wanted me to state the obvious so she couldn't be sued for libel, fined by her station—or worst of all, fired!—but she wasn't going to get it from me.

"Wow, that's a whole lot of assumptions," I said, blinking. I was trying to appear naive and hoped I didn't simply look foolish. "For one thing, the authorities have yet to officially declare that Sean Powell was responsible for Uncle Alec's death."

"But he left a confession—"

"Please let me finish," I said over Julie's interruption. "The two murders might have no connection whatsoever. But perhaps Kevin Powell can help you on that score. Did you ever consider interviewing him?" I opened my eyes as wide as they would go.

Now Julie was seething. "Thank you very much, Carrie Singleton."

The spotlight and mic were turned off.

"Thanks a lot, Carrie!" she all but growled. "You could have been more cooperative."

"Really? After the way you ambushed me?"

"You know as well as I do that Torres killed Sean Powell."

"Only you couldn't say so on television so you expected me to do it for you."

She stormed off. Evelyn appeared, something she never did when other people were around. "I think that's the end of the Dynamic Female Duo."

"I sincerely hope that's true. I need to talk to you," I said.

My brisk tone startled Evelyn, but she said nothing as we headed for my office. I knew I didn't have much time before Trish arrived so I got right down to business. I glanced over at Evelyn, who was perched in her usual position on the corner of my assistants' desk.

"I'd like you to tell me how you were able to help Alec—how you knew when he couldn't move on and when he finally could go wherever he's supposed to go."

She cocked her head. "Why is that so important?"

"It's obvious you never want to tell me anything about your existence when you're not here in the library. But I have to know. I have to know if—" I swallowed. "If there's a chance you simply won't show up one day and I'll never see you again."

Was that a look of relief on her face? At any rate, Evelyn smiled. "No fear of that, Carrie dear. And I suppose, given our relationship, you're are entitled to know a bit more."

"Because you know more, don't you?" I said, realizing the truth. "Last year, when I was about to turn down the library position, you told me you weren't sure why you were here but you knew you were supposed to help somehow."

Evelyn nodded. "My visits to the library became more frequent just about the time you started working here, reshelving books and doing whatever mindless tasks Sally gave you."

I stared wide-eyed, barely able to breathe. This was the most Evelyn had ever told me about her life after death. "And now you know how you're supposed to help?" I asked.

"Isn't that obvious? I'm here to look after the residents of Clover Ridge and those who visit here."

"Like Alec," I murmured.

"Like Alec."

"And do what exactly?" I asked.

Evelyn pursed her lips. I was expecting one of her acerbic comments, but instead she simply nodded. "A good question. One I often ask of those above me. And each time I'm told that my function is to help find solutions for hostile situations."

"Through me," I said.

"Yes, through you and with you."

"Oh." A feeling of awe mixed with dread shot through me. Why was I put in such a responsible position without my approval or input? "Is this because I'm single?"

Evelyn smiled. "I think we've covered enough ground today. And don't worry about losing me anytime soon. I'm here for the long haul."

She disappeared before I could answer.

* * *

I called Marcella to tell her and Albert that Sean's murderer had been apprehended.

"Old news," she informed me. "Right, Albert? We've been watching Julie Theron."

"Tell Carrie she did good, jumping on that killer and stopping him from getting away," Albert shouted from a distance.

I heard the excitement in their voices as I spoke to each of them in turn. I supposed knowing Julie and me brought them closer to the incident.

"Will this slow down the work on the new library addition?" Albert asked me.

"I don't see why it should, with Buzz Coleman and Kevin Powell on top of things. The renovations should be finished in November as planned. We'll have a dedication ceremony soon after. I want you both to be part of it."

They thanked me and I promised to stay in touch.

* * *

A few hours later I was sitting across from John in his office in the precinct. After the hectic morning I'd had, I was glad to leave the library and quietly discuss last night's events in a place where no one could contact me. Though his eyes were red-rimmed, no doubt from being up most if not all of the night, John seemed relaxed. I'd just filled him in on Julie's surprise visit when Gracie Venditto, who oversaw the running of the precinct, entered the room with two steaming cappuccinos on a tray.

"What's this?" I asked.

John grinned. "I must have complained loudly enough to a few citizens because they gifted us with a new coffeemaker. As you can see, it makes all sorts of coffee."

I sipped the frothy drink and smiled. "This is delicious. I'll have to stop by more often."

"Any time, Carrie." Gracie winked and closed the door behind her.

"So, backtracking to last night," John said. "Mind if I tape it?"

"Go right ahead."

I told him how I was half-asleep when Julie called and wanted me to go with her to find out who Kevin Powell was meeting so late at Tootsie's. I repeated as much of his conversation with Rafe Torres/Victor Ramas as I remembered.

"Rafe seemed very intent on learning what Sean had told Kevin about him. At first Kevin acted like he didn't know what Rafe was after. I certainly had no idea. Now, of course, I realize Rafe wanted to find out if his secret was safe. Once he knew that Sean had told Kevin about his phony architect license, out came his gun. I have no doubt—now or last night—that he intended to kill Kevin."

"How exactly did you and Julie Theron stop that from happening?"

"I was feeling desperate—not knowing what could be done to stop him. I turned to Julie. The next thing I knew, she jumped on Rafe Torres and knocked him to the ground. Even when Kevin joined in and tried to hold him down, Rafe managed to get up. Which is when I rammed into him. That did it. I imagine one of them took away his gun while I called you."

John asked me a few more questions about what happened when, then had me run through the events all over again. It was his way of extracting every bit of information, including tiny details an inexperienced interviewer might consider unimportant.

He drained what remained of his cappuccino. "What do you make of the encounter between the two men?"

"You mean why was Rafe ready to kill Kevin?"

John nodded.

"To shut him up."

"About?"

"About the fact that he was working as an architect with a phony license. I believe that was why he murdered Sean."

"But they'd been working together for years," John said. "Why suddenly do this now?"

"Because either Rafe was getting sloppier or he was simply incompetent. I heard Sean arguing with Rafe a few times about mistakes in Rafe's designs. Could be Sean felt that Rafe was an actual liability. He knew he was dying. I'm thinking he told Rafe he would no longer guard his secret."

"Why do you think he'd kept Torres's secret all this time?"

I drew a deep breath. How best to tell John what I knew but had no way of proving? "I think Rafe knew Sean accidentally killed Alec Dunmore and eventually Sean found out Rafe's secret. They were blackmailing each other."

"Thank you, Carrie." John grinned and switched off the tape.

"I don't see how that can be of any help," I said.

"Actually, it confirms what Victor Ramas told me. He said he was present when Sean Powell and Alec Dunmore got into a fight and Sean landed one on his chin that sent him reeling into the wall. Ramas pressured Sean into getting him jobs and Sean, being nobody's fool, decided to look into Rafe's background.

"Ramas admits he fiddled with Sean's truck after Sean told him he was calling the state architectural board about his phony license. When he heard that Kevin Powell was taking over the construction company, he wanted to know if Sean had told Kevin his secret."

We chatted a bit longer. "I'm glad you caught Sean's killer," I told John.

"With some help from our local Nancy Drew and her friend." I was glad to see he was grinning. "I'm sorry it was Sean who killed Dylan's uncle, then hid the body like he did."

I stood, ready to go back to work.

"Have you and Dylan set the date yet?"

"Not yet," I said. "We've been too busy. But funny you should mention it. My dad just called and asked the same question."

"Don't wait too long," John said, sounding ominous.

"Do you know something I don't know?" I asked.

"No. Just go ahead and do it." He grinned again. "You'll be glad you did."

Chapter Thirty-Five

"You are the cutest little puppy!"

I stroked Scampi's silky coat as the adorable Maltipoo nestled in my lap. She stood on her back legs and reached up to lick my face.

"No, no, no!" I laughed as I wiped away her kisses.

It was Saturday evening, and Dylan and I were sitting with Angela and Steve in their living room. We had just demolished a huge takeout dinner from our favorite Indian restaurant. I was stuffed to the gills and totally relaxed.

"She loves you, Carrie," Angela said.

"She loves everyone," I said, though from the way Scampi had sought me out, I was secretly pleased to be one of her favorite people.

"Potty time," Steve said.

I handed him the puppy. They were trying to train Scampi to make on wee-wee pads. She had drunk some water twenty minutes ago, so now would be a good time for her to go. Steve joined us a few minutes later with Scampi traipsing after him.

"Any success?" Angela asked.

Steve shook his head.

I burst out laughing.

Angela scowled at me. "Not one word about cats and their litter boxes."

Dylan, who was sitting next to me on the sofa, put his arm around my shoulders. "We'll have to go through the training process when we have dogs."

"Dogs?" I said. "Like more than one?"

Dylan shrugged. "Sure. Why not? We don't have to get both at the same time."

"I suppose not. It's just that we never talked about getting a dog."

"Steve, look!" Angela pointed at Scampi, who was circling. "She's ready."

Steve scooped her up and ran with her to the wee-wee pads in the hall. When he joined us, he was grinning broadly. "Success! I left her chowing down on her treats."

"Very good, but next time just say 'potty' and lead her to the pad," Angela said.

"I was afraid she wouldn't get there fast enough, and I didn't want her going on the rug," Steve said.

"How will she learn if you carry her to the pad each time?"

"I don't plan to carry her each time, *dear*."

While her parents bickered about her bathroom training, Scampi ran over to me and I lifted her back onto my lap.

"I would love to have a dog . . . eventually," I said to Dylan.

"That's great. It's one of the things we need to talk about."

My cheeks grew warm. Weeks had passed since we had last discussed our future. Dylan had brought up the subject a few times and each time I'd been preoccupied with some pressing issue. When we first got engaged, Dylan had assured me he wouldn't pressure me to set an immediate date for our wedding. But that didn't give me a free pass to postpone our marriage plans indefinitely.

"We will. I promise." I clasped my hand in his. "We'll talk about things this weekend."

To my surprise, Dylan, who was never demonstrative in public, leaned over to kiss me on the lips. "I'll hold you to it," he said as if to seal the deal.

* * *

About half an hour later when Angela asked if anyone would like some ice cream, we all discovered we weren't that full and could manage a small portion. Seated around the kitchen table, we got onto the subject of the two murders.

"Both cases are considered solved," I said. "The district attorney decided to accept Sean's confession regarding the events of the night Dylan's uncle Alec died. He said Sean had no reason to lie."

"That makes sense," Steve said. "And it finally puts the matter to rest."

From the way he looked pointedly at me, then at Dylan, it was obvious that Steve knew about Alec's ghostly presence in the library.

"Angela, you told Steve," I said.

"I'm sorry, Carrie. It just slipped out one evening."

"I thought she was losing her marbles when she told me," Steve said.

"I almost crashed the car when I found out . . ." Dylan didn't finish his sentence because he had no idea if Angela had told Steve about Evelyn, too.

"Yeah! Weird," Steve commented. "Still, it gave you a chance to chat with your uncle before he, er, took off for good."

"It did," Dylan agreed. "But it sure felt strange, knowing he was dead, only there he was—not quite solid but talking to me."

"I hope the four of us can agree to keep this subject private," I said.

"Absolutely!" Angela said.

Steve laughed. "I won't tell anyone. Besides, who would believe me?"

Angela glanced at her watch. "It's almost nine o'clock. Time for your new best friend to make her news flash announcement."

"Julie's not my new best friend. You are, Ange. Well, not so new."

Dylan laughed. "Carrie's been ducking her calls."

"I can't understand why she makes me sound like a hero every time she talks about that night at Tootsie's," I said. "She's to be commended for saving Kevin's life. Sure, I helped a bit, but Julie is the real deal."

"Julie got what she was after—breaking a tremendous story," Steve said.

"She's capitalizing on the fact that you're Clover Ridge's favorite daughter," Dylan said.

"I am?" *Why are they all nodding and grinning?* I felt my ears grow warm. "Anyway, I'm glad Victor Ramas aka Rafe Torres finally confessed to murdering Sean Powell. He never broke when John told him what Julie and I overheard him say to Kevin, but when John surprised him by telling him why he had to stop Sean—that was the final nail in the coffin."

Angela laughed. "It's helpful when a ghost fills you in on vital information."

"It would have been more helpful if Uncle Alec could have told us everything that happened to him when he first came to Clover Ridge instead of remembering it in dribs and drabs," I said.

Steve switched on the kitchen TV and we moved our chairs around so we could see the screen.

Julie looked fresh and wide awake as she brought us up to date on the Sean Powell homicide. I had to admit that her narrative was spot on. She glossed over how we'd ended up at Tootsie's, but I supposed she had to protect her informants. Once again she downplayed her role in stopping a murder and disarming Ramas, insisting that the three of us each played important roles in taking him down.

"And now we have a final resolution to the homicide investigation. Victor Ramas aka Rafael Torres has been charged with first-degree murder in the homicide of Sean Powell. He has been remanded to prison to await trial."

Another reporter appeared and asked Julie questions. I was surprised at how calm and measured she responded. There was no trace of the willful madwoman I'd been forced to deal with.

The other reporter left and once again Julie had the stage to herself. She smiled into the TV camera, managing to look pleased with herself and saddened at the same time.

"I've one more surprise for you, one that's both joyful and bittersweet. Just when I've grown so terribly fond of the people of Clover Ridge, my bosses are sending me to Chicago, where I'll have my own half-hour show twice a week." Julie grinned. "An offer I couldn't refuse."

"Thank God!" I said as Steve clicked the remote and Julie's face disappeared from view. "I won't have to deal with her ever again."

Dylan and I left soon after. As we were driving home to the cottage, I said, "I think if we're going to have two dogs, I'd like them to be different breeds. And different sizes."

After a minute, he said, "I'm okay with that. Have any breeds in mind?"

"Nope. Maybe we can visit a few breeders."

"Good idea." Dylan glanced over at me. "Did you ever have a dog when you were growing up?"

I laughed. "Are you kidding? My mother take on another living responsibility?"

"My neighbor had a golden retriever. His name was Charlie. I used to walk him sometimes."

I turned to study Dylan's profile. "Is that what you'd like us to have—a golden retriever?"

He nodded. "I think so. Maybe we'll visit a few breeders like you said."

"Fine with me. I've heard goldens are sweet, gentle dogs."

"Charlie sure was."

"I was thinking—let's adopt our second dog from a shelter."

"All right. As long as it has a good disposition. And gets along well with children."

"Of course."

Dylan glanced at me. "Keep in mind, babe, any dog we adopt will require training. Even if we get a trainer, we'll need to put in hours of work on this."

"I'm up for it." I slipped my arm through his. It was fun talking about getting dogs sometime in our future. "I hope Smoky Joe won't have a problem adjusting to living with dogs."

"Maybe Angela and Steve can bring Scampi along for a visit. Get Smoky Joe used to having canine pals," Dylan suggested.

Allison Brook

"What a great idea!" I thought a minute. "But let's wait till Scampi's toilet trained to go outside. We don't want any accidents."

"Good thinking," Dylan said. He turned into the entrance of the Avery property.

"Let's talk more about this—and other things—tomorrow," I said. Now that I'd gotten started, I was eager to make plans about our future. I'd broken through a wall I hadn't realized I'd constructed.

Dylan shot me a grin. "Nothing would please me more."